Mike Grist is the British/American author of the Chris Wren and Girl Zero thrillers. Born and brought up in the UK, he has lived and worked in the USA, Japan and Korea as a teacher, photographer and writer.

HAVE YOU READ EVERY CHRIS WREN THRILLER?

Saint Justice
They stole his truck. Big mistake.

No Mercy
Hackers came for his kids. There can be no mercy.

Make Them Pay
The latest reality TV show: execute the rich.

False Flag
They framed him for murder. He'll kill to clear his name.

Firestorm
Is the new President a traitor?

Enemy of the People
There's a target on Wren's back. Everyone's a hunter.

Backlash
He just wanted to go home. They got in the way...

Never Forgive
5 dead in Tokyo. His name's all over it.

War of Choice
Russia renditioned his friends. This means war.

Hammer of God
A US city annihilated. All bets are off.

HAVE YOU READ EVERY GIRL 0 THRILLER?

<u>Girl Zero</u>
They stole her little sister. Now they'll pay.

<u>Zero Day</u>
One little girl dead in Haiti. More will follow.

Kill Zero
The past isn't dead, but it can kill...

SAINT JUSTICE

A CHRISTOPHER WREN THRILLER

MIKE GRIST

SHOTGUN BOOKS

SHOTGUN BOOKS

www.shotgunbooks.com

Paperback ISBN - 9781739951115

For Su & Sej

QOTL

C hris Wren stood in a dried-up gully under the beating Mexican sun, wondering how many deaths it would take to get out of the CIA for good.

Maybe thirty. Maybe just one.

The gully's sloping banks focused the baking midday heat like a lens, and Wren shuffled his shades, scanning the sun-battered landscape. There was nothing but withered desert scrub rooting through rust-red sand to the left, a couple of long-necked ocotillo stalks rising toward splintery orange rocks on the right. This was just another gouge in the epic landscape of the Sonoran Desert, one hundred miles south of the US border.

The only visibility lay dead ahead, where a few miles on the gully bled out into a desert plain beneath a chemical blue sky, broken now by a tiny plume of dust rising like a distant signal fire.

Incoming vehicles, at last.

Wren laid a hand on his Sig Sauer P320 ACP .45 pistol. Eight rounds to a mag, incredible stopping power with a powerful recoil, but nothing his solid 6' 3" frame or his conscience couldn't absorb.

"Agent Wren," came a voice in his tactical earpiece. The Kid, as Wren called him. Samuel Regis, 27 years old and son of a senator. He'd been fast-tracked into the CIA with management seniority over Wren, just as his father was warming up for a presidential run. A political appointment.

"That's Officer to you," Wren growled.

"Sure, Officer," Regis allowed in his plummy Harvard accent. "You have eyes on?"

"I see them," Wren confirmed. "Qotl cartel outriders coming up the creek. Five minutes ETA."

"Play it cool. This is a big deal."

Nothing Wren needed to say to that. With twenty years' experience, you didn't much listen to the latest newbie on the block. This was his op anyway, until the senator had gotten involved. It was meant to be a simple back-channel anti-terror deal with Qotl leadership, headed by Don Mica. Wren knew all about Mica, had almost assassinated him once. A harsh operator, he was most famous for feeding his enemies alive to rabid dogs.

He wasn't an ideal partner, but Wren lived in the gray spaces, and had done so for twenty years. The Qotl cartel brought in drugs and destabilized the border, but they weren't waging terror wars or blowing up buildings. That made them semi-allies in Wren's book.

Then the senator had gotten involved, his son came in, and Wren's deal was nixed.

Now he'd been sent out here for a solo mission, to restate the primacy of the War on Drugs. Put the Qotl cartel on notice. Put Don Mica on notice. It meant burning a fair chunk of his Qotl intelligence network, all on some order passed down through a silver spoon punk who'd never gotten his hands dirty.

Wren didn't buy any of it. Hadn't bought it from the start. The senator was up to something.

Regis began talking. "In case-"

Wren cut the line. The dust plume was thicker now. Four minutes out. He'd already set certain precautions in motion. Now he brought up his phone, reset the line to his earpiece and dialed a number from memory.

"Hector," he said.

"Christopher Wren, my boy!" Hector Gutierrez crowed down the private line. Gutierrez was a fringe Qotl cartel informant, a connection Wren had made when first going undercover with the cartel fifteen years back. He was a Baja-Mexican raised half in LA and half the shanty towns of the peninsula, complete with diamond teeth grille, teardrop cheek tattoos and, bizarrely, a set of red suspenders he never went anywhere without. "What you don't know might get you killed, cuz."

Wren grunted. "You think I don't know what's coming my way?"

"Latest I heard, Santa Justicia's about to get his ticket punched." Gutierrez sounded far too happy with this prospect. And there was that nickname. 'Santa Justicia', or 'Saint Justice'. Wren gritted his teeth. It was stupid, but you couldn't pick what they called you.

"You're saying my people sold me out?" he asked, checking the incoming vehicles. They should be coming within range of the Kid's snipers now, but if this whole thing was a set-up, then the snipers weren't going to fire under any circumstances.

"Maybe I am," Gutierrez teased. "Word is you're on the outs anyway, cuz. Don Mica, you know he's got a thing for taking out the CIA's trash. Two birds with one stone, you feel me?"

"Three minutes," Wren said. "Give me something solid or stop wasting my time."

Gutierrez laughed. "Something solid, pendejo, like a knife in the ribs? What you think I know?"

Wren watched the trucks rolling closer. A Humvee. A couple of heavy black trucks, like a presidential motorcade. In back rolled a black panel van, which could be filled with starving dogs. Maybe Mica planned to watch 'Santa Justicia' get eaten alive.

"Looks like Mica's brought his dogs," Wren said. "What's he planning here, Hector?"

"Walkies?" Hector tried. "I hear the Sonoran Desert's lovely for a stroll this time of year."

Wren grimaced. Gutierrez was an idiot, but unfortunately for Wren, he was the only idiot he had in this particular pinch.

"Look at it this way, Hector. If I'm for the dogs, guess what happens when I mention your name as I go down?"

"I bet it ain't good, homes," Gutierrez cheered. The man was positively giddy, holding Wren's life in his hands. Maybe high on his own supply. "Glad I ain't there."

"You've got one minute, Hector. My lips are feeling real loose. It's now or never."

Gutierrez held out, and the Humvee entered its final approach up the gully, the trucks flanking either side. Exactly how Wren would take down a high-value target like himself, if it came to that. Maximum overkill.

"Make a decision," Wren warned. "But bear in mind, if I get out of this alive, I'm coming for you."

"Fine, ese," Gutierrez said, sounding bored, "but only 'cos you asked so nice. I got some documents."

"Documents saying what?"

"Bad stuff. That Don Mica made a deal with Regis to foment a coup in Argentina. Political crap aimed at generating some BS hit pieces? Goal was to help Regis become President by taking down his opponent." Gutierrez took a breath. "Was all good, until Regis got cold feet and

4

pulled out. Now Mica's mad. I seen him, he's been pissed for weeks, Chris. Talking all kinds of crazy, drug war stuff, about exposing Regis as a charlatan, on the take." A brief pause. "Looks to me like you're the peace offering."

Wren snorted. Peace offering meant sacrificial lamb, just to placate the cartel. It figured. It made for an easy retirement plan for his CIA handlers, who would just look the other way. "You're lying to me, you know what happens?"

"What lie, Christopher?" Gutierrez replied. "He gonna sic them dogs on me too."

That was true. Wren killed the call and took a step forward.

The trucks pulled up. Cartel soldiers got out, solid men bristling with rifles aimed right at Wren. Don Mica followed seconds later, a thickset, vigorous man in his fifties with a bald head and a thick black beard. Wren ran the numbers. Mica was a hundred yards off. A do-able shot with the Sig .45, but not so easy if Wren was pin-cushioned by about twenty bullets from the rifles trained on him already.

"Don Mica," he called, "I hear you've come to kill me."

The Don raised a hand in greeting, spoke in low Honduras-accented tones. "Christopher Wren. I heard all about you. Looks like you're a chip in this game, now, one I'm happy to cash in."

Wren smiled, took a few steps closer. "Cash me, my team drops a bomb. Look up if you like. There's a Predator C-class drone circling at ten thousand feet, though you'll never see it. Hellfire missile, hundred-yard blast radius, this whole gulch will be a crater. You kill me, blammo, out go the lights. One less scumbag drug mule to deal with."

The Don didn't look up to the sky, though some of his men did. Instead he smiled back. "I heard about your tricks." His low, nasal voice fit perfectly with the dusty desert backdrop. "Bluffs and sleight of hand bullshit for Las Vegas tourists. But there are no backcountry yokels here. There's only teeth."

He gave a signal, and the back doors of the panel van opened. Crazed barking erupted as a clutch of froth-mouthed dogs sprang into sight, yanking at their leashes.

It looked bad.

"So maybe I am bluffing," Wren said. "One way to find out. In the meantime, let me get this straight. I almost took a CIA task to assassinate you, once upon a time, but I didn't. Now Regis bailed on your coup, and you're feeling jilted. I get that, but somehow you're not trying to collect on him or his son, who's even now half a mile away. Instead you're collecting on me."

Mica raised an eyebrow. "You're well-informed. I like how resourceful men die. Always grasping for one last way out." He paused a moment, wheels turning. "But the son. You say he's here?"

Wren pointed. "That way half a mile. His team booted my standard back-up, sent me out to run point alone. If you ask me, he should never have come out here, but I guess he wanted 'battlefield experience'." Wren made air quotes. "You know how that goes."

Mica snorted. "The general on the hill. Rich men always send poorer men to fight."

"I'm as poor as they come. Born in a hole in the ground, raised by wolves. I think it's the same with you."

The dogs barked madly. Don Mica stared at Wren. Making his own calculations. "If I let you live, say I went after the son instead, I would be taking on a US senator."

Wren marked that as progress. The guy was listening, and that was half the work done. "You're either looking for payback or you aren't. No room for shades of gray, and I'm faint charcoal at best. A mile out from this coup deal. I never even took that contract on your life, and you know why? Same reason I came here. Cut a deal. You're more useful to me as an anti-terror asset. The coup idea was stupid, burning a whole country for one man's political ambition." He let a beat pass. "You know that. I know it. Civil war's great for arms traders, but not so hot for the drugs business, am I right?" Mica just stared. "The coup was Regis' deal, and he stiffed you. Not me. Place the blame where it lays."

Silence reigned for a moment.

"Or put it on me," Wren went on, "and everyone here talks about what they saw. You got bought off by an American stooge. Revenge and honor didn't mean squat to you when the big money talked. You sold yourself out for a payday."

Mica nodded slowly. "This is more like your reputation. The man who persuades. Tell me, is there really a drone overhead?"

"Let those dogs loose and find out. I figure about the time they reach me, the payload's surpassing terminal velocity, twenty seconds 'til impact. You think you can clear this gulch in time?"

Mica scratched his beard.

"The CIA's got many hands," Wren went on, "each blind to the other. I wouldn't have made it twenty years without an eye on every angle. You think I mean to die here?"

Mica took out a fat cigar, rolled it between two fingers. "You're saying I take out Regis, leave you alive." He raised the cigar, scented along its length. "I'd be doing you a favor."

"Wrong," Wren pressed. "I'm doing you the favor. You want to hold the leash, not be the dog, am I right? Deal with me here, we're equals. Deal with him, you get starved until you're rabid, he sends you after the other Dons, make more civil wars when he's ready. Chaos south of the border. Regis cheerleads a crackdown, gets your head on a pike. Looks

7

good for his presidential run. He flipped on you once, next time will be with a bullet."

A long moment passed. Wren's life was on the line, but the equation had just shifted. Less likely it was going to be thirty dead, now. More likely it would just be one.

"Who you want for your business partner?" Wren closed.

Mica waved the cigar. "A man who'll take orders. All right. Here is my counteroffer. I leave this with you, Christopher Wren. The fabled Santa Justicia. Kill the senator's son and make this right. Send a message for me."

Wren shook his head. "I don't take orders. I make deals. I kill him, that's my part done. Justified, because he just served me up. But you claim it. That's good for us both. Your reputation. Mine too."

Don Mica didn't blink. "It'll mean war."

"It already is war," Wren said. "Unless you want to be Regis' dog."

Mica frowned. Tucked the cigar back into his jacket pocket unsmoked. Nodded. "You have ten minutes. After that, we come for anyone left."

"It'll be done in five," Wren said. "Start firing. Give me cover."

He spun and started running. He crested the gully's side in seconds, already working the phone to open a line back to the Kid. Behind him a storm of rifle fire erupted.

"I'm on the run!" Wren shouted down the open line as he sprinted full tilt across the desert sands. "Don Mica came in guns blazing, something's twisted here, we need an immediate evac!"

It took seconds. Regis had to be trying to figure out what went wrong. "Agent Wren, repeat, we can hear ordnance. Are you under fire?"

"You hear gunfire, don't you?" Wren barked. "They're

8

herding me south; I need a helo out of here right now. The guy's got wild dogs!"

Another long second. South was the opposite direction to the sniper's blind; a camouflaged hut set on a low hill in the rolling desert landscape. South wasn't the direction Wren was running, but there was no way they could know that. He'd picked the gully, even picked out the location for the blind, and left himself an alley of approach he could take unseen. Regis had let it all slide by, too arrogant or inexperienced to imagine his own double-cross might get double-crossed.

"Checking," Regis said.

Wren ran, then at just the moment he'd emerge into their sightline, he threw himself forward and began crawling through the baked dirt. He'd scoped it all out from the blind's location. There was enough scrub-brush cover to take him right up behind them without them seeing. They'd never know he was coming.

"What on Earth are you checking?" Wren shouted, keeping up the pretense. "Get me out of here!"

"Reading you," the Kid came back. "Scrambling a helicopter immediately. Hold out for ten minutes, we'll have you out of there."

"Did I mention they have dogs?" Wren called, letting his roughened breathing sound through. A quarter click covered already. He just had to sell it for the rest. He finished up the crawl then sprang back to his feet. "I shot one, but he got me pretty good. His damn tooth's stuck in my butt!"

"Stay alive, Agent Wren, that's an order!"

Bullshit. Wren had read it right from the start. The Kid was a fool. His father was a bigger fool. You didn't bet table stakes with men willing to go all-in. If Regis had wanted his stupid coup, he should have followed through.

"Working on it, sir," Wren said, throwing the 'sir' in there to be kind. The Kid didn't have long left.

He circled. More gunfire was spreading from the gully now. The dogs were running wild. Don Mica was making a good show of it.

"Wait, one of the dogs seems to be coming north," the Kid said. No doubt watching through a sniper monocular.

"You think I care about that?" Wren cried, running up the slope. The blind was just ahead. Ten men, all-in. Enough to secure the safety of a senator's son. "I've got teeth in my ass; I'm not keeping track of every mad pet on the Sonora!"

"Right, but-"

Then Wren was there. He burst through the tan camouflage strip sealing the blind and saw CIA intelligence people he'd just met a few hours earlier, each hand-picked by the senator. Now all of them were a party to betrayal: three sat clustered around a laptop, four were at the sniper's slit looking down to the gully, with twin snipers proned out side-by-side with a spotter and Regis between them.

All facing the wrong direction. All waiting on the moment Qotl cartel took out Christopher Wren.

It took a second. Wren strode over to Regis, put the Sig .45 against the back of his head, and paused for a millisecond to balance the scales. The Kid had sold him out. Worse yet, he'd sold out his country's safety for his father's political ambition, and there was no greater crime.

Half a second, and Wren pulled the trigger before the Kid knew what was happening. No need to talk. The Action Express did the job and then some. The reverberation was enormous.

Executed.

Wren turned. Let the Sig hang from his index finger. Already pistols were trained on him.

"You all wanted to hand me over, or you didn't know it was happening?" Wren asked, letting his anger burn through as he glared at their eyes one by one. Marking them all.

"Either way, those dogs are coming. You want to die when Qotl cartel gets here, or you want to live?"

Nobody fired.

"That's what I thought. You crossed me here. Do it again, I'm coming for you. Now let's go."

He ran back out the way he'd come. He didn't put it past Don Mica to kill anyone he found hanging around. Not Wren's responsibility.

Twenty years' service. All it took in the end was one death. A pretty good deal.

2

OUT

A flight, sleep, shower and new suit later, Wren sat outside the Manhattan office of his boss Gerald Humphreys, Director of Special Operations at the CIA. The furnishings made it look like some hip smartphone store, with lots of designer slate on the walls, chrome desks and blond wood flooring.

He was ready to make it happen. He'd never felt more certain of anything in his life. It was time. Twenty years of masking the truth: telling his wife he was away on business trips that lasted months; making excuses for why he couldn't call his kids every night; telling the neighbors BS stories over weekend BBQ about the state of play in Kazakh oil futures - his cover story as an international hedge fund trader.

"Come," came Director Humphreys' deep, authoritative voice.

Wren stood up. He went in. Even in a suit and minus his Sig .45, with his hair barely tamed and his scraggly black beard tied in a knot, he cut an imposing figure. Bigger than Humphreys, who rarely even bothered to stand.

This time he did. He looked pale as a cadaver straight out of his coffin, propped upright against a cream wall marked with five copper stars. Like the stars at Langley, Wren knew, each one a fallen CIA agent, though these were Humphreys' own. A wall of honor or of shame; he'd never asked.

"I can't let you go, Christopher," Humphreys said.

Wren looked at him. Late fifties but cropped sharp as a cold razor, Humphreys' only concession to personal style was his thick mustache. He was old enough that he'd be thinking of packing things in or making the next move up the ladder, to CIA Secretary or into politics.

Wren sat down unceremoniously. "Aren't you going to offer me a whisky, talk about old times?"

Humphreys stared hard and didn't sit. He was a stickler for the rule book, except when he wasn't. He'd been instrumental in Wren's last five years of deployments. He'd overlooked the chaos of Wren's psych profile, keen to get the world's pre-eminent black-ops specialist on his 'Special Operations' team; a legend in the field, more like a boogey man to America's enemies.

Saint Justice.

"I hear that maybe you killed the Senator's son," Humphreys said, like a shot across Wren's bow.

Wren waved a hand. "That was Qotl cartel. Whole thing was a set-up. Who's telling you otherwise?"

Humphreys glared, standing stock still. "I know you did it."

"So press charges. Court-martial me. Let's blow the whole thing sky high. Bring down Regis senior too. Maybe you, if you had something to do with it?"

Humphreys paled a whiter shade, nearing translucent. "How dare you accuse me?"

"Easy to dare," Wren said. "Twenty-four hours back I was in a canyon staring down a Qotl firing line. You're child's play next to that."

Humphreys' knuckles whitened. Ready to blow, maybe,

and pull whatever trigger he had lined up to shut Wren up forever.

"You know this has been coming," Wren followed up. "I'm out. Dishonorable discharge me, if that's what it takes, hammer another star up on your wall. Nobody'll ever know either way. Fact is, it's time. I've got a family. My focus is them."

Humphreys laughed, deep and harsh. "It doesn't matter that you have a wife, Wren, even children. You are no family man."

Wren shrugged. Easy to take insults like that, too. He hadn't gotten this far without a plan to see it through. "So black-bag me. Make me disappear in a secret prison south of the border. It'll just bounce back on you."

Humphreys frowned. "How's that?"

Wren pointed at him. "Your star's risen because of me. I've cleared more open terror cases than anyone in Company history. Brought down more jihadis, cultists, cartels, gangs and domestic terrorists than you even had listed. Topple me, all that goes away too. Your stellar record. No top-of-the-heap Directorship for you. No political role at the end of the line." Wren clicked his fingers. "Done."

Humphreys fumed. "I should never have taken you on."

"So kick me to the curb now. Make this easy on both of us. We part ways today and never cross paths again. What do you say?"

"That last part sounds ideal," Humphreys said, teeth gritted. "I never want to so much as hear your name again."

"Likewise," Wren answered. "Sign me up."

The meeting went fast after that.

Wren felt dazed on the drive home. Out of downtown Manhattan toward Great Kills, Staten Island. The end of an era. But it felt right. He couldn't keep on lying. His first duty was to his wife and kids.

They weren't expecting him home so soon. He was in Thailand, as far as they knew from his latest cover story; out there for a banking deal. He stopped at a coffee shop and bought cakes. Blue frosting for Jake, red cinnamon swirls for Quinn, and a bottle of red, a Shiraz, for Loralei.

Their place was a beautiful, spacious detached home overlooking Siedenburg Park on the edge of Staten Island. In the winter the lake shone like a pearl, in the spring the sassafras trees erupted in yellow flowers.

Walking up the drive, his heart beat like he was going to propose again. Telling Humphreys had been one thing; it would be another entirely to tell Loralei. That he would be home more. That he'd put more time into therapy, to deal with his night terrors. She knew only the smallest part about his past, that he was an orphan who'd struggled to find his place in the world. He didn't tell anyone more than that.

At the stoop, he realized he'd forgotten his house keys somewhere, maybe left them with all his bags at LaGuardia after the rush back from Mexico, but he couldn't stop himself from grinning as he stood at the door. Short of breath. Vision tunneling to the spy hole, wondering what she would think. He cursed softly: flowers! He'd forgotten flowers. But the cake and the wine would do.

He knocked.

The door opened.

It wasn't Loralei.

3

WHAT YOU SOWED

Looking at this woman standing in his doorway, Wren's brain short-circuited.

Maybe his wife had hired a maid? Maybe this was a friend, though he didn't recognize her at all. Blond hair. Cream paint splatters on her dungarees. Beyond her even the house looked different. A new oak-paneled mirror. A new potted plant.

He smiled. "Hi, I'm Christopher. Loralei's husband."

The woman stared. "OK."

"I'm home early, forgot my keys, is she in?"

The woman's eyes narrowed uncomfortably. "I'm sorry, Loralei, you said? I think maybe you've got the wrong house."

Wren frowned and checked the house number. It was correct. He saw the familiar chip in the door frame's paint where Jake had dinged his tricycle. This was it. But they weren't here.

It sent him operational. Someone had taken his family. It was a trap.

"Where are they?" he asked coldly. He had no weapon, but he wouldn't need one for this.

"I, uh, don't know," the woman said, reading the change in him and taking a step back, ready to slam the door.

Wren didn't give her the chance, striding in and past her. Down the hall he went, where many things looked the same, but many weren't. The same walls, floor, ceiling, but new paintings. He rounded the corner to the den and saw-

A man was standing in the middle of the room wearing white overalls, holding a paint roller. There was white sheeting on the floor, a ladder, and all their old furniture was gone.

The man stared. Wren stared.

"Get out," came the woman's voice from behind. "I don't care who you are. I'm calling the police."

Wren tried to figure it out. This was some strange kind of trap. What foreign agency stole your family then started redecorating? This was...

His stomach sank. This was something else. Something he'd never even considered, though he should have. Director Humphreys' words came back to him, 'You're no family man, Wren.'

He blinked. The guy was still standing there, but now the woman stepped in front of him holding up a gun. Wren clocked it, a Glock 9mm, overpowered for home defense. She might sprain her wrist firing it.

"Get out," she ordered.

The bag holding the cake and the wine dropped from Wren's hand. The bottle smashed, red wine sloshing out and staining the white sheet. The woman's eyes turned to the mess and Wren used the moment to lean off-line and take her gun. One hand swiped the barrel, the other locked her wrist and the weapon plucked free like he was picking an apple.

She stared at him in disbelief. Wren clicked the magazine absently out and put it in his pocket, pulled the slide to eject

the chambered round, caught it mid-air, then handed the disarmed weapon back.

She stared at the gun in her hands, suddenly useless. "Get out of here right now!" she shouted.

Wren put the pieces together. "I'm sorry. I didn't know. I thought maybe you'd taken my family, but maybe you're renting the place from my wife? Loralei Wren?"

The woman frowned. "Mrs. Wren? I, uh, yes. I think that's the name." She looked to the man. He nodded mutely. "But I don't know anything about your family. You need to leave. This is our place now. You don't just stamp in. I have more ammunition."

"How long have you been here?" Wren asked. "Last question."

"I don't have to answer any questions!"

Wren turned to the man. "How long?"

The guy cleared his throat. "A month," he managed, looking uncertain. "It's our first place," he added weakly.

A month? Wren had spoken to Loralei nearly every night, even while he was undercover. If she was going to rent out their family home, surely she would have told him?

"Last warning," the woman said. Now there came the drone of sirens drawing near.

Wren didn't know what to think. Either way, he wouldn't get any answers here. He looked down at the dropped bag. "Sorry for the mess."

He walked out. He tucked the magazine and the loose shell into the mailbox at the end of the drive, lifted the flag then kept walking past several police cars as they raced in. He placed a call to Loralei, but she didn't pick up. After five more tries and several messages he began to worry.

He brought up the number for her family in the UK, tapped it and waited for the connection to land. The call went through. A groggy voice came online. It was the middle of the night still, across the Atlantic.

"Hello?" said Loralei's dad.

"It's me," Wren answered. "Where's Loralei?"

A few seconds passed. "Christopher?"

"What's going on, Charlie? Where is she? Where are my kids?"

A low sigh followed. "It's over, Chris. She found out. What you do, all this CIA business? It was too much for her, and now you're done."

That froze him. She found out? A dozen questions burned through his head. How? Why? Who told her? Only one that mattered, though.

"Where is she?"

"I'm not going to tell you that, am I?"

The words landed like blows.

"I'm out of that life," Wren said hurriedly, like it could turn things around. "I quit the Company. It's over, I swear."

"It is over." The old guy heaved another heavy breath, gearing himself up. "I can't help you, son. We always got along OK. But you weren't there. You lied. I respect what you've done, protecting your country and all, but it's no life for them. For a family."

Silence. Wren wanted to argue but he knew it was true. There was no point repeating he'd quit.

"Where is she?"

"Not here. Come out and check, if you like. Gone, Chris. A clean break. It's been coming for years. Surely you saw it?"

He hadn't. He'd been so bound up in his own lies that he hadn't seen the lie building up in her.

"My advice is to respect this," Charlie went on. "Don't try to find her. She won't like that. If you want to see your kids, you need to get yourself straight. Get out and stay out, prove you're trustworthy. Do that and she'll reach out, get you visitation with your kids."

He didn't know what to say. Visitation? "I deserve better. This is wrong."

"So did she," said the old man.

Wren's mind leaped. He had no doubts he could find Loralei. He could find her in less than an hour, most likely, but would that help?

"How long?"

"How long what?"

"How long am I out in the dark? Can't see her, can't see my kids?"

"How long?" Charlie repeated. "I don't know, Chris. But I will ask her. I'll get you an answer. But not for at least a month. OK?"

Wren almost choked. A month was impossible. How would he do a month?

"OK, Chris?"

"OK," he found himself answering.

"I'm hanging up now. This is what you sowed, Chris. Reap it."

The line clicked and went dead. Wren was left standing in the middle of the road, alone.

4

VIKINGS

Wren got in his truck, a modified Jeep Wrangler Unlimited, and started driving. He didn't know where at first. Into the night and out of New York; he just had to keep moving to outrun his father-in-law's voice in his head.

Reap it.

By dawn of the next day he was already halfway to Loralei's destination, some podunk town in Delaware called Frederica. One call to some hacker friends and they had her in forty-three minutes.

But halfway down, pulled over by the roadside looking out at the sea, he stopped. Charlie's words came back to him, that his days with the CIA were the cause of all this. It was true; he had lied. He'd lied since the start. How would it look now, to use the fruit of those lies to track her down?

And what would he do if he reached her, just demand to see his kids? He couldn't imagine that playing out well.

The truth was, he owed her. Charlie was right about that. He had to respect her.

A month, he'd said. He'd waited longer before.

He got back in the Jeep and hit the road with no

destination in mind. He wasn't looking for anything but to kill time. The first day was hard, cruising back west and getting a good look at the country he'd spent his adult life defending.

The next day was easier. He ate in diners and slept in motels or the Jeep. He read books and watched movies, but mostly he kept moving. For thirty-one days he roamed the country, until at some point in the wilds of Utah, pulled over by the side of I-70 beneath sweeping starry skies, the month was almost up. It was late, but coming up for dawn in the UK.

Just a few hours to go.

Wren sat at the wheel of his Jeep, gazing out at the silhouettes of buttes against the purple sky. The stars scrolled overhead, the engine's cooling vents clicked until they were cold and receding taillights on I-70 melded into one seamless red tracer round in the rearview mirror.

On the passenger seat next to him lay dozens of wrinkled pieces of paper, all covered in bright crayon scrawls. A house, a horse, a family. These were drawings from his kids, and he carried them on every mission, wherever he went. They were worth more than anything else he had.

He looked at the clock.

Just an hour until dawn in the UK, now. He closed his eyes just for a moment.

A sudden, sharp sound woke him from a doze. It sounded like metal on the window, right by his ear.

Maybe highway patrol?

He blinked and rubbed his eyes. It was night still, but ahead lay bright floodlights from multiple vehicles, with more behind him. He peered closer. Not cars, he realized, but bikes, and all pointed at him with their engines rumbling low.

This wasn't highway patrol.

Through the side window he saw a guy with face tattoos and a thick black beard, wearing a leather motorbike cap and a white wifebeater. He was in his forties and built solid. Wren recognized one tattoo on his cheek: a blue skull with blond dreads and a hammer of Thor.

His stomach ran cold.

Vikings. Dry memories from his last FBI intelligence confab on extremist groups rose up: the Vikings were a mid-sized biker gang based across five states, involved in drugs and illicit porn. They were infamously anti-government, with several members linked to failed domestic terror attacks in the past.

Wren swiftly checked their spread in his peripheral vision. It looked like a whole cavalry, maybe a dozen. Three bikes sat in front blocking his route, with four to the rear and a handful on each side.

They had him trapped. The tap on the glass came again. It was metallic, and he noticed something gleaming across the man's fingers; a brass knuckle-duster twinkling in the white high beams.

"Open up the door, boy," the guy called through the glass. "Let's have ourselves a talk."

Wren blinked. Boy? "What's the problem?" he called back.

"Your night just got real interesting. Now step out."

Wren grimaced. There was only one reason a gang like this wanted him to step out, and that was to preserve the Jeep. No need to jack the door and damage the paintwork; it'd be better to resell if Wren handed it over easy.

"The Jeep's yours," Wren said, keeping his hands on the wheel. He didn't even glance to the glove box where his Sig Sauer P320 .45 ACP lay, eight in the mag and one in the chamber. Tempting, but he wasn't looking for firefight. "I'll walk."

"We've already got the Jeep," the guy said, and Wren's mind spun faster. As the first to approach, this man had to be the gang's enforcer; the muscle that did the most violent work. "What we want is you." The brass knuckles tapped on the window again.

He was enjoying this. Wren looked into his eyes and saw the sadism. This wasn't just a carjacking. "Tell me first, though, you some kind of banker out of Salt Lake, getting high off the big money bailout?"

Wren looked into his eyes. "Banking of a kind. I specialize in liquidations."

The guy frowned. "And a comedian? Even better. Boy, we'll all laugh ourselves sick when you're cracking jokes from a cage."

From a cage? Wren looked the enforcer square in his blue eyes. One direct, clear warning would be fair.

"You don't want to do this. I'm a Force Recon Marine. Until recently, I was CIA. Back up, I walk, you can have the Jeep and nobody gets hurt. That's the best you can hope for here."

Someone tried one of the rear doors, but they were locked. The enforcer leaned in so close his lips almost touched the glass. "Nobody gets hurt, that's real neighborly of you, looking out for us like that." He hawked and spat. "So let me return the favor. Go easy, and I'll help you learn to love the collar. Failing that, we drag you behind a bike at forty for a spell, really tenderize that tough streak."

Somebody laughed. The enforcer grinned, revealing crooked yellow teeth. "What's it to be, boy?"

Wren considered his position. He'd given a direct warning. As far as he was concerned, that put him in the clear.

"Don't call me boy," he said, and shoved the door out like a punch, left arm extending with all the strength of his 6' 3", two hundred fifty-pound frame. The door caught the enforcer mid-sentence in the chest, maybe cracked a rib as Wren followed through, then he staggered back and Wren keyed the ignition with his left hand.

The V6 engine burst to life and he hit the gas, even as his right hand went for the glove box and curled around the SIG's snug grip.

The Jeep burst forward, the bikers' mouths opened in shock then he hit their bike blockade and plowed forward. A Triumph Bonneville lowrider clanged to the side and a Harley Fat Boy went under his chassis and stuck, shredding sparks from the highway shoulder as he pushed the Jeep up to fifteen miles an hour.

The Vikings opened fire. Wren ducked low, steering as best he could as gunshots hammered into the truck, spidering then shattering his rear window. A lucky shot blew out his back right tire and halved his torque.

He wasn't going to make it, not dragging a Fat Boy with a junk tire. He looked in the rearview and saw the bikers catching up already, their guns training in and bullets continuing to spattering the Jeep's bodywork.

Wren saw just one choice, and swung hard right off the shoulder, beyond the sweep of headlights and into the desert's wild dark of low creosote bushes, boulders and cacti. The tires crunched, the chassis juddered then the Fat Boy caught on something in the undergrowth and gut-punched the Jeep to a halt.

He'd made some three hundred yards distance into the darkness, and maybe it was enough. Wren scrambled to the passenger side door, something they wouldn't expect, and slipped out onto the cold sand seconds before their floodlights pulled up on the driver's side.

Engines revved and voices clamored, calling out what they were going to do when they caught him. Wren hustled on his belly like a sidewinder, snaking away through the grit and desert dirt.

"You ever been hung and quartered, boy?" someone called nearby, maybe the enforcer. "Burned on a cross for your sins?"

Wren dodged a barrel cactus to stay out of their high beams, then came up against a heavyset guy looming right in front of him in the dark. His head was as a gallon jug, with his bulbous belly silhouetted against the starry sky.

He saw Wren, opened his mouth and Wren surged up into a big uppercut, thighs driving his left fist square into the big man's chin; hard enough to drive the girdle of his jaw up around his cheeks like a slipped pair of shades.

The big man's head shot back like an ejected shell and his body dropped, the scream dead on his lips.

Wren dropped to one knee, took five seconds to palm his wallet, then plunged back into the dark just as headlights wheeled across him like nightclub strobes.

A man ahead was bringing a rifle to bear, and Wren shot him with the Sig. He dropped, but a chain whipped down across Wren's wrist, smacking the gun from his grip.

Wren grabbed the chain and twisted, jerking the holder off balance, then tracked the chain back to sweep the man into a big judo throw that pounded him into the ground. A muzzle flare sparked to Wren's left but he was already darting away, right up to a guy winding up a big swing with a baseball bat.

Wren scooped the bat under his left arm while evading an incoming blade aimed for his eye, then fired a big right elbow against the first guy's temple and a snap kick to the second guy's balls.

They both dropped. Wren scanned for his Sig but it was lost in the dark.

Then the enforcer was there, the brass knuckles on his right fist catching the light for a second before it swung into Wren's gut with a meaty thump. Wren managed to slip some of the impact, but the metal caught his solar plexus and drove the breath from his lungs.

He couldn't breathe, but ignored the ensuing panic and sent out a front kick that caught the enforcer center mass and sent him reeling away.

Then he ran.

Lights wailed and bullets barked. A bike growled over the rocky ground nearby but the terrain blocked it. Another biker came from the dark and flung himself at Wren like an offensive lineman, tackling his legs so they tumbled together through a stand of creeping cacti.

Wren's back thumped against a boulder, the guy managed to get a hand around Wren's neck, but he answered with a haymaker punch to the man's groin that put him out for the count.

Then he was up again and running into the night.

5

THAT GUY IN THE MOVIE

Wren woke to a deep rumbling, closing in fast. He opened bleary eyes from one of the old nightmares, flashes of his dark childhood in the Arizona desert, to see white lights rushing toward him. He rolled, and an eighteen-wheel semi-trailer truck thundered by only feet away, juddering the sandy blacktop beneath his hands.

It took him a second. Side of the highway?

More trucks followed.

He shifted further from the edge, into the shoulder amongst peeled-off rags of tire rubber and old crinkly chip packets, breathing hard. For a moment he lay flat on his back looking up at the stars, pushing the nightmare down.

Still alive.

Flashes of his flight through the desert came back to him, staggering by moonlight while staunching blood from various shallow wounds, making a beeline for the whirring lights of the Interstate. At some point he'd limped up to the roadside, laid himself down and passed out.

He rolled up to a sitting position, steadying a flush of dizziness with both palms on the cool blacktop. Everything hurt. He ran down a mental checklist. His jaw felt loose but he could grit his teeth. His back and sides were stiff and his breathing caught on bruised ribs. He extended his legs and arms carefully, like an infant born on the roadside shale, but there were no breaks, no bullet holes, nothing worse than cuts and scrapes.

On his feet, he checked his front pockets. His wallet and phone were gone, must've been ripped clear in the fight. The Vikings would have taken the Jeep now too, breaking it down for parts. The engine, tires and electronics would be worth a few grand. That was a blow, but the true loss only hit him a few seconds later.

The pictures from his kids on the passenger seat.

Drawings they'd made over many years; all the moments he'd missed while he was out fighting the exact kind of stupid, tribal violence the Vikings represented. For years he'd collected them and carried them with him. They were the purpose for all this.

Now they were gone.

He checked his back pockets and came up with the wallet he'd palmed from the heavyset man whose jaw he'd cracked. He opened it and looked over the contents by the strobing white light of passing cars. There were some crunched-up notes, some receipts, a social security card, a kid's prom picture behind a clear window, and a driver's license with an address.

Paydirt. The guy's name was Eustace. You couldn't make that stuff up.

Wren stuck a thumb out and started limping along the shoulder. A few cars slowed down to check him out, a huge, bedraggled hitchhiker on the Interstate by night, but nobody stopped. Wren didn't blame them.

He reached the gas station maybe two hours later. Across the stained concrete of the well-lit forecourt, the kid behind the counter watched him push through the glass swing door with wide eyes.

"What happened to you, man?" he asked.

"Alien abduction," Wren said. "You got ice?"

"Aliens? What?"

"I'm kidding," Wren said, and flashed a smile. "Just fell over out hiking, now my car wouldn't start." He shrugged. "Tough day, tough night, but I'll be fine. How about that ice?"

"Ice? I got, uh, yeah," said the kid, watching blankly as Wren started plucking products off the shelves. He craned his neck to follow. "In back, bottom of the chest freezer. Did you say hiking?"

"Uh-huh. I'm a big hiker."

Wren picked up a box of bandages, a hand towel, a tube of superglue, a pack of Tylenol, a couple of hot quarter-pound cheese burgers and a local map.

"Where were you hiking?" the kid asked. "I didn't know there were even any trails out around here."

"I like to blaze my own," Wren said, and fished a couple of big water bottles out of the fridge followed by a bag of ice from the freezer. He caught a glimpse of himself in the mirrored back. The bruising wasn't too visible yet, but the blood was. One of his eyes was shot through with red, and there were scratches on his cheeks and forehead.

"Like that guy in the movie?" the kid asked. "Who got stuck in a crevasse under a boulder, and had to cut his own hand off?"

Wren couldn't stifle his smile, and raised both hands. "Like that, yeah, but I made it out intact."

He paid for the shopping with Eustace's money, took the bag then nodded at a set of keys on the side of the register. "Those for the restroom?"

The kid handed them over and Wren thanked him and headed out.

The restroom was clean enough. He got the hot water going in both sinks then stripped and washed with the cloth. His back was a tapestry of rising purple, and his arm had a welt where the chain had struck, but nothing was too serious. Hard cords of muscle had absorbed most of it. His legs were much the same, bruised and cramped but basically OK.

He doused the washcloth with disinfectant and swabbed himself liberally, enjoying the clarifying sting. Next he used the superglue to seal up a few nastier cuts and topped them with bandages.

He looked in the mirror. He didn't look all that bad. His eyes drifted to the names tattooed on his broad chest, each done on the day they were born. Jake and Quinn. His kids. Now they felt like testaments from an earlier life. Standing there, his father-in-law's words came back to him, burned into his head after a month of repetition.

This is what you sowed, Chris. Reap it.

Now the month had passed. He could call Charlie at any time, but not yet. First he had to get the pictures from his kids back.

He cleaned up the restroom nice and neat, dabbing up all the blood and putting the trash in the wastebasket. No sense leaving it for the kid at the register to do. At a payphone beside the store he called a cab, then popped two Tylenol out of their blister pack and washed them down with two bottles of water.

After that he sat down on the forecourt to wait, munching on his burgers and holding the ice pack to the back of his head.

6

EUSTACE

The cab took an hour to arrive. Wren sat out front of the station looking over the forlorn gas pumps and the road, savoring the cold of the ice against his thumping head.

Wren climbed in, and the driver surveyed him in the rearview mirror.

"Hot dang, man," he said. "You get run over or something?"

"Came off my horse," Wren said, "out roping cattle," then closed his eyes and drifted through the ride. Soon enough they pulled in at the bottom of Eustace's road, in a tiny town called Emery. He stepped out.

It was a beat-down neighborhood, all cracked blacktop with duplexes lined side-by-side like neglected herd cows, overgrown with poison oak and sprayed with desert dust. Street cleaners didn't come out here, he bet.

The cab sped away. Wren walked unevenly up the road, favoring his left side. Old trash lay in the gutters, soda cans and fast food chicken wrappers bleached from long days of sun. It was coming up for dawn now and people would be rousing. Political lawn signs sprouted from weed-clumped lawns. Big, rusted Chevy trucks were the order of the day on broken-flagged drives, trailing dark oil marks.

Eustace's house was the same as any, with a toppling telephone post at the corner, cables trailing down around head height. The front porch had peeling white paint that showed cheap beech boards beneath. There were holes in the roof felt, dozens of dry clay wasp nests under the rotten eaves and the porch swing hung by only three chains.

Probably Eustace's family home. A story of loss. Already the air felt hotter and drier out here. The only well-maintained item was Eustace's bike, parked on a neat cement pad by the wall. Twin heavy-duty security bolts anchored the wheels and frame to eyelets in the cement. His prized possession.

Wren walked around back. The yard was overgrown, a swing set smothered in weeds. No kids here now. The slide door was open a crack. Wren slid it further and stepped in. Kitchen, den, hall. At the bottom of the stairs Wren could hear Eustace snoring above. Each breath came with a pained catch. Up the stairs he saw family photos, Eustace with a wholesome-looking lady around the BBQ, their two cute kids playing in the yard. Hardly the standard set up for a biker gang initiate

Wren entered Eustace's room. Inside it was sparse, not even a TV. He sat on a magazine stack at Eustace's side. The big guy was blacked out on his single bed. His face had bandages, but what did a bunch of bikers know about advanced jawbone disorders? After the knee to the chin Wren had delivered, Eustace would likely suffer stroke-like symptoms all up and down his body. Without proper care he'd go undiagnosed and bad habits would make it worse. He'd get a hunch, twist a knee under the extra weight then never walk right again.

He wasn't going to give Wren any trouble. Still, he probed for a gun under the pillow or down the side, but there wasn't one. There was nothing dangerous within reach. For a moment he sat there, studying the big guy. He had an uneven shave on his scalp, half-masking recent Viking tattoos that were red at the edges. It filled in the rest of the story.

Not a patch member. Just another lost soul, reaching out in a dangerous direction.

"Hey Eustace," he said, and flicked him lightly on the temple. "Wake up."

The big man came to with a snort. One hand went up to rub his chin, then came back with a delayed whimper of pain. His eyes rolled as he tried for focus. Wren figured they'd put him out with some generic opioid.

"Wha-?" the big guy asked, then winced.

"Where's my Jeep, Eustace?"

Eustace blinked and peered. It was dim in the room, so Wren pulled the curtains open. The sun was rising pink outside, a new day. In the fresh influx of light, the bloodstains on Eustace's pillow and sheets stood out.

Eustace's eyes grew a little sharper. Recognition came, and he started shuffling as the panic came on, trying to get the covers off and get up. Probably he hadn't done a sit-up in a decade, though, so it didn't take much to hold him down.

"Shh," Wren said. "Calm down. Your momma's in the next room. Let's not wake her."

That worked as a caution and a threat, and Eustace stopped struggling. His eyes burned through the opioid fog.

"Id's you. You tug by wallet." He winced with every word, and his eyes shone with rising tears. He probably thought he was about to die.

"I did," said Wren, and tossed the billfold onto Eustace's chest. "There you go, I brought it back. Now it's your turn. Where's my truck?"

Eustace stared defiantly. Wren chalked that up; he was ready to suffer, if not die, for his new 'family'. Wren had

34

come across it a hundred times before. 'Don't be a snitch', that was the first thing they told you on joining any gang.

"These guys, they're opportunists, Eustace. They'll dump you the first chance they get. You're a nobody in their eyes. So what are you being loyal to?"

Anger spiked Eustace's eyes. Wren read it and adjusted. it was no good going head-on any further, the guy would just clam up, and torture was unreliable at best. Better to try a different tack.

"Nice Triumph," he said calmly. "I know what a bike like that costs, and it's more than you or your momma has.

That sparked Eustace's eyes with confusion. "Whu?"

Wren gave him a second. There were many routes to breaking a man. "I was thinking about taking it. Part-exchange for my Jeep. I'd cut a mean figure on it, don't you think? Cowboy rides off into the sunset. But I think if I did, you might kill yourself. Is that about right?"

Eustace just stared at him.

"You'll drink and moan, you'll make excuses, but in the end, you'll eat a gun." Wren scratched his chin. "I've seen it a thousand times. Wife left you and took the kids, leaving you with some crappy job cleaning toilets or flipping burgers for college kids at the drive-through. Then one day the gang rolls through, maybe somebody makes overtures, and you figure it's a way back to pride. You sink the last of your savings into the bike, get the tats and start working on your patch membership, but then if you lose the bike?" Wren whistled low. "That's like a cop losing his gun. A great shame, am I right?"

"Ged tha hell oud of by houth!" Eustace grunted.

"Trust me, I've been there," Wren went on casually, "and I don't want to cause your death. So let's make a deal. You tell me everything you know about the Vikings, right now, and I give you a better gang to belong to. One that'll help you out and give you something to aim for, not drag you down. Good clean fun, basically. What do you say?"

Eustace said nothing, maybe too bewildered, but at least he was listening still.

"Either way, I'll be watching," Wren went on. "See, Eustace, I collect people like you. I've got an organization called the Foundation with over a hundred members based around the world; all people on the edges of some real bad decisions. I check in on them often, make sure they're staying on the right side of the tracks, give them a bit of help when I can. Pass your one-year with the Foundation, no bad mistakes, you get a coin, like AA. Pass your three-year, your five, your ten, all come with coins, which bring privileges and benefits, like a loyalty program. I've negotiated some great discounts at the mall." He winked. "Backslide, and you go down a coin. You're on coin zero now, because you stole my Jeep and tried to kill me, so back a step means you're into the red and I take the bike. Probably leave you in hock, but that's your choice. It's how I roll. It's on you to make better choices."

Eustace just stared. "Who de hell are you?"

"My name's Christopher Wren. I was born into a gang that makes your Vikings look like toy soldiers, so I know what I'm talking about. Ever hear of the Pyramid?"

It took a second, then the big man's eyes widened.

"Yeah, the death cult," Wren said. "We were based out this way, in Arizona. America's biggest mass suicide event, with a thousand people burning themselves alive. That rings a bell, doesn't it? As far as I know, at eleven years old I was the only survivor, but I saw it all. As you can imagine, I've about had my fill of suicide."

Eustace's jaw dropped open slightly, which caused him to whimper.

"After that I drifted for a while, then found a new gang to

36

join. The Marines. Soon I graduated into Force Recon special operations overseas, then I worked for the CIA in black-ops, and now…" he paused, looking around the room trying not to think about his family or the future he'd hoped for. It seemed a dramatic comedown after that resume. "I guess I do this."

Eustace said nothing, though his eyes were wide. Wren figured it was a real moment of revelation for them both.

"So cough up," he went on. "Admission to the Foundation doesn't come for free. For extra credit toward your first coin, tell me where the Vikings stowed my Jeep. Don't leave a bit out, Eustace. You're complicit now, and both our lives depend on it."

BRAZEN HUSSY

E ustace spilled like a split bag of meal.

The Vikings had a roadhouse off I-70, name of 'The Brazen Hussy'. As best he knew, Wren's Jeep would be there, cooling off until the gang broke it down for parts and arranged for a fence out of state.

A clean hit, Wren figured. If the place was lax enough, he could walk right in, knock a few heads, get his kids' pictures and his Jeep, maybe steal a bike or two by way of compensation, then call in the sheriffs and roll out. Get back on the road, make that call to Charlie and get back on track to being with his family.

First though he needed a car and a gun.

His second cab of the day rolled up, and the driver didn't even look in the mirror as Wren climbed in. Just the way he liked it. Wren slumped back in the seat and closed his eyes.

"Here," came the driver's cigarette-rough voice some time later. Maybe he'd said it twice.

Wren sat up. Maybe an hour had passed already. He looked out into blazing sunlight and saw the tumbled metal heaps of a junkyard. He paid the old guy and climbed out.

Orangeville. Wren sampled the air but didn't taste much

other than the iron of his own blood. Out here on the fringe it looked much like Emery. Maybe a little bigger. Wider roads. Less trash.

The junkyard gate had a bell and he rang it five times, until a ropey lady with beaded dreads came out cursing and spitting brown chaw.

"What you want?"

"A truck. Whatever you've got that'll run. Plus a thousand dollars, cash. You take Bitcoin?"

She laughed. "You trying to stick this place up?"

"I lost my gun. I'll pay you two thousand in crypto coins, plus another thousand if you throw in a pistol; anything made in the last twenty years, I'm not choosy. Or you wanna pass up easy money?"

She spat more chaw. "This look like a gun store to you?"

"That's three grand for junk."

She chewed hard, staring at him. "One man's junk's another man's treasure. And crypto? That ain't worth a thing."

"Tell that to the banks."

She smiled. "You a narc? You look like a narc. You have to say, if you're a narc."

"I just quit the CIA. Some punks jumped me in the desert. I think you see that on my face, right? I'm just looking for a little divine retribution."

"CIA?" Now she laughed. "You're full of crap. But amen, brother. God will have his vengeance. Wait there."

He ended up with a beat-up Ford 25 Super Duty truck. The radiator was part-fried and the engine was on its last legs, but the plates were legit for another three months, and Wren had no intention of driving it longer than a couple of days.

The gun was a Rorbaugh R9 Series pistol, snub and black but worn to silver at the edges. Wren checked the serial number, but it'd already been filed off. He checked the breech and the magazine.

"Hollow-points, brass casing," the woman said. "That there's the NRA gun of the year, 2005."

"It's a beaut," Wren said, and tucked it into his waistband.

It took a few minutes for the Bitcoin transaction to go through, then a few more as the woman checked and double-checked it on her scrappy rubber-bound tablet computer.

At last she looked back up at Wren, holding up the truck's keys in one hand and a wedge of dirty bills wrapped with a rubber band in the other. "And if the po-lice scoop you up? What you gonna say about this vehicle's provenance?"

She stretched out the word provenance like it was hillbilly French.

"Found it by the side of the road," Wren said. "Must've just bloomed there like a mushroom, gun already in the glove box."

"I expect that's about what happened," she said, then handed over the keys and the grubby cash. Wren pocketed the bills, climbed into the truck and set off for the Viking's bar.

A rattling, shaky forty-minute drive followed. East along I-70 through the desert scrub, buttes scrolling by in the distance, cacti blooming a riot of purple flowers. Wren almost felt good.

The roadhouse lay just where Eustace had said, an adobe block with a CCTV camera and a small parking lot set out in the middle of nowhere. On the roof was a pink neon sign with a 'hussy' kicking her legs.

Wren rolled off the highway onto sandy gravel beyond the range of the camera. There were ten Viking bikes stationed out front in the middle of the day. Ten was a lot; at least that was one way to look at it. On the other hand, it didn't really compare to storming mujahideen camps in the caves of Afghanistan, one of a five-man squad against an army of terrorists.

He popped the door and stepped out. The sun beat down,

the desert was still. His head throbbed. From a quick survey, there was no sign of his Jeep. Either Eustace had lied or he was just too junior in the gang to understand how they worked.

Wren figured it was the latter.

Time to go.

He approached the roadhouse from the side, staying away from the camera. An AC vent in the clay wall ticked and dripped. He circled to the rear, where a couple of trash boxes buzzed with flies, beer crates lay in piles and a dog lay asleep in the meager shade, chained to a post.

It was an Alsatian and big, but with its ribs showing starkly. Wren cursed, reminded of Don Mica back in Mexico. He liked dogs, and the Vikings were starving this one just like the Don did, most likely to keep it mean.

He'd explicitly asked Eustace if there was a dog, and the big man had said no. They were going to have words about this at their first coin meeting.

Wren considered a retreat, a run over to the nearest Walgreens to buy steak, but he'd spent enough time on this already. Instead he padded softly over to the trash boxes, where the buzz of the flies grew stronger. He opened the first and a fog of hot fetid air rose up. He picked out a couple of pizza boxes and some takeout chicken buckets, dropped them on the floor and spread the contents.

The pizzas were pepperoni, about three slices' worth left over in crumbs and crusts, and there were shreds of chicken left on a twelve-pack of drumsticks in the bucket.

He tossed the meatiest to the dog. It mustered from its slumber as the bone bounced near its nose.

"Good boy," Wren called softly.

The dog looked at him, then sniffed at the chicken bone, then its lips pulled back in a snarl.

"There's more where that came from," Wren said, and

tossed a chunk of pizza. The snarl faded as the smell spread, then the dog wolfed up the slice. Next it went for the bone, then it strained against its chain with its head high, waiting for more.

Wren had plenty, tossing scraps as he smoothly advanced. He'd always been good at making friends.

8

ENFORCER

The back door opened with a creak, the sound covered by pumping heavy metal music from the front bar. Wren recognized Korn, a nu metal band from the early 2000s. Their single 'Dead Bodies Everywhere' raced ahead as he entered a greasy, filthy kitchen.

The floor was cracked terracotta tile, the walls were splashed with old black stains and the stainless steel worktop wasn't living up to its name. Stacks of pots and pans lay in the sink festering. A tall fridge-freezer stood against the near wall, the small door to its ice box hanging open, the power cut. Wren padded over to look inside.

It was filled with ammo boxes. A rudimentary armory. He opened the fridge-freezer's big door and found the shelving removed, replaced with several rifles and a shotgun. Now he smiled at the thought of spending a thousand dollars on the gun in his waistband.

He pulled the shotgun, a Remington Versa Max in desert camouflage colors. It was already loaded with 20-gauge lead buckshot; Wren pocketed another box of shells from the icebox. A swift reconnoiter of the kitchen cupboards turfed up several rolls of cash and a swatch of plastic zip-ties, which he pocketed then advanced toward the sound of thrashing metal.

Along a short corridor stood a swing door with a small glass porthole. It was dark and murky beyond, but Wren picked out the bar, the barman and a cluster of men sitting around a table in an open dance floor. Most were in leather jackets, though one wore a bright white wifebeater, all looking off to the left. Wren cracked the door and peered through the gap.

There was a low stage with spotlights, where two girls were dancing jerkily around a single silver pole. They were both naked but for dark metal collars around their necks, from which heavy-looking metal chains stretched down to eyelets in the floor.

Wren's eyes narrowed. That wasn't good. Of course, it was possible this was some kind of S&M show, all consensual with the girls getting compensated appropriately, but the more Wren watched, the less certain of that he felt.

The girls were thin, like the dog, and there was something strange about the expanses of pale skin on display. It took him a few seconds to distinguish between the rippling shadows cast by a tacky colored mirror ball, then he figured it out.

These girls had been beaten grossly. Their backs were marked with livid red weals, as if they'd been battered with a long, thin hammer head. Their chests and thighs were a mottled black and purple. Add to that, Wren felt pretty certain they were barely out of their teens.

His jaw tightened. Eustace hadn't said anything about this either, but Wren's mind cast back to what the enforcer had barked at him the night before, something about collars and cages.

Something about tenderizing the meat.

He'd figured that was just big talk, but now he

44

recalculated. He'd intended to go in non-lethal; maybe beat them up, load a few of their bikes into the Super Duty as compensation for the Jeep, then call the sheriffs in.

Now that no longer seemed nearly enough.

Now the starving dog out back seemed like the least of their crimes, because if there was one injustice Wren hated more than any other, it was human enslavement.

He pushed open the door and advanced.

In the dark and the sound, they didn't notice him coming. He reached the table and brought the Remington's grip swinging hard into the head of the man on the right with a great crack, knocking him from his chair.

Before anyone could react, Wren hammered the man on the left too, then stepped back and leveled the shotgun.

"The way I see it," he called in a loud bass voice, "the burst from this will take half of you. The rest I'll finish more slowly. Either that or we talk about your business model."

The men stared. Some slid their hands off the table; reaching for weapons, Wren figured. He tracked them but kept his eyes on the man in the wifebeater.

Up close, he recognized him. This was the enforcer from last night; shadowed with tattoos and rippling with oversized muscle. He didn't reach for a weapon like some of the others, but then he didn't need to; he was still wearing his brass knuckles. Wren imagined the length of those knuckles would perfectly match the marks on the girls' backs.

"The comedian," the enforcer said, his face hard. "I wondered if we'd see you again."

"Not in a cage," Wren said.

"Not yet, anyhow," said the enforcer, and his eyes flicked to the left over Wren's shoulder.

Wren had been expecting it, and sidestepped sharply to the right. A nail-studded baseball bat swung through the air where his head had been, followed by the barman, staggering as his blow didn't land.

The table burst into action as weapons whipped up from pockets and holsters, but none got off a shot faster than Wren.

Sparks burst from the shotgun's barrel and the table erupted as lead pellets shattered bottles, chewed into wood and obliterated flesh. Men screamed and fell, their bodies shredded. Wren took a step back, angled right and let rip with the second barrel, spraying a slightly wider halo of lead at the three men still standing. One took the bulk of the blast in his chest and was instantly cored through, while the other two took the scatter and dropped from a dozen wounds each, clutching their arms and faces.

The barman swung the bat at Wren again, but Wren was ready again, bringing the shotgun to block the blow like a bo staff. Nails clanked off the barrel, and Wren dropped his right hand off the grip, pulled the Rorbaugh and fired point blank into the barman's head.

His head exploded backwards.

Then something crashed against Wren's temple.

He fell sideways, both the pistol and the shotgun dropping from his grip. His hip thumped off the pulverized table, his hands failed to catch him off the backs of tumbling chairs and he hit the ground amongst the bodies of fallen bikers. His vision blurred and he almost blacked out, but instinct and muscle memory made him roll, which saved his back from the enforcer's spine-powdering stomp.

Now the enforcer stood over Wren with his fists raised, brass knuckles sparkling in the mirror ball light. Wren's head rung like a tolled bell, and he realized he'd just taken a hit from one of those knuckles.

He kicked out automatically, catching the enforcer's ankle just hard enough to send him staggering backward and buy Wren the time to surge to his feet.

He met the enforcer on the sticky dance floor, with heavy metal thundering and bodies flailing underfoot. The enforcer was jacked on adrenaline already, his eyes flaring wide, and now there was a Luger 9mm in his right fist. Wren got one hand on his pale wrist and the other on the gun and yanked, aiming to snap a finger and strip the weapon.

The weapon discharged sideways and the barrel grew unbearably hot, but Wren didn't let go. For a moment they wrestled, then the enforcer sent a headbutt at Wren's face. Wren saw it coming and tucked his chin in, flattening the guy's nose across the top of his skull.

The Luger pulled clear with the shock and clattered along the floor. The enforcer bounced back onto the balls of his feet, blood pouring down his face and staining his wifebeater vest, but showing no signs of backing down.

"Not used to a target that punches back, are you?" Wren asked through gritted teeth. The enforcer raised his fists and Wren did the same.

Brass knuckles flashed as the enforcer launched a blistering attack, but Wren sidestepped just as quickly and launched a high elbow toward the man's neck. He blocked it with his shoulder and spun, sending a low answering hook into Wren's belly. It almost caught Wren's solar plexus, but he rolled most of the impact and sent an instinctive snap kick across the enforcer's chest.

It hit hard and the man staggered back, almost tripping over one of his fallen comrades. Wren followed with a hook-jab-uppercut combination that the enforcer weaved through, throwing his own jabs in return that caught only air.

"Who are you with?" he rasped, spraying blood now. "FBI?"

"I'm freelance," Wren panted, and sent another snap kick. The enforcer caught it on bristling elbows, knocking him briefly onto his heels, and Wren took the chance to dive at his ankles, locking them together and toppling him to the floor in a wrestler's hold.

The enforcer tried to spin free, but Wren flipped and swiftly worked a heel hook lock on his left ankle, twisting it across his body and up into his armpit. He ignored the enforcer's frenzied kicks and screams and pulled until the knee hyper-extended with a meniscus-bursting pop.

The enforcer shrieked but somehow slithered free, climbed to one foot and sent a huge right haymaker at Wren's head. The ferocity of the attack surprised Wren, but he managed to sway just far enough back for the enforcer to over-balance.

He caught himself on his left foot, but the knee gave way immediately and he fell into Wren's waiting arms. Wren wrapped his right arm this time, twisted it over his own shoulder then snapped down hard.

The enforcer's elbow shattered and he bellowed.

Wren released his wrist. The enforcer hopped and panted. It was a wonder he was still standing.

"Those girls," Wren said, barely out of breath and pointing at the stage, where the girls were now huddled close together with the pole between them. "Are you keeping them in a cage?"

The enforcer's eyes lit on something on the floor, and too late, Wren realized it was the Luger. The man dived. Wren had no choice but to send out a field-goal kick with his right foot. The enforcer's head lined up perfectly, Wren's foot swept in and the two connected with a meaty, bone-jarring crunch.

The enforcer's neck jerked the wrong way and he hit the ground with a slap, already dead.

Wren stood for a moment, looking over the carnage he'd wrought. Nobody was moving, at least not much, though the girls on the stage were shuddering.

"It's going to be OK," he said, as gently as he could. "You're safe now."

Then he brought out his zip ties and set to work hog-tying the men who were still alive. There were a couple of questions he needed answering before he called in the sheriffs.

9

CALLED TO ACCOUNT

The Brazen Hussy was dark and silent, bar the occasional groan of a Viking, after Wren ripped the plug out of the jukebox's socket.

No more Korn. No more rotating mirror ball. The girls were gone, their iron collars removed and their pockets full of Viking cash. Wren had brought them something to drink, and found them clothes, but they hadn't spoken much. He'd asked some questions, but maybe their English wasn't good enough, or maybe they just didn't want to stay there a second longer. He couldn't blame them, not after what the Vikings had done.

"Leave town," he'd said. "Go far away from here, at least for a while. Stay together. Stay safe. Can you do that?"

They'd nodded then run. They hadn't trusted him. That was understandable.

Now he stood in the midst of the bar, surveying the damage.

Five men were dead, three were circling the drain and three more, including the barman, wouldn't be fighting fit for months. All the living were hog-tied and gagged. In another life, their deaths might have bothered Wren, but not now.

50

These men had made their decision the night they'd come for him, and so had he, like he had so many times before.

This outcome was on their heads.

Wren picked one of the older bikers, a guy with a gristly beard and shotgun pellet wounds spread across his right shoulder and chest, and leaned down.

"Where do you keep the girls?" he asked.

The guy cursed up at him. He was no Eustace, that was for sure. He was harder, a patch member.

"It's not here." Wren put one foot on the man's shoulder and pressed. The biker's jaw tightened but he couldn't prevent a moan escaping his lips. "I already checked the back. There's no cages, no cells. So where are they? Where's the operation based?"

"Go suck a-"

Wren pressed down harder. "I already sent five of your friends to the big roadhouse in the sky. Do you really want to follow them over a two-bit human trafficking gig?"

The man opened his mouth to speak, then abruptly a divot chipped out of the floor by his head and a loud gunshot filled the bar. A fraction of a second passed then another gunshot followed, spraying the man's brains across the vinyl.

Wren was already in motion. He dived, rolled and came up behind a fallen table top, pulling his Rorbaugh and beading in. There was a young man in what looked to be a three-piece suit standing behind the bar, which momentarily baffled Wren. He'd already cleared the whole structure, and there was nobody else.

Shots thumped into the table top. Wren rose and fired back, taking the man in the right shoulder on the second shot. He slammed into the liquor bottles arrayed along the back bar, shattering glass and spilling spirits, then fell.

Wren circled the bar, swaying back as the man in the suit

fired from the floor; six more shots until his pistol clicked empty.

"You're out of ammo," Wren said, and stepped back into view. The man was clean-shaven, slim and clearly terrified. "Who are you?"

"I'm... I'm in accounts."

Wren frowned. "You're an accountant?"

"I do the books."

"What books?"

"Uh, for the bar."

Wren regarded him. "You do the books for the bar. In a three-piece suit. Just for this bar?"

"I do, uh..."

"More than the bar, right?"

"I, uh, I can't-"

"You know about the trafficking?"

The guy's eyes went so wide Wren thought they might pop out, just as his skin blanched pale. He'd be no use to Wren passed out from shock, so he tabled that line of questioning.

"Where did you come from?"

The young man nodded toward the front door. "I just arrived. I come once a week."

Wren considered. "So you're an accountant with a gun. That already tells me a lot. You saw a situation here and you thought you'd insert yourself, but pretty inexpertly. That's manslaughter against one of your own already. Why fire at all?"

"I, uh, I don't know. It seemed like a good idea."

Wren shook his head. Everything about the Vikings screamed amateur hour. He heaved a breath. "Listen. I don't care about you, or about that guy you just executed. Maybe you're neck deep in whatever bullshit these bikers were up to, maybe you're not, but I need to know right now. People trafficking and enslavement, do those ring any bells?"

The guy blinked and looked wildly side to side like he was looking for a way out. Wren pointed the Rorbaugh at his stomach to focus his attention.

"That's a tell, just like almost passing out. Tell me now, where do the Vikings keep the girls, or I put a bullet in your belly and we watch your lunch leak out."

The guy's mouth opened, closed, then opened again. "You'll never catch them," he said.

"Catch who, more Vikings? I caught plenty already."

The accountant shook his head. "I already warned them before I fired. They'll be coming here in force. They're clearing the warehouse right now, and-"

That got Wren's attention, and he stepped closer, put one foot on the young man's shoulder and squeezed. "What warehouse?"

10

WAREHOUSE

I n forty-five minutes Wren was there, after a thirty-mile rush along I-70 then another five miles off-road along gravelly tracks into the desert.

He'd passed incoming sheriff's vehicles from Orangeville along the way, sirens and lights blaring. He'd called them in, but that wasn't his business anymore.

The Vikings' warehouse lay before him.

It sat in a shallow valley flanked by sandstone ridges and low bluff mesas, encircled by a razor-wire fence. It looked brand new; a squarish, flat-roofed, windowless structure in corrugated aluminum. The razor wire posts were new too, the lines glinting rust-free beneath three tall security lamps. In all there was only a single entrance, barred with hefty plate-metal roll shutters.

Six bikes with Viking skull decals were parked in the lot. That was strange, and didn't seem to match what the accountant had said about delivering a warning.

Why hadn't they come back to the Hussy?

Wren opened the window wide and took a long pull on the hot desert air. He smelled freshly laid tar, desert sap and a high sweet stink that took him back to a field hospital for local villagers in Syria, south of Palmyra.

He'd been working a CIA psy-ops propaganda campaign with rebel Kurdish forces against the national Ba'athist Syrian Arab Army, looking for an informant. The camp had been filthy, filled with people lying sick and exhausted in makeshift tents and on gurneys, fuming off old sweat and despair, excrement and urine. Floating over all those foul smells, though, had been the saccharine stink of baby formula.

It was ever-present in refugee camps, where UN workers tossed it out in huge bales of silvery packets for people to fight over. Adults drank it, babies drank it; the sour stench of dehydrated milk floated in the air wherever a large mass of humans were trapped together in poor conditions.

Now here it was in the middle of the Utah desert.

Wren blinked sweat out of his eyes. His heart hammered in his chest. The accountant hadn't mentioned the scale of the operation, but Wren knew just from the smell: this was massive. There had to be a hundred people caged within that warehouse, waiting to be shipped on.

There was nothing Wren hated worse. His knuckles tightened on the wheel. Maybe they were waiting for him inside. Maybe they were watching him right now.

Time to find out.

He flicked on the radio, cranked up the volume and gunned the van off the track and onto the scrub, accelerating through clusters of sage and low whipple cacti. Halfway there he reached fifty miles an hour, another twenty yards and he hit the outer razor wire fence. It pulled taut, strained against its pilings then snapped across the grille. At eighty yards he realized his trajectory was off: he was going to hit the shutter's side column, likely reinforced with thick rebar, and get himself splattered on the inside windshield.

He reacted fast, a switchback yank on the wheel which sent the Ford screaming across the sandy blacktop and against its own momentum. The truck hydroplaned to the right on burning rubber for a giddy second, ate up a four-foot dodge to the side in a squall of burning brake fluid then hit the roll shutters head on. The front grille punched the plate metal clear out of its housing with a tremendous bark.

Wren rocked forward on impact, the seatbelt snapped hard across his ribs, then he lurched back into the seat as the shutter whiplashed upward like a matador's cape and the Ford careened into pitch black within. His floodlights illuminated a mass of wire cages to the left and tall rows of metal shelving ahead, then he was in amongst them.

The shelves hammered off the Ford like bodies in a crowd, ripping a mangled path through four rows before his momentum finally stalled and the wrecking ball of his vehicle finally rocked to a halt.

Wren took a breath. Bruce Springsteen was singing 'Born in the USA' at full volume on the radio, suddenly unbearably loud in the contained space. He kicked the door open and slithered into darkness, running low away from the truck's island of sound and light, accompanied by a sudden cascade of incoming gunfire.

Wren kept count as he sprinted for cover, four blasts that echoed maddeningly off the aluminum walls and roof. He stopped running at the end of a long row of twenty-foot-tall shelving, holding the Rorbaugh high in his right hand.

"Born!" yelled Springsteen from fifty yards away.

Another shot came and pinged somewhere near the truck. Wren edged around the huge shelf, keeping his profile hidden by the stacked boxes, and scanned the dark interior. The Ford's headlights were the sole illumination, radio blaring like a wounded animal panting at the end of a rampage.

To the left lay cages.

Lit only by the red glow from the Ford's taillights, they filled the left half of the warehouse, made of diamond-lattice steel wire and standing seven feet tall. There was only one thing you needed cages like that for.

They were empty, bar a tawdry mass of sleeping bags, mylar blankets and clothing wadded in the darkness. Wren cursed under his breath.

He was too late. The warning had come and they'd shipped everyone out.

Another shot zipped through the dark, punching through boxes on the rack nearest him and trilling off the metal frame. He'd been spotted, but the muzzle flash of the sniper gave the guy away too. He was up on the cages somewhere, standing in what looked to be a guard tower, using a long rifle that was barely visible in the faint light from the truck.

Wren ran quick numbers; the guy had already fired five times now, and a standard long gun packed three to five shells in the magazine. That would make him due a reload.

Wren charged.

A shot rang and sparked just to his right. Maybe a six-shell option or a second shooter. 'Born in the USA' ended and the radio host drawled into darkness as Wren plummeted through the cages' open door.

A seventh shot came, closing the range now, and Wren felt the bruised air to his left. Had to be a large capacity mag. He raised the Rorbaugh and fired up into darkness, five discharges as he ran, until he was standing near directly underneath the guy.

A thud came from above as he fell.

High ground wasn't always the best.

Wren spun and moved.

Another shot came abruptly, skittering sparks off the cement floor where he'd been standing. He beelined for the cage chokepoint; the door. The guy out there would know it too, and a second shot ripped through the air, homing on Wren in the red glow of the taillights. There was no time left, and Wren had to act fast. Plays ran through his head. The Rorbaugh had plenty in the magazine.

He locked his stance and fired four times straight through the cage wire wall, hitting the Ford's taillights and killing them. The cages fell into darkness, giving Wren cover, but within seconds an answering hail of bullets tore through the air where he'd been.

He sprinted through the cage entrance and circled toward the sniper. All that mattered now was speed and silence. Around the Ford he went, stopping beside the headlight beams and firing into the shelving ahead.

The sniper fired back but missed; that was his mistake. Wren's muzzle flashes were obscured by the bright headlights, but not the sniper's. His shots pinpointed him perfectly.

Wren's blood pumped and he sprinted on tiptoes, undetectable beneath the riot of the radio. Maybe he could take the guy conscious and get some answers. He circled one of the shelves and saw him lying there, proned out with the rifle still targeting the truck.

Wren was about to leap but a second too soon the guy must have sensed him and jolted upright, trained the rifle and fired. The shot whiskered by and Wren returned fire. He took the guy in the cheek, drawing a red dot, and back down he slumped.

Wren kneeled by his side and put a hand on his throat. Dead at once.

He listened for a long second. Now Meatloaf was crooning for all he was worth. No more shots came. No movement. That was two men, when there should be six on sentry, judging by the bikes outside. That left four more.

It didn't take long to find them.

11

PROFESSIONALS

Wren found the warehouse lights by the door and flicked them up. They blinked on musically across the warehouse, filling the cavernous space with harsh white illumination. He scanned the cages and shelves and was immediately drawn to the guardhouse.

He climbed a ladder, stalked along a rooftop patrol way above the cages and found the man he'd killed, alongside two other bodies.

Wren had only killed one of them.

He knelt beside the group, amped by adrenaline and hearing now the drip of blood through the cage roof like a drum roll. The man Wren had shot didn't look like a Viking at all. He was pale with short blond hair, tall and solid in all black like a special ops tactical Marine. Wren checked his pockets but there was nothing, not even a phone.

A professional?

That was bad news.

The other two wore faded leather jackets with the Viking logo on the back, and were big like Eustace, but full patch members. Wren rolled one and saw two stained holes in the chest, one through the head.

Definitely these were not Wren's wild shots out of the dark. This was an execution up close and personal, from someone the guy had known and trusted. Possible explanations raced through his head, but none covered all the bases. He needed more data.

He jogged along the walkway to an elevated office tucked in the upper northwest corner. From the doorway he looked back out, picking out more dead Vikings gunned down amongst the shelving.

He'd stumbled into something bigger. A cleanup operation?

Through the door, the office had been stripped. Cables sprayed where tower computers should have been, monitors sat forlornly, there were pale marks on the walls where planners would have hung and a filing cabinet hollowed out.

In a corner, clutching a Glock and surrounded by bullet holes in the drywall lay another Viking. He was a patch member with plenty of tats, marked by three random shots to the body that had been chased by two in the chest, one in the head.

The scale of the cleanup clicked into place.

Wren had seen hits like this before, cartels mopping up their local partners after an operation went south. Dead men tell no tales. He wound back the record to the moment in his head, to when the accountant must have called it in.

Wren had hit the Hussy and overpowered every Viking there, and this group had assumed he was not a single man, but a government strike team. Their response had been to empty the cages and burn their entire local operation.

They'd cleaned up the Vikings and exported the 'human cargo', leaving no evidence behind.

Except.

Wren's chest went cold.

He checked the pockets of the dead Viking, but they were

empty. He ran back down to the floor level and checked every other Viking he could find, including one crushed beneath the shelving his Ford had knocked over.

All their pockets had been emptied. No phones, no scraps of paper, nothing. By the roll shutter entrance he saw twelve gallon jugs of gasoline, and realized what he'd interrupted. This cartel, or whatever they were, had slaughtered the Vikings and was just about to burn the whole warehouse down. Nothing would've been left.

But something was left.

Evidence remained. The Vikings from the Hussy had to know about the warehouse too, and the group running it. Their phones would have calls and numbers and chat logs. But Wren had brought local sheriffs down on the Vikings; they'd all be locked up in the local PD right now.

Did that mean..?

His mouth went dry. It was possible. If this wider organization were anything like the cartels Wren knew, they wouldn't let a little thing like a police station stand in the way of cleaning up their trail.

They were professionals with incredible resources and the ability and the will to rub out local partners on a moment's notice, trafficking hundreds of enslaved people at a time, and he'd never even heard they existed.

This operation had just gotten out of control.

Sprinting now, he found his Jeep in a motor pool on the other side of the shelves. It was shredded with bullets and the engine block was already gone, the dash gutted for electronics. The passenger seat was empty and his kids' pictures gone.

All that seemed very distant now.

He dropped back into his Ford Super Duty. The engine was still running and he cranked it into reverse, pulling away from the shelving and shooting back out through the dangling plate metal shutter and onto desert scrub.

If an attack on the Vikings in police custody was coming, it would be soon, and a hundred miles lay between him and the nearest police department in Price. Wren didn't care about their lives, but he needed to know what they knew.

Already he was behind. He needed to get a warning through.

Racing at eighty back along a gravel track through the red sands of Utah, he called a number he never thought he'd call again.

12

HUMPHREYS

"Yes," came a male voice on the other end of the line. You got nothing else when you called through to the switchboard of the Special Activities Center of the CIA.

"This is Christopher Wren, codeword clockjaguar3, looking for Director Gerald Humphreys."

There was a moment, then a polite, "Please hold."

The tracking on his phone line would have already begun. Doubtless his name was on blacklists up and down the nation's intelligence agencies already, each one usually a walled garden desperate to hold in its own secrets. They'd make an exception for Wren.

Thirty seconds passed, then a voice came on the line. Director Humphreys, the by-the-book king of his own government fiefdom, and chief oversight officer on Wren's activities for the last five years.

"Wren," he said. "We had a deal. What do you want?"

There was nothing much to say to that. They'd already have his location by now, much good it would do them. There wouldn't be enough cell towers nearby to triangulate him precisely, maybe they'd just get a rough spread of a few thousand square miles.

Basically, they knew he was in Utah.

"This is a sidebar to our deal," Wren said, dismissing so much in a few words. "I'm not calling to talk about the past. I've got a new urgent issue here, and a request."

"A request? You abandoned multiple intelligence operations midway through, you don't get to make requests. Worse yet, I've been looking into the cult of personality you've been building for the last twenty years, Christopher. The 'Foundation'? When were you going to announce to your colleagues that you were a cult leader?"

Wren frowned. "How do you know about the Foundation?"

"Don't worry about how I know. Worry about the treason charges this exposes you to. Wherever you are, stay right there. I'll send someone to pick you up. You built a private cult army, and now you're going to pay the-"

"It's not a cult," Wren interrupted. "I'm not a cult leader. There's nothing illegal about it, nothing I needed to announce. It's a support group, Gerald, that's all. But listen, the thing I need to-"

"A support group? Do you really think I'll buy that line of bullshit? Who the hell even are you?"

"It's not like that," Wren answered, tightly controlling his anger. "But it doesn't matter right now. Listen to me, Gerald; I think I've uncovered a major terror threat to the homeland here, and I need to get a warning out on an imminent attack, plus a new status so I can take action on the ground."

That took Humphreys a few seconds to absorb. "Terror attack? And a new status? Wren, you're so far out I'd be raising your profile if I dunked you in a black site for the rest of your life. There's no status."

"I want AWOP," said Wren, then spelled it. "A-W-O-P, Agent WithOut Portfolio."

"What?" Now there was danger in Humphrey's tone. "There hasn't been a freelance Intelligence agent in fifty years."

"Forty-five," Wren corrected. "Those were Cold War sleepers, undercover with Russia for decades, but it's basically what I've been doing for twenty years already. This will just formalize things. The attack's coming within-"

"I don't care if it's five centuries," Humphreys spat. "I'm sending three squads after you as we speak. Your best option is to quit running and turn yourself in."

"I'm not running. I'm going to the site, but I'm thinking this group will hit it before I arrive, so-"

"I don't buy any of this, Wren. What am I supposed to think, when you deny running this 'Foundation' then call in a major terrorist threat? For all I know, the threat is you."

Wren gritted his teeth. This was going the wrong way. "So talk to the FBI or the National Guard and send those squads. Borrow some Black Hawks too, stock them with Marines, I'll lead them right to the target location. I believe the attack's coming within the hour, most likely at the police department in Price, central Utah. They'll be holding members of the Viking biker gang, and I expect this organization is going to wipe everyone there out to silence the Vikings."

That stopped Humphreys for a moment. It was such specific intelligence that he couldn't just dismiss it. "What kind of setup is this? Is this a threat?"

"This has nothing to do with me. We're looking at a big organization here, Gerald, human trafficking on a large scale, maybe bigger than anything we've seen domestically so far. The Vikings were their local partners, and I just found six of them dead at a warehouse being used for human trafficking in the desert. Now the larger group is clearing house and wiping out the evidence. I expect a paramilitary response at Price. The level of professionalism tops anything we've seen with the cartels, Gerald. You need to get eyes in the sky scouring the desert for a semi truck transporting up to one hundred trafficked people. You also need to get those Black Hawks to Price PD and lock it down. They're not prepared for what's coming."

"What's coming? How can I trust any of this?" Humphreys asked. "You're a confirmed liar, Wren, and with your pedigree?"

That stung, and they both knew what it meant; the childhood Wren never talked about in the Pyramid, the mass suicide he'd barely survived at 11 years old. It didn't matter how young he'd been at the time, some still believed he'd been complicit.

"So let this be the proof. I'll bring them down with or without your help, but I can't protect Price if I'm not there."

Silence followed, apart from the SuperDuty's engine and wind whipping through the open window. Humphreys would be weighing the threat, likely chewing on his mustache. Despite the way Wren had left the agency, he'd been an exemplary agent.

"A trafficking operation in the desert," said Humphreys. "A hit on Price, Utah."

"That's it. Find that truck and make the police department secure. Tell them I'm coming. Those Vikings are witnesses to this terror group and we need them alive."

Humphreys chewed. "I'll talk to Price. We'll see."

13

PRICE

Wren gripped the wheel like he was throttling a snake, counting the minutes and miles as he raced west. Bare desert raced by either side, the windows down and a rain-smelling wind blowing dust into his eyes.

His mind charged ahead, running calculations. Over three hours had passed since he'd kicked things off at the Hussy, and the adrenaline buzz was fading, leaving his body aching from the desert beating and his head rolling from that brass knuckle punch in the head.

He angled the rearview mirror; his head was swollen on that side and his left eye was bloodshot. He cursed. A month on the road had dulled his reactions.

That was just a taste of the family life he'd set himself up for; losing his instincts, getting soft.

His phone sat on the dash. His father-in-law, Charlie, would be expecting a call, but Wren couldn't face that now. Not with hundreds of lives on the line, rattling in the back of some iron semi truck trailer passing through the desert, with nothing good lying ahead of them.

Wren gritted his teeth. This had always been the choice,

between his own family and justice for others. He'd never been good at making the distinction.

Price came on fast.

At ten minutes out confirmation came in from Humphreys as a text message; it had been sent a half hour earlier, but he'd finally regained cell tower signal.

NOTHING ON THE TRAILER TRUCK. I WARNED PRICE AND SENT REINFORCEMENTS. THEY HAVE YOUR VIKINGS, BUT THERE'S NO SIGN OF AN ATTACK.

Wren wasn't surprised about the first part. Finding a single truck in the desert was probably an impossible task. As for the second part, time would tell.

A sign for Price whipped by.

Wren brought up Google maps on his phone and zoomed in on Price PD. The station was a single-story new build situated on a residential dead-end, backed by low hills of old construction dirt. A strike force might struggle to attack from the front, especially if the sheriffs had put out a vehicle barricade fifty yards out, as Wren would have.

But across those hills? A strike team could get in and out unobserved.

A creeping fear rushed up his spine. He found the number for the police department and placed the call, but nobody answered.

His chest went cold.

It was happening right now.

He tore through downtown Price topping a hundred, cannoning into a neighborhood of residential streets, beyond which lay the low brown hills. At the sign for Price PD he spun the wheel so hard he almost tipped the pick-up.

Ahead lay a cordon of five police cars, broken open down the middle. One of them had a crumpled, smoking hood where it had taken the brunt from a much heavier ram vehicle. Two officers lay on the ground that he could see, not moving.

Wren flew through the gap and hit the brakes as he breasted the department's red brick front. The building's metal and glass front had been shattered inward by a ram vehicle, but there was no sign of it now, or the strike team.

Wren killed the engine and sprang out of the Ford, Rorbaugh drawn, one in the chamber. Cubic skitters of glass on the floor showed the treads of the ram vehicle, a broad wheelbase with thick tires like a Humvee.

Wren ran through the crunching glass. A tall desk for the duty sergeant dominated the lobby, overseeing rows of plastic seating that had been shoved into a chevron. A water fountain jug lay on the floor, magazines were scattered, and there were bodies.

Three dead police officers lay on the floor. Wren ran by with the Rorbaugh held high, registering double shots to the chest, one in the head on each victim. The rounds were placed neat and tight, signaling a professional hit despite what must have been a chaotic assault.

Wren's heart pounded. He'd been on hundreds of strikes before this but the edge never went away. Thick wafts of gunpowder smoke hung like swamp gas in the air. Two doors hung open and Wren broke left.

An office spread before him, with desks in rows, bullet holes in the walls and five more bodies.

Wren saw red.

You didn't get to just do this. Not to the police, not in America.

He backed out and sped to the second door, a secure door of thick metal that hung on one hinge now, with blackened scorch marks where an explosive had chewed through its steel frame. Beyond lay a concrete corridor with a few bright posters explaining the after-effects of meth.

At the end of the corridor he found the cells, crammed full of the dead.

It was the Vikings. Their black jackets lay in spreading pools of blood. The air hung heavy with gunpowder smoke and the AC whirred hard to clear it. Wren counted eleven bodies, mowed down behind the bars like sitting ducks.

Wren judged from the splatter pattern of blood and the tight grouping of bullet holes in the far wall that there'd been three men with automatic weapons and they'd just let rip. Judging from the carnage, they'd expended hundreds of rounds, meaning they'd stopped to reload several times.

The door to the cell hung open and Wren pushed through, delving into pockets, but every Viking he checked had nothing. He spun back and ran to the evidence locker, but it had already been raided; plastic trays and baggies strewn everywhere.

No phones. No evidence.

On a desk nearby he saw the paperwork for the Vikings, and an officer on the floor beside it with a bullet hole in her head. Miraculously, she was still breathing.

Wren dropped to one knee. "Stay with me," he said, checking her for other injuries. He moved her jacket lapel, and saw the familiar two shots in her chest, blood soaking through the blue fabric.

"Help's coming," Wren said, feeling his rage surge. "You'll be OK."

She breathed out then didn't breathe in again.

Wren ran back to the Vikings and surveyed the scene. All dead. Whoever had done this, they'd been fast and thorough. There was nothing left to go on. No leads.

Then Wren heard it, even above the whine of the AC. The sound of distant helicopter blades.

He kicked through a heavy metal door in back, which led to a changing room for the jail guards, lined with lockers.

One officer lay sprawled facedown on the floor beside another metal door with three open deadbolts, beyond which lay the parking lot.

Wren dropped to one knee by the dead officer. The entry wound in the back of his head was small and scorched, which helped explain how this assault had gone so smooth and fast.

This officer had opened the rear door and let his killers in. He'd turned his back to open the inner door, and they'd put him out of his rat-bastard misery at close quarters. A squad had started flaming the Vikings, even as the ram vehicle struck the front. They'd attacked on two fronts simultaneously, with a man on the inside.

Price PD hadn't stood a chance.

He checked the traitor officer's pockets, but of course his phone was gone. Wren cursed and pushed out through the open door into the lot. The air was clear of gunpowder smoke here, but that came as no relief.

Sirens were drawing in, reinforcements from another sheriff's station, probably Orangeville, along with the low, deep thrum of helicopters approaching from the west. Moments later twin Black Hawks appeared over the horizon, getting larger every second.

Wren cursed again.

This looked terrible for him. The Vikings were dead. Price PD had been slaughtered, and now Wren's fingerprints were everywhere. The warehouse full of people had been moved on and there was on onward trail.

He considered his two choices for maybe three seconds: stick around to explain all this to trigger-happy Marines backed by the CIA's trigger-happy Director of Special Activities, or don't.

He didn't like his chances with the former. Humphreys would hate him now more than ever.

That only left option number two.

14

TURNAROUND

W ren ran for the low brown hills, took cover and sprinted south. At the end he pushed through a copse of oak trees then emerged onto a quiet residential road.

At the second house along, with a rusted RV and two pickups on the drive, he strode to a beat-up Dodge Ram. He was in luck; the door was unlocked and the keys were in the sun visor. The engine coughed to life, and he rolled out smoothly, heading back south.

The Black Hawks hovered over the PD, deploying Marines down fast ropes. Wren backtracked the way he'd come, mind spinning as he tried to puzzle through what he'd seen.

Back in the warehouse the size of this organization had been a rational but distant fear; now it was real and undeniable, powerful and ruthless enough to slaughter a whole police station just to get to the Vikings.

This was big. It was ugly. At least one cop in Price PD had been crooked, which meant bribes and a network of influence that spread who-knew how far. It surely involved more than just the hundred or so souls they'd shipped out of the warehouse a couple of hours ago.

Wren placed the call to Humphreys as he traveled east at the speed limit. As he passed through CIA verification, a steady stream of emergency vehicles tore by heading for Price, blue lights flashing.

Humphreys answered.

"Where the hell are you, Wren?" he shouted by way of greeting.

"Heading back to the warehouse, Gerald. I know how this looks. I know you're going to-"

"You don't know anything, you sick son of a bitch," Humphreys interrupted. "What we're seeing here, it's too much, Wren. I knew you had a chip on your shoulder, sore about your wife shipping out, but going Unabomber on us?"

Wren blinked. He hadn't expected Humphreys to know about Loralei and the kids. They must have been watching him. "That's why I'm calling. This wasn't me, Humphreys. I'm the one who warned you about it!"

"So you're a sadist," fumed Humphreys. "It's not a warning when you call me as the hit's going down. It's not enough, how you left things in New York? Now you're bringing us all down with you. Just what is your endgame here?"

Wren squeezed the wheel harder. He tried to think of a way through. Everything Humphreys had just said would check out. They had him at the scene, with prior knowledge and a motive, plus a secret 'cult' willing to follow his orders.

It was a perfect storm. His troubles of a day ago seemed positively sunny by comparison.

"This wasn't me, Humphreys. I'll find the people who did it and wrap them up with a bow."

"Bullshit. You're having a psychotic break, Christopher.

Come in, we can help. They've got medicine these days that'll keep you high for the rest of your life."

"I'll give you the warehouse."

"Your warehouse? We'll just find whatever you want us to." A second's pause. "You shouldn't have screwed with me here, Wren. We're coming with everything we've got. You're going to regret it."

The line went dead.

Wren stared out the windshield.

The turnaround was fast. He knew he should run there and then. Break north for the border, get into Canada and take a crab boat across the Bering Strait. He could be in some tiny Inuit burg off the east coast of good old mother Russia within a few months. That could be his life.

Except there were lives on the line here, and he couldn't just walk away. A hundred-plus pitiful souls ferried out on a semi, heading God knew where. His Foundation would be left in shambles without their leader, a hundred lost souls unraveling without the coin system to structure their lives. Maybe he'd never see his wife and kids again.

He couldn't run. He didn't have it in him.

He had to make this right, and there was only one possible place left to pick up the trail.

15

CAGE

By 11 a.m. Wren was back at the Vikings' warehouse. The oblong entrance hung wide open like an open mouth, and the red roll shutter lay on the bare blacktop like its severed tongue.

Wren stopped the Dodge by the entrance and went inside.

Silence reigned.

There had to be something here. They'd cleared the warehouse in only an hour or two; how thorough could they have been?

Wren started with the shelving, pulling down box after box and spilling their contents. Soon the floor was coated in a foot-thick layer of everything a large-scale human trafficking organization would need: cartons of disposable burner phones with non-consecutive SIM cards; box after box of MRE Meals Ready to Eat; giant tubs of vitamin pills and fish-oil capsules; bottled water, mylar heat blankets and cushions; clothing in all sizes and for all ages; thousands of boxes of baby formula, medicine and first aid gear.

Wren took a handful of burner phones and kept searching.

The fog of baby formula and human waste hung in the air. After an hour, with hunger pangs tearing at his belly, Wren peeled the seal off one of the MREs and ate it cold as he moved on to the warehouse's motor pool.

There were four vehicles: a sheriff's car, a white panel van, an old beater truck and his bullet-torn Jeep. Nearby, in a chemical barrel being used as a fire pit, he found ashes: some rags of clothing, some fragments of paper, and a small, singed corner with just a fleck of bright red crayon. Wren recognized it; his foot from one of his kids' drawings.

He set the empty meal tray down on the beater's roof and moved to the bodies. He'd already checked them once and found all their pockets empty; now he took photos of the three professionals, in case he got access to NCIC or Nlets and ran a facial recognition search.

No leads.

One place remained.

Wren stood in front of the cage's wire mesh wall. It filled half the warehouse, stretching away in a rumpled landscape of sleeping bags, dirty clothing, mylar blankets and upended cots.

It sickened him.

The lives of enslaved people were filled with brutish violence, humiliation and death. A single trafficked human could sell for a hundred thousand dollars, making the slave trade a gold mine, and one that had never gone away.

Wren knew as much from personal experience. In the Pyramid he'd only been a child, but they'd still put him in a cage and treated him like a slave. He'd done manual labor all day, every day, as far back as he could remember. He'd been beaten. He'd been humiliated. He'd almost died.

Looking into this cage brought all that back. Sweat ran down his back and his heart rate sped up.

He strode through the open gate.

The warehouse lights were bright, but his intense focus shrank the world down like a spotlight in a pitch-black cave.

76

Moving swiftly and efficiently, Wren rifled through every thread of clothing, bedding and mylar. He scanned every scratch, indentation and blemish in the cement floor, looking for the secret places.

There were always secrets. Even in the Nazi concentration camps, where the slightest infraction was punished by instant death at the hands of the SS, inmates had found ways to record their experiences and hide them away. Some had even stolen cameras to capture images of the truth; not with any hope of saving themselves, but for posterity. They buried them, or hid them in drainpipes, or slotted them under roof tiles and into fence pipes, or secreted them in the lime of mass burial pits.

After forty minutes he found it.

In the middle of the floor, the raw cement flooring was broken by an embedded power socket, and within one of the plug pin holes lay a twist of yellowed paper.

Someone had inserted it.

Wren took it out carefully, careful not to rip it. The paper was thin, like a tissue, and he unfurled it gently.

It wasn't what he'd expected. It was a receipt from a convenience store, printed in faded blue ink. It had no address, but there was a phone number which Wren recognized as the area code for Chicago. One item was listed, 'Discount Flowers, $2.99'. A two-word message had been scrawled across it in what had to be blood.

SAVE WENDY

In the corner there was a date, September 27. Wren did the quick calculation.

Eleven months earlier, and half the country away in Chicago.

He let out a breath. Eleven months meant this was most likely a dead trail, not from the latest batch of people. Still, it was something to go on. Chicago had to mean something. He tucked it carefully into a plastic baggie then into his pocket, then looked up and around the cage.

This place was done. He hated it.

On the way out, he brought up his phone. Normally he'd reach out to his team with the CIA or FBI to run down this lead online, but he couldn't do that now. However, he did have two Foundation members in Chicago who were perfectly suited for a task like this.

Theodore Smithely III and Cheryl Derringer. They were denizens of the city's seedy underbelly, and kept their ears to the ground.

He wrote them a message as he passed back through the warehouse.

I NEED YOUR HELP. PLEASE CANVAS YOUR CONTACTS FOR SIGN OF MASS-SCALE HUMAN TRAFFICKING MOVING THROUGH CHICAGO. BE DISCREET. POSSIBLY LARGE NUMBERS OF PEOPLE GOING MISSING ON A REGULAR BASIS, INCLUDING A WOMAN CALLED WENDY.

He sent the message then ran a quick reverse check on the phone number. It belonged to a convenience store on Chicago's south side.

Time to go.

Amongst the jumble of clothing and boxes by the shelves, he found a black ball cap and pulled it low over his eyes. Back out in the burning Utah light he climbed into his Dodge Ram and started the engine, but before he could drive off, his burner phone chimed. He brought it up.

It was a response from Cheryl.

WHAT DO WE GET FOR HELPING?

Wren snorted then tapped out his response.

I'M COMING TO YOU. WE'LL DISCUSS IT TOMORROW. FIND WHAT YOU CAN.

Last of all he wrote a message to Humphreys on another

burner phone, sent it, then placed the call so they could track the location.

THIS IS NOT MY WAREHOUSE. SCOUR IT.

He tossed the phone out of the window and left the warehouse behind.

16

CHICAGO

The sprawl of Chicago began twenty miles out, as the expansive fields of grain, wheat, hay and broom corn of rural Illinois intensified into an eight-lane expressway bounded by narrow green risers, boring directly into the city's heart.

Wren looked out from the backseat of a Greyhound bus, ball cap pulled low.

He'd slept through the night, after driving across the state line into Grand Junction, Colorado, where he'd paid a Greyhound driver two hundred dollars to let him on without going through the ticketing system. He'd gone to the back of the bus with a pair of jumbo hot dogs and a large bottle of water, laid down on the gritty floor and sank into blissful darkness straight after eating.

The sleep had done him good, only waking once or twice to check news sites on one of his burner phones. All anyone was talking about on CNN, FOX, MSNBC and others was the major terror attack on a police department in Price, Utah. They had Wren's photo next to it, with variations on a theme for their scrolling banners:

PYRAMID SURVIVOR & CIA AGENT WAGES
DOMESTIC TERROR ASSAULT

Not good. If anything, it cemented his trajectory. There was no going back now, no return to Loralei and his kids possible, at least until he'd cleared his name. Humphreys would have a squad sitting on his family, no doubt.

It's what Wren would do.

He watched the structures of Chicago rising around him, nearly 10 a.m. in the windy city.

He hadn't been back to Chicago for nine years, not since breaking the Ripper Crew copycat murderers, seconded with the FBI. Five women had died by then, dumped in the city's wastelands. Wren had been called in to break the gang, and swiftly gotten to know the dark side of Chicago: the satanic gangs, the 'vampire' clubs, the S&M groups that took their ritualized humiliation right up to the edge. So Chicago had become a place of violence and cruelty for Wren.

The Greyhound pulled off the Stevenson Expressway and Wren strode up to the front, forking over another hundred dollars to the driver to let him off at the exit road.

On the grass verge, Wren looked out at the city. The sky was a leaden gray over the Willis Tower, scarred by blurry white blemishes of lighter cloud, like burn marks on a bloated body. Off to the right was a rental place and he walked up.

With his wallet back, containing several credit cards under fake names, it was easy to rent a white panel van. In Chicago, he figured that would render him near invisible.

The Foundation app on his burner phone chimed as he started to drive. At a red light he brought it up. A message from Cheryl, one of his two contacts. She had been a sex worker and dominatrix when he'd met her, harvested from that dark time of his life. Once she'd been a major feature in the 'vampire' blood-letting clubs, before Wren brought them all down in a cascade of torture charges. Still, she kept her finger on the pulse of the city's sordid side.

TEDDY SEEKING A LEAD ON YOUR HUMAN TRAFFICKING GROUP, the message read. WILL BE IN TOUCH

Teddy was his other Chicago member; a wealthy once-banker, now he lived with Cheryl in a curious platonic union. He'd been a leader of an S&M vampire club, until Wren ended that era. He'd joined the Foundation in tears then done everything he could since to get out.

I'LL COME TO YOUR PLACE SOON, Wren wrote, and pulled away as the light turned green, bound for the South Side. He passed through Wentworth Gardens along West Pershing Road, skirting Fuller Park. Here gangs of young men hung around at corners and on stoops. Gang signs were everywhere, evidenced in uniform colors in bandannas and graffiti tagged on railway tunnel walls.

The gas station and convenience store that matched the number on his receipt sat on West Pershing, near the Dan Ryan Expressway, two blocks south of the White Sox field. Wren drove by massive empty parking lots, rail tracks running over sallow tunnels, blank-faced aluminum warehouses and construction yards heaped with mounds of gravel, then pulled into the store's parking lot.

To the left stood a Louisiana Fried Chicken place. Opposite was a dead end of new-build duplexes. Wren sat for a moment, windows down, taking in the sour Chicago air. A woman ran past in sneakers and jogging sweats, dragged by a foam-mouthed Alsatian. By the gas pumps a little boy was crying about his ice cream, splatted and steaming on the blacktop.

Wren took out the receipt encased in its plastic wallet. Wendy, it read. Had she come to this store? Had she lived around here, maybe?

He tugged his cap lower and opened the van door. It was hot out, late summer in Chicago, enough blocks in from Lake Michigan to not feel the breeze. The air felt dead and condensed, like the dusty stink of a stale attic, unopened for a decade.

Wren walked into the store.

There were two kids on service, maybe college age. Wren noted the flower display in the window: wilted Calla lilies, roses, some cuttings and other flowers he didn't recognize. He studied the label on one.

Discount Flowers, it read, $2.99, just like the receipt.

The kid at the checkout desk had a tattoo on his neck and was tapping at his phone. Wren pulled his CIA badge. That was a risk, with him being hunted by Humphreys, but he didn't think the kid would take note of his badge number and call it in.

"I'm looking for the person on shift eleven months back. Were you here then?"

The kid looked up, ready with some sarcastic remark maybe, then saw the badge and peered closer. His eyes widened. "Uh, what?"

"Eleven months back. Was it you, or should we call the manager?"

"I, uh. I don't know. I'll call the manager." The kid placed a call and had a short dialog. "He says he'll meet you in the chicken place. The manager, that is. Felipe."

"I'll wait here," said Wren.

The kid shifted uncomfortably. He was clearly not keen on Wren standing there, watching him. "The chicken's real good over there. You'll like it. Right, Shelley?"

He looked to the girl. She nodded. "It's delicious."

Why not? He hadn't eaten since the MREs in the warehouse fourteen hundred miles earlier. "Chicken, then."

He almost heard the sighs of relief as he strode out.

83

Across the street he went into the Louisiana Fried Chicken. It was greasy and smelled delicious. Wren ordered a five-piece basket with fries and sat down to enjoy it. In the corner the TV clicked over to the news.

It was about him. The newscaster on CNN said something about developments in the Price, Utah warehouse murders and terror assault on an entire police station. Wren's picture popped up in the corner of the frame again, and he pulled his cap down again.

The chicken guy, some kind of Israeli-African mixture behind the counter, looked at Wren, looked at the TV, but didn't bat an eye. Maybe he was used to wanted criminals chowing down in his shop, or maybe he just didn't care.

Wren tucked into the chicken. It was good, rich and greasy. He watched the coverage on the TV; now they were saying Price was America's worst terror attack since 9/11. Thirty-two dead, including the warehouse. They had dramatic footage of the smashed PD's front wall, half-enclosed by white forensic tents swarmed with FBI lettermen. A reporter enthusiastically ran up the brown hills in back, pointing out recent tracks and theorizing about the rumor of spent shell casings found by the police.

Soon enough Felipe came in. Wren knew it was Felipe by the way he homed in on Wren; the description from the kids in the Convenience store would be easy. The big dark guy with the black cap.

Felipe was short with slick, combed dark hair that looked like a hairpiece but probably wasn't, just unfortunate genetics. He came over and sat down.

"What is this about?" he asked. He had a Mexican accent with teardrop tattoo falling from his left eye. Clearly he was no stranger to violence in the barrio himself.

Wren explained without any mention of Utah. He was an FBI agent pursuing a missing persons case, which somehow involved flowers bought at his store, as evidenced by an old receipt.

"Let's see it then, ese," Felipe said, seemingly not phased in the slightest. Judging from the teardrop tattoo, he'd been a gang member. In his own neighborhood, he wasn't afraid of anything.

Wren produced the receipt and laid it on the Formica table between them.

"Wendy," Felipe said, reading the letters written in blood. His eyes took on a far-off look. "Yeah, I remember selling those flowers. I remember who I sold them to, too, that kid who was always stinking my place up. I registered him missing eleven months back. Some homeless vet called Mason."

Wren leaned in. "You registered him missing? What happened?"

"I don't know that, ese. You want to see?"

17

HOMELESS

Felipe led him out of the chicken shop.

Wren followed. Felipe was a shade under six foot, which gave Wren a good view of the top of his head. Definitely not a piece, just a badly combed hairstyle. Five minutes passed as they headed west, past the convenience store and the open lot to the right, toward the railway line.

Felipe stopped and pointed under the railway bridge. It was narrow and dark, with tight pedestrian walkways either side of a two-lane road bounded by railings. "There. Mason was some homeless punk, come with a whole crew. He told me his name on his first swing around the shop. He was simple, you know? My name's Forrest, Forrest Gump? Yeah. Sweet, in a way."

He lapsed into silence.

"So Mason lived here?" Wren asked, looking at the tunnel. There was no sign of a homeless encampment.

Felipe waved a hand. "Yeah, so they all came at once, some time at the start of last year; I heard they got booted from under Lake Shore Drive. You know, they put up those fences under the highway to stop homeless camping out?"

Wren grunted. "I think the term is 'the unhoused'."

Felipe laughed. "Yeah? Well, this was a whole town of them. I hated it, man. They came in the store and stank it up. Some of them high, some trying to lift whatever they could. It's not worth calling the five-oh on homeless, like calling extermination for cockroaches. You just deal with them yourself."

"Except Mason bought flowers."

Felipe sighed. "That damn kid. Twenty-something, scars all around the top of his head like some kind of crown. I reckon he was a vet living on Uncle Sam's dime, PTSD, injury in the line of duty, the whole nine yards. He'd stop by the window and just drool. Didn't matter how much I poured threats at him. Kid was too dumb to know he was being threatened. Kind of got him a free pass in the barrio."

"Looking at the flowers," Wren said. Putting the picture together.

"Like a dog for a bone. He'd beg over at the L, few blocks east, then come by. Sometimes carrying food; they give sandwiches out at the Revival Faith church on Indiana. I'd see him counting his change."

"Revival Faith?"

"Huge place. You can't miss it."

"And then?"

"Then one day he saved up bought flowers for his girl. Wendy." He pointed at the receipt.

"Who's Wendy?"

"No idea. Never met her."

"OK. Then he went missing?"

"Sure did. The same day he bought those flowers. That was it, I was happy. But something was off about it. A couple days later I came over here and had a look around. All their gear was left. Cardboard dens, tents, junk like that. The city cleared it away later, they're pretty good about that, but no

Mason. No Wendy either." He gestured again at the receipt in Wren's hand.

"So you reported it?"

"I tried. Like I said, who cares? The homeless are here, the homeless aren't here, it's like they're invisible. The 'unhoused' sorry. Of no fixed abode means you can't go missing. You already are."

Felipe sighed.

"And you don't think they just got moved on again?" Wren asked. He had to be sure, despite the quickening of his pulse. "Like under Lakeshore Drive?"

"You tell me. Everything you've got in the world; would you leave that behind? It was a week before sanitation cleared it all out. Where did they go that they wouldn't still need a tent or a sleeping bag? Why didn't they come back to get it?"

Wren could picture it already. The space under the bridge could easily house up to a hundred people. To snatch them all, presumably at night, would have taken at least one semi-truck trailer. If he had to do it, he would hit them while they were sleeping, maybe 2 a.m., blocking off the road on both sides so they had nowhere to go. Then he could just scoop them up.

They wouldn't put up much of a fight, at least not against seasoned operators with weapons. He looked around, but the location was perfect; there was nobody nearby to witness, just the empty lot, a theater supplies warehouse and empty construction yards. Any sound of the snatch could have been covered by a long freight train passing overhead. The whole thing could've happened in minutes.

But what good were homeless to slavers?

That was the problem now. They were hardly prime material. Often they were malnourished, likely many were junkies, probably riddled with disabilities. Each would sell for only pennies on the dollar, making them not worth the cost and risk of acquisition.

"About a hundred here, you say?" Wren asked.

"Maybe. I didn't count 'em."

"The train comes through often?"

"Every thirty minutes, maybe. And yeah, it's loud and it goes on for maybe five minutes, slowing down into the station."

Wren turned and looked up, scanning the lamp posts near the bridge.

"There's nothing there," said Felipe. "I asked them to put up some cameras. This is not downtown."

Wren looked farther afield to intersections. He knew from past experience that there were plenty of cameras dotted throughout Chicago, as with any major city: traffic cams, surveillance outside banks and other high-security facilities, but how many of those would keep their footage for eleven months?

Dead-end.

"And you don't know anything about Wendy?"

"Like I said, I figured that was his girl. Mason. He talked about her a few times, but I mostly tuned him out. I see that receipt now, though..." Felipe petered out. "Who took him, you know? For what?"

"Bad things," Wren said. "But I'm going to find him. Find them both."

"So that's it?"

Wren nodded. "That's it. Thanks. You've been a big help."

Wren walked under the tunnel with his chest thrumming. Felipe remained behind.

"Will you let me know?" he called after Wren. "If you find him? I bought him his flowers, actually. I felt sorry for that poor bastard, counting out his pennies so damn slow. The dumbass needed them more than I did."

Wren looked back. That was unexpectedly touching. "You bought the flowers?"

Felipe looked uncomfortable, like he'd been caught out having a heart. "Yeah, man. He was a vet, you know? Thank you for your service, all that. Looked like nobody had taken care of him in years. Three bucks was nothing."

"I bet it wasn't nothing to him. Thanks Felipe. You've been very helpful. I'll let you know."

Wren kept walking into the shadows. It was easy to forget, doing what he did, that there were good people out there too, people who acted right even without the coin system and the threat of coin loss to stay in check.

18

REVIVAL FAITH

There was nothing to find in the tunnel. City sanitation had done a good, neat job of cleaning it all up. Not a scrap of cloth remained, not a shard of glass, no bullet tracks in the walls. Mason had been there, and Wendy too, presumably, but no sign of them remained now.

Wren laid down on the sidewalk. There wasn't a lot of walking room left. The railings basically hugged the wall. A gang of kids cruised by, laughing and pointing.

He ignored them and closed his eyes, thinking again how the strike might have gone. The two trucks either side, pulling up in the night as a freight train rattled overhead while the homeless were asleep. Using bean bag guns, Tasers or hypodermic darts, they could pacify them swiftly. There was no CCTV nearby, and any cameras that had captured the trucks as they left would've long erased their footage; only compelled by law to hold footage for thirty-one days.

A freight train went by overhead, probably bringing in gravel and lime for mixing into concrete; building high-rises was one of Chicago's biggest growth industries. It was loud, like Felipe said, and it lasted a long time.

Wren was building a picture. Altogether, each factor

suggested an MO, a modus operandi, the group's standard way of operating: homeless sites under freight bridges, in decrepit areas, with no CCTV and easy access to a highway.

Chicago was a mass of old rail lines as well as the more modern L, with various elevated highways that would serve just as well for cover. There had to be some thousand blocks in the city on the whole, with hundreds of sites just like this one, and all of them naturally appealing to the homeless.

An endless supply. But why the homeless? They were easy to snatch, easy to cover the theft, but hardly valuable as human chattel. So what were they for?

No answers came, just the familiar anger.

Wren opened his eyes and brought up maps on his phone. It was simple to locate the church Felipe had mentioned, Revival Faith, along with a spread of others that most likely catered to the homeless. A quick search told him Chicago had up to sixty thousand of the unhoused at any given time.

Sixty thousand people was a lot. Maybe the slavers were selling them in bulk for labor? Chicago was as good as a bottomless font, and clearly the trafficking operation was still a going concern.

Another thought struck him. Since it was ongoing, could there have been a strike somewhere in the city in the last thirty-one days? That might leave a truck sighted on CCTV somewhere, giving Wren a lead to follow.

He got to his feet and returned to his van.

The Revival Faith church filled half a block, ten blocks east on Indiana Avenue: a huge older building of corrugated red brick with a newer portion in pink cladding and glass. It looked like a sports center. Wren knew a little about the Revival Faith; a black church focused on community and missionary work for Jesus.

He parked in the lot and went into the lobby. Inside it was cool and white, with marble floors, a few marble plinths set with flowers, wood detailing on the walls blending into artful constellations of crosses. A security guard stood by a row of turnstiles, blocking further access. In chairs a few old-timers were sitting in their Sunday best.

One of the old ladies sprang up as Wren approached, a lady who had to be eighty years old, wearing an African pattern power suit with a fantastic slope-brimmed hat.

"Welcome to Church, go in the light of Christ, my name is Gloria," she said with the bright joy of mission in her eyes. Wren had seen it many times before and smiled back.

"And you, ma'am. I'm not of the congregation at present; I'm looking for information on your outreach to the community."

"Oh, we do many good works here," Gloria began enthusiastically, and turned to her friend seated on the nearby couch, "Anastasia, weren't you just saying to me how delicious those crumb cakes were, at the park bake sale?"

"Mighty fine," said Anastasia, a heavy lady in purple finery, eighty-three if she was a day.

"This is more about missing peoples. The unhoused in particular. Could I speak to your outreach director?"

"Oh, I expect so. They have their office upstairs. They'll let you up." She motioned to the security guard. The guard just stared. Wren knew his CIA ID would get him through. Likely it would also bring Humphreys down on his head within the hour, hitting harder than a Ford Super Duty.

"Can you call her instead? I'd appreciate discretion."

"Discretion?" asked the woman. "I suppose I have the number."

"I'd be much obliged." Wren sat down beside Anastasia. "I'd rather go through unofficial channels. It's a sensitive matter."

"Oh I see," Gloria said, then made the call and bumbled through it merrily, mangling Wren's intent but remembering to request the outreach director, while Anastasia sized him up.

"You're not from around here," she said.

"You're right in that, ma'am. I'm from out of town."

"How far out of town?"

"Arizona on one side. Heaven alone knows the other."

Her generous features curled into the slightest frown. "Are you a Revival Faith man? Have you been saved?"

"Once upon a time," he said, with a smile. "Now I may have lapsed somewhat."

That confused her for a minute. "Lapsed?"

"Like Saul on his Damascus Road. Like I'm waiting on a resurrection." Wren smiled, working his encyclopedic memory of names like a well-oiled slide on a Glock 19. "Like your name. Anastasia. That's from the Greek 'anastasi', it means resurrection, if I'm not mistaken. It's a beautiful sentiment."

Anastasia blushed slightly, confusion mingling into pleasure.

"She's coming," said Gloria, coming off the phone with such a satisfied expression Wren thought she might burst from the inner light. You couldn't find a more direct opposite to his old days in Chicago than that.

"The gentleman says he was saved, but waiting on a resurrection," Anastasia said, off-balance now. "Apparently that's my namesake in Ancient Greek."

"Oh, Ancient Greek?" Gloria cooed. "The Revival affords eternal salvation to all through the Good Lord's resurrection!"

Wren listened absently while she spoke. Anastasia seemed to be warming up, which was good. He didn't want anyone dialing in a suspicious-looking stranger asking strange questions.

After five minutes an attractive woman came through the turnstiles at the far end of the lobby, and Wren stood. She wore a stylish navy suit and her heels clacked across the marble. She held out one hand and beamed a high-wattage smile.

"I understand you have questions about our outreach program, Mr....?"

"Nightingale," he lied. "Thank you for seeing me."

"My name is Nancy Mbopo. Shall we?" She gestured toward a couch a little further over.

"Thank you."

They sat down.

"Ms Mbopo, I'm concerned about the disappearance of large numbers of the unhoused across Chicago. I first noticed this with a missing encampment under the West Pershing bridge. I knew several of those people, in particular Mason, an Iraq-war veteran, and Wendy, his girlfriend. I met them panhandling outside the L stop and we became friendly, then one day, they were gone. Their whole camp was gone, and I can't find them anywhere." He paused to take a breath, then lowered his voice. "I'm worried this is part of something bigger. A government scheme to remove 'undesirables', maybe bussing them out of state, maybe something worse. I'm looking for any sign that the unhoused population near you has dropped in recent months." He paused a brief moment. "I'm assuming you keep records of attendance at your soup kitchens. Any kind of fluctuation in numbers would help."

By now, the director had laid the clipboard across her knees and rested her hands on top. "May I ask in what capacity you're making this request, Mr. Nightingale? Isn't this a matter best left to the police?"

He nodded. It would be so much easier with his badge. "I agree that this is a matter for the police, but left to the police it will be neglected. I already reported the disappearance of my friends, and it was briefly investigated then brushed aside." He leaned in slightly. "We're talking about hundreds of invisible people, Ms. Mbopo, simply vanished, and nobody knows where they went. Nobody cares what happened to them. In some ways it's a net win for the city."

She shifted uncomfortably in her seat. "That's a callous way of describing it. I'm sure the police..."

"Are overwhelmed with other matters. But not you. This is a church. You help the least of these. So please, help me, so I can help Wendy and Mason."

She opened her mouth to respond, and Wren knew what was coming. The politest shutdown: she wasn't convinced. Time for a redirect.

"Did you know Mason and Wendy?"

She was ready for that. "I don't often go to the soup kitchens myself, I-"

"Manage on the macro level," said Wren, and smiled. "I understand. But somebody keeps records. This is a large church. That amount of food, I'm sure you treat it professionally. I'm only asking to see those records." He gave it a second. "Please, what could the harm be?"

Her eyes took on a guarded edge. "I suppose I could speak to the church director. He'll be in tomorrow. That's the best I can do."

"I don't believe that's your best."

She stood. "I think we're done talking today, Mr. Nightingale."

Wren rose as well. "I didn't mention my profession."

"You didn't," she confirmed.

"I'm a freelance reporter. I've already had interest from major newspapers in this story, and I guarantee, when it goes to press there will be heroes and villains. This is your chance to be a hero."

Her gaze hardened. "Is that a threat? I help you right now or you'll make our church the villain?"

Wren shook his head. "I have no intention of doing that. The villain is whoever took them. But your chance to take the limelight as a hero? I've got a long list of churches I'm going to visit today. You're the biggest by far."

Her brow wrinkled. Maybe she was hooked again. "What newspaper showed interest?"

"I can't say, but one of them includes the letters P O S T."

Her eyes narrowed. "The Washington Post?"

"I didn't say anything."

She studied him. He knew he looked beaten up and rough. "Have you got a press badge?"

"This is not the kind of investigation where I flash a press badge," he countered. "As you can see, I've already taken a beating for asking too many questions. If I'm right, serious heads are going to roll. I don't want to join them,."

She studied him a moment longer, then sighed. "All right. I'll get you the figures. I should have something for you tomorrow morning."

"Tonight would be better."

"Tonight then," she said through gritted teeth. "A guard will hold a packet for you at the door."

"Thank you."

She walked away.

"Jesus' light be with you," said Gloria sunnily as Wren left the building.

"And also with you," he replied.

19

BRIDGE

The other churches were easier.

St Thomas Episcopal. Zion Grove. Prayer Band Pentecostal. South Park Baptist. Tabernacle Baptist. There was almost one of them per block, denser than just about anywhere Wren had seen, but then it seemed this area needed a lot of faith. While he was talking to the pastor at Turner Memorial, the CNN caption on the TV in back flipped to news of a shooting over in North Kenwood, barely five blocks away.

It was a lot of information, by the end of the day. Wren had pages of notes and data to sift through.

By the time he returned to Revival Faith, it was nearly 10 p.m. Gloria and Anastasia were long gone, though the lobby was lit up bright and white. The same security guard stood inside the doors glaring out.

Wren knocked on the glass. The guard unlocked one of the doors and held out a manila folder. Wren took it.

"Pass my thanks on to Ms. Mbopo," he said.

The guard just slammed the door.

Back in his rental van, he opened up the folder. It contained three sheets of paper: one with registered names of the unhoused, one with head counts for the last nine months of soup kitchens, and one with stock counts from their food supplies across the same period.

None of the other churches had provided him as much. At best he'd gotten estimates. A few kept loose records, but the homeless were always moving from place to place as the city chased them around, like the last few crumbs of dust refusing to hop into the dustpan.

But put together with the Revival Faith data, his notes amounted to something solid. He got out a pen and started to annotate the three sheets with intel from the other churches.

A pattern began to emerge. His pen scrawled faster as it took shape.

It seemed there'd been massive drop-offs across the city over the last year, spread across various homeless soup kitchens. Hyde Park had steadily been decimated over a month-long period starting six months back, after which it had stabilized. Bronzetown was next, with the drop-offs lasting several weeks four months ago. Wren brought up a map on one of his burner phones.

Next was West Town, then Lincoln Park. Each time the drop-offs persisted across several weeks of soup kitchens. Wren's mouth grew dry as he brought the data up to the present moment.

Chinatown numbers had started dropping just two weeks ago.

The pattern was right there.

Wren drove to Chinatown, a ten-minute buzz up the expressway, with his anticipation building. If he could find an abandoned encampment, and wind back nearby CCTV footage, then he could get ID on a truck.

That could lead him right to them.

It was gone 11 p.m. by the time he arrived at Chinatown and the streets were quiet. There weren't many bars in that part of the district, not a lot of nightlife, just residential and schools.

Wren knew what he was looking for now, the strike MO, and began a fast, weaving patrol of the night streets, looking for the needle underneath the haystack of rail lines and expressways. There were tunnels everywhere. Chicago was a city in transit.

Soon his eyelids were drooping. At one point a police car fired its sirens in back and he thought he was going to get picked up for cruising, but it fired them off just as swiftly; maybe just running a red light.

Around 2 a.m. he pulled into an all-night ramen bar on South Archer Ave, across from a strip mall with a little five-level red pagoda on top. A few people were walking by and a drunk lay slumped next to a trash can, drooling. Wren drank strong black coffee in a window seat and wolfed down kung pao pork noodles, watching the traffic go by, feeling the anger turn cold in his stomach.

Nobody cared about homeless people getting swept up.

The noodles were hot and salty, just the way he liked them. He left a tip. The TV on the corner played his face on repeat maybe a dozen times in the ten minutes he was there. When he was done he checked his darknet foundation page again for updates.

There was a message from Teddy and Cheryl.

MAY HAVE NEWS SOON. WILL CALL IN A FEW HOURS.

Easy for them to say. Vampires at heart, they both still kept nighttime hours. He itched to call Humphreys and find out what they'd uncovered at the warehouse, but didn't want to call without something to offer in return. It would mean burning his present location, and he wasn't done with Chicago yet.

At the counter he asked the server about homeless people nearby.

"How's that?" the guy asked. He was Asian-American and young, with a drooping hipster mustache that made him look like the Chinese Errol Flynn.

"Homeless," Wren repeated. "The unhoused. I've got a friend said he was sleeping rough around here. Where would he go?"

The guy thought for a moment. He actually tapped his head, like it would help, then shrugged. "I'm drawing a blank. Sorry."

Wren got back in the van and drove. As the minutes ticked by, the whole idea began to seem like a long shot. Just because the Mason strike had left bedding behind on the street in Wentworth Gardens didn't mean they'd leave it here too, and even if they had, the city might have picked it up faster.

Then he found them.

Sometime after 3 a.m., with the city entering that fuzzy time just before dawn, when the streetlights were still on and the drunk night owls were crossing paths with the morning litter crews, Wren found the longest tunnel yet. It ran under a railway interchange, six tracks overhead with a whole abandoned village of sleeping bags, tents, cardboard forts and makeshift washing lines below.

But no people.

Someone honked behind him. He drove to the end, parked on the shoulder then came back through at a jog. This was it. He was standing in the midst of an abandoned encampment. Well over a hundred people could have fit here, maybe two hundred. Probably they were getting moved on constantly by the city, but this was more than that, just like Felipe had said. If this was the city, they'd have taken their stuff. This had to be a strike, but it could still be weeks old.

His heart hammered. He felt he was getting closer to Mason and Wendy. Wren picked through tents and cardboard shells, upturning plastic bags and rooting through wallets of tatty documents and weathered family photographs, looking for something to give him a date.

He found a sandwich wrapper, ham and cucumber, only a day old by the sell-by date. It was recent.

He ran back out onto the street. There were no CCTV cameras overlooking the tunnel, but there had to be plenty elsewhere, like the onramps to the nearby expressway. He kept on running until he was staring right up at a dark digital eye mounted high on a lamp post.

CCTV of the exit ramp.

Bingo.

Now he just needed to get access to that footage.

He took a breath. This was progress, but it was still the middle of the night. He wasn't going to access anything right now. Besides which, he was exhausted. The city turned around him; lights, sound and vehicles in motion. He felt dizzy and realized how weary his legs were, barely holding him up.

He was no use to anyone like this.

He walked back into the homeless camp. Rocked by passing traffic to the side and freight trains above, it stretched ahead in a wonderland of reeking bedding. Wren was too tired to care, and it wasn't like he had anywhere else to sleep. No motel would be safe now, with his face on every watchlist. In the Chinese restaurant they'd been calling it the worst terror attack on home soil in nearly twenty years.

This was OK. Nobody noticed the homeless.

He rolled himself up in cardboard and fell asleep in seconds.

20

MS-13

S ome time before the dawn Wren was dragged from sleep with a pair of hands around his throat.

He tried to bolt upright, but couldn't. A face hung over him, bleary in the artificial light under the bridge. He heard laughter and felt impacts landing on his legs, but it was hard to focus with his airway constricted.

Still, he smelled gas. He felt the cold liquid seeping through his clothes. Whoever this was, they were preparing to set him alight. On some level it registered as ridiculous, the second time in two days he'd been attacked in his sleep.

On another level, all he thought about was ending the threat. His mind skipped into operational overdrive, logging details in a hyperaware state.

He recognized the blue bandanna of the young man throttling him. It signified MS-13, or Mara Salvatrucha, a legendary drug gang out of Los Angeles, formed in LA in the 80s of Salvadoran immigrants. From the sound of laughter and the flickers of movement he caught around the edges of his assailant's face, he figured there were six of them total.

This wasn't a targeted attack, he felt sure, not the same people who'd swept up the encampment. These were just gang punks picking on a lone straggler, looking to have a good time. They'd only understand one language.

Wren's right hand shot up into his attacker's crotch, grabbed hold of meat through the thin fabric and wrenched back down. Instantly the hands fell from around his throat as the punk squealed and dropped.

Wren burst up in a cloud of bedding and cardboard.

A handgun discharged but Wren was already behind another gang member, whipping his head around so hard that his neck broke. Another shot rang out and there were shouts, but now there was a freight train passing overhead like a thunderstorm. No sound would carry far from here, no cameras would capture it.

Wren charged two of the skinny gang members and hoisted them both in the air, into the railing dividing the sidewalk from the road and over. They slapped down on their heads and shoulders.

That left one. He trained his gun on Wren and fired, but Wren had already stepped off-line and forwards neatly, sweeping his left arm up and around to knock the barrel off target. His hand closed around the punk's wrist and the gun discharged again, this time hitting one of his fellow gang members in the belly, just as Wren brought his right elbow crashing down onto the punk's shoulder.

His clavicle snapped. He screamed and the gun dropped, then went for a knife with his left hand. Wren brought his elbow backwards into the guy's right ear, knocking him stone-cold unconscious on his feet.

He fell. Wren collected the gun. The two gang members who'd toppled to the road were running now. Wren vaulted the railing, muscles bathed in adrenaline now, and fired twice.

Both men dropped.

Wren let out a breath and turned.

The stink of gasoline was all over him, rising off his

clothes, in his hair, making his eyes sting. He surveyed the scene as the train continued to hammer along above. Two dead from shots in the back, one on his side and bleeding out from a bullet in the gut, one unconscious with a broken clavicle and likely a skull fracture, and one curled around his dislocated testicles.

Wren saw the red gas canister. He saw a lighter where it had dropped on the floor. A thought occurred to him. Maybe this wasn't such bad luck after all. Maybe he could use this.

First he dragged the two bodies off the road and buried them in filthy bedding and newspaper alongside the one with a broken neck. He covered up the man dying from a bullet in the belly, ignoring his feeble cries for help, and the one with the busted head too.

He focused on the man who'd woken him. His eyes were screwed tightly shut now, both hands clamped between his legs. Wren had a solution for that, though, and poured the rest of the gas can over his head.

He screamed. Nobody heard. Wren ripped off his sodden blue bandanna and slapped him with it until his eyes opened.

"One question," he said, "if you want to live."

Then he flicked the lighter, sparking a gas jet of flame. The man's eyes focused. Wren waved it back and forth. One mistake now and he'd set himself on fire too.

"The homeless here," Wren went on, speaking slowly and clearly. "They were taken in the last few nights. Did you see anything?"

The man just stared, so Wren asked him again, then brought the lighter in close. The guy couldn't have been more than twenty years old, but twenty was enough to be a poison on society. He shrieked a little then nodded, gulped and words spilled out of him in a torrent.

"No man, we didn't see nothing, one day they're here, next

they ain't, now what you gonna do with that flame, brother? We was just teasing, having some fun, you know?"

Wren narrowed his eyes. "Isn't it still fun? Aren't we having fun now, you and me?"

The guy took a second to catch on, then nodded rapidly. "Yes, yes my man, we're sure having fun. Whatever it takes, this is fun, just tell me what else you want to know and I'll let you have it, maybe we stop playin' then."

Wren nodded. He hadn't expected an answer to the first question. Whoever the people were sweeping up the homeless, they wouldn't have let any witnesses live. But maybe he could narrow his search window.

"OK. I believe you. One more question and we're done. Is that cool?"

"Cool, man, yes it's cool! We're cool, name it!"

"The people under here, when did they disappear? Yesterday? The day before. One day they were here, the next they weren't. Think hard. A lot's riding on it."

"What? How'm I supposed to know that? I ain't keeping track of-"

Wren brought the lighter right up to his eyes. "Bullshit. You cruise the streets looking for fun, right? You see these people. When there was a hundred of them you wouldn't come in with your gasoline can, would you? They stand guards, some might have guns, it's not worth it, right? But when it was just me, you came. Some torture, some fun, set me alight. You've done it before, haven't you?"

The guy's eyes rolled. Stress and pain were getting the better of him. "It ain't like that at all. I-"

"How many times?"

"I don't know! It ain't hardly a crime, is it? Folk like that are half-dead anyway. We're doing them a favor!"

Wren shook his head. "Listen to me very carefully. The people here, when was the first night they were gone?"

"What?"

"What night? When did they disappear?"

The guy shuddered. "I, uh. Maybe two nights back? Two, I think."

"So Tuesday," Wren said. "Tuesday night they weren't here? So Monday night they were?"

"I guess! I don't know man. No, wait. We swung by Monday and they were gone. Or, wait. No! Monday early, maybe 'bout 9, they was here. Monday late, like now, they was gone. Weirdest thing."

He smiled. He had white teeth.

"Monday night," Wren mused, "between 9 p.m. and, what time is it now?"

"'Bout 4 a.m, brother."

"4 a.m. That's useful."

"Thanks, man. So, we good?"

"Sure, we're good," Wren said, "I'll even do you a favor." He stepped back and touched the gas jet to the man's chest. Instantly he went up in flames, a bonfire flaring yellow and orange, screaming and jittering until the pain and asphyxiation knocked him unconscious.

Wren walked away and the fire spread behind him. He barely heard the cries as the flames carried through the remains of the encampment and found the others. He'd never burned anyone alive before, but it felt strangely familiar.

He tossed the lighter over his shoulder, stripped his soaking jacket and tossed that too, then kept walking until he reached his van. Back in the driving seat, he drove ten blocks north until he found a quiet rest area at the edge of an industrial estate, then climbed into the back, laid his dizzy head on his wadded, gas-drenched pants and fell back to sleep.

21

CHERYL

Wren woke just after the dawn, and for a little while lay still in the back of the van, haunted by uneasy memories of the past. Maybe it had come from burning that MS-13 member alive.

He shouldn't have done that.

In the moment it had seemed like justice. It was what they were going to do to him; what they'd likely done to other unhoused people before.

That wasn't the regret, though. The regret was how it took him back to the end of the the Pyramid, when he'd stood at the head of the cult compound's main street out in the deserts of Arizona, with a thousand dead and smoking bodies laid out before him. With his father's hand on his back, telling him he was a good boy.

They'd all burned. The men, the women, the children. Some had gone willingly, some had been forced, but they had all burned. All except Wren. Even his father, 'Apex' leader of the cult, had burned in the end.

But not Wren.

It was a bad memory, one he hadn't dreamed of in many years. It left a dark feeling lingering over him, like everything was ending and he was just the last person to know it. On that day he'd lost every member of the only family he'd ever known. He'd only been 11 years old.

It felt like things weren't so different now.

The sounds of traffic grumbled by outside. Wren forced the dream away, got up and opened the van doors. Pale morning light poured in, washing away the phantoms of the past.

The homeless camp was gone, ten blocks south and now doubtless a cinder heap. That realization presented a sobering reality; all those people were really gone, every sign of their past existence erased, doubtless undergoing the worst experience of their already harsh lives right now.

Wren had to save them. That mattered more than six dead MS-13 members who'd deserved what they'd got. He hadn't been able to save the Pyramid. He had to save Mason and Wendy.

He rose to his feet, rolled stiff shoulders and stepped out of the van. Mid-morning sun beat down on the blacktop, releasing the pungent aroma of summer dust and tar. The city rolled on around him; cars bustling, people in suits rushing to work, the expressway roaring nearby. He drank a bottle of water and checked his darknet messages.

A dozen messages had come in from Teddy sometime in the night. Wren scrolled through them, each growing increasingly frantic.

WE HAVE TO MEET!

I HAVE WHAT YOU NEED!

CHRISTOPHER COME NOW!

That was convenient. Wren's plan to access the CCTV footage involved both Teddy and Cheryl. He tapped a simple response, 'COMING', then climbed back into the van's front seat and set out. Teddy and Cheryl lived uptown. Better to hear this in person and set the CCTV ball rolling in a place he could grab a shower at the same time.

Two birds with one stone.

The morning traffic wasn't so bad, with Wren out before the worst crush of commuters. Soon enough he was up in Old Edgebrook, a few switch-backed residential streets zigzagging through the forests of Dahla Park in the northwest of the city. Baby mansions stood on small but doubtless expensive plots, each boasting a distinct architectural style straight out of a magazine: French shutters, round picture windows, colonial turrets.

Teddy was rich, his fortune made in investment banking, and had one of the biggest houses in the neighborhood, with a yard screened by tall fences that once hid his dark parties from the eyes of the world. Now, Wren knew from past visits, the pair of them mostly laid around on inflatables in the pool all day, after nights spent carousing the downtown gentlemen's clubs.

Wren parked the van and knocked on the oak front door. Cheryl answered swiftly. Her face was as impassive as ever, giving nothing away. She was beautiful and incredibly pale, with thick lips and wide eyes, but there was a cruel slant to her resting expression. She wore jeans and a snug t-shirt that accentuated her curves.

"Christopher," she said, like seeing him was a terrible disappointment. "Teddy's getting desperate." She stepped out of the way to admit him, then added as an afterthought, "You stink."

Wren chuckled. "Pleasure to see you too, Cheryl."

They'd dated briefly in his Chicago days, inadvisably. Cheryl was anhedonic, a medical condition which meant she felt no sense of joy in anything. It had forced her to seek thrills from the vampire groups instead. The first time Wren had seen her he'd been entranced, as she stood on the stage like a queen of the night, her generous curves heaving as she drank pig's blood from a gallon vase.

"Did you roll around in gasoline or something?" she demanded, eyes screwing tighter.

"Something like that."

"Take a shower."

"That's the plan. Can you run a wash on these?"

Cheryl looked at his clothes. "I can throw them out. You've been sleeping in trash again, too?"

"I think a wash will do it." He stepped through the door and studied her. "You're looking well."

She snorted. "I've been spending a lot of time on social media, gaslighting people. It's wonderful for my complexion."

Wren laughed. That didn't seem to please her, but pleasing Cheryl would be a mistake. It bred contempt. Ever the vampire, she lived off the strong emotional reactions of others, whether in person or filtered through the Internet, and had clearly aimed to annoy Wren with that. For him to simply laugh would give her nothing.

"That's dangerously close to breaking the terms of your coin level," he said.

"Is this my coin meeting?" she asked sharply. "Are you here to help me, or for my help?"

Wren nodded but couldn't stop the smile. "I do need your help, Cheryl. Do you still have your blackmail list?"

"My what?"

"Let's skip the dance and tickle and get to the list, if that's OK? Last time we had a coin check-in, you had several Chicago PD officers in your little black book. Men you'd danced for, men in the vampire clubs, men who might've paid you for things they shouldn't have. I said you should dump it and you said yes but meant no. I'm thinking you've still got it."

Cheryl regarded him coolly. "You really need that shower, Chris."

"Pick a cop in traffic or one close and ask them to pull some CCTV footage for me. I've got the camera number, date and time range written down." He fished in his pocket and held out a piece of paper. "I want all the semi trucks, probably two in convoy, and I want ALPR, that's Automated License Plate Recognition, on where they go. I need that ASAP."

She stared at the piece of paper like it might be infected. "That's a lot of acronyms."

"It's all written down. Will you do it?"

"What's in it for me?"

Wren smiled again. "The knowledge that you're helping hundreds, maybe thousands of innocents go free."

She frowned. "I said for me."

Wren had expected that. "I'll give you a coin bump. What are you, coin three now?"

She cocked her hip. "Are you asking or telling?"

"Coin three. I'll jump you to four."

"Four?"

"At four you get access to the coin four support groups. You get one more coin meeting with me per year. There's also a really nice five percent discount at Arby's."

Her face puckered. "Arby's?"

"I'm just kidding. There's no discount."

She chewed the inside of her lip. "You think one more coin meeting with you is going to persuade me to help?"

Wren shrugged. "It does or it doesn't. The coin four groups are great, too. A lot of breakthroughs happen in those groups, a lot of hard-earned wisdom and fellowship. It's worth it if you think it is. You know that's how the Foundation works. I'm not here to persuade you."

She chewed harder. Cheryl, right along with Teddy, was one of the more challenging members of the Foundation. At times they both realized the benefits membership brought them: the structure, the sense of belonging, the guard rails on a life they'd been living with destructive abandon, the support from the groups. At other times, they hammered against those guard rails with everything they had.

"Just take the paper, Cheryl," Wren said. "Call the cop or don't. If not, I'll find another way to get that footage. Now, I'm going for a shower."

She took the paper. "What about Teddy?"

"What about Teddy?"

Cheryl perked up slightly. "He's waiting for you in his temple. He's been furious all night that you were ignoring him."

She was trying to provoke him. "I wasn't ignoring him, I was asleep. He can wait five more minutes. This way to the shower?"

"Sure," she answered sullenly.

22

TEDDY

Wren had been in their house once before. It was beguilingly normal, and everything was spotlessly clean. The downstairs bathroom was immaculate; he expected they had maids in every day. He tossed his gasoline-soaked clothes out the bathroom door and stepped into the rejuvenating steam of their walk-in shower. Jets from the walls massaged his bruised skin.

In a full-length mirror opposite the shower, he surveyed his injuries before the steam clouded the glass. Most of his body was darkened with black and purple bruising. It hurt, but he was used to that kind of thing. He parted the scruffy black hair on the left side of his head, and saw the tender weal where the enforcer had punched him with his brass knuckles.

It hurt, but scabs had already formed. His left eye was no longer bloodshot, though the bruising spread down to his cheek like a port-wine stain birthmark.

It would heal soon enough. He splurged a healthy dose of Teddy's caffeine-infused shower gel and worked up a lather. It did feel surprisingly refreshing.

At some point the door opened, but Wren ignored it. He

cleaned his injuries, then brushed his teeth with the corner of a face cloth, then stepped out of the shower and saw Teddy with a gun in his hand, pointing it at him.

It was a ridiculously overpowered Sig Sauer P226, finished in black satin. It made Teddy look small, and Teddy was no slouch; at six feet two he was just a shade shorter than Wren and bulked up from working out. In most company he dominated. Yet here in his own bathroom, with a gun in his hand and facing a naked man, something was missing.

"Hi, Theodore," Wren said casually, picking up a dry towel. Right then, he didn't much care if Teddy splashed his brains across the beautiful slate tiles. The last time Teddy, or Theodore Smithely III, had pulled a gun, he'd fired it. Wren still had the scar in his arm.

Wren dried his face and chest then wrapped the towel casually around his waist.

"You ignored my messages," Teddy said.

"Has Cheryl been pushing your buttons?" Wren asked. "It was night, and I was asleep, except for when I was getting set on by MS-13 idiots. They're all dead now, by the way. But I came as soon as I saw your text."

"Too late."

"Too late for what?"

Teddy just snorted. "Christopher Wren. On the run. Needing my help. Where's your all-controlling coin system now?"

"Theodore," said Wren, part-soothing, part-chiding, then reached up and slowly tapped his own temple. "It's all in here. You know that."

Teddy raised the barrel. "One shot and it's gone."

Wren gazed into the gun's black hole, not even for the first time that day. "You want to sit down and talk? Or will you execute me in your downstairs bathroom? I don't know what your maid will think of that." He looked at the walls appraisingly. "You'll never get the brain fragments out of these cracks."

Teddy trembled. He was angry, that was obvious. Wren wondered if today was the day. "Put some clothes on," he said.

"Cheryl's washing them. They were covered in gasoline."

Teddy made a pained face.

"They're on a hot wash," came Cheryl's voice through the door, making no effort to hide that she was listening in.

Teddy sighed.

"It's nothing she hasn't seen before," Wren said. "You too."

"Use the towel. Damn it, Christopher. Take this seriously."

Wren carefully wrapped the towel around his waist. "Serious enough?"

"Come on."

Teddy backed up. Wren followed, dripping on the thick shag carpet. They went like that through the house and up the stairs, with Teddy carefully shuffling backward, holding the gun on him while Cheryl followed.

Teddy's 'temple' lay behind a triple-bolted door. He opened each bolt carefully, like a ritual. Inside it was dim, but Wren picked out the mannequins. The attic space was cavernous, taking up the whole home's square footage. The walls were papered with newspaper clippings divided into zones, and each zone had its own diorama of figures spread in various poses, specifically built to Teddy's specifications.

Wren recognized this from Teddy's coin meetings. All of these were re-enactments of past murder scenes. He had a morbid fascination about violent death, and these mannequins were Teddy's methadone, a way to act out without hurting anyone.

"No," Teddy said to Cheryl as she tried to slip in, closing

the door in her face like a little sister kept out of the 'boy's den'.

Wren and Teddy looked at each other for a moment.

"You said you had something for me," Wren said.

"First, I want out of the coin system," Teddy said. "Out from under you. No more controls. No more rules. No more threat of getting minus coins for 'backsliding'. I want to be free again."

"So you're free. I release you. I never forced you into the system."

Teddy shuddered at the memory. After he'd shot Wren, he'd lost two years of coins because of it, setting him back to zero. Then he'd spent the days of Wren's recovery begging to be allowed back to coin 1.

"Not enough. I want your blessing."

Wren sighed. "Listen, Teddy. I can see you're unhappy, but I'm in the middle of something here. Something important, something with hundreds of lives at stake. Kill me, you're killing their best chance of getting free. So shoot or get off the pot."

A bead of sweat ran down Teddy's cheek. "I've got something you're looking for," he said, licking his lips. "A trade."

"Information on the traffickers?"

"Right. After you sent that message, I put the word out in some of my more unique chat groups. The kind only I've got access to? Anyway, I've got a guy. He's crazy, but I think it's real. I'll trade you, him for a release."

Wren leaned in. Teddy leaned back. "Trafficker or slave?"

"Trafficker," Teddy said. "Big numbers of people, he said, moved through Chicago and headed north." A long moment passed. "Well?"

23

BUTTERFLY

"What does he know?" Wren asked.

"A place," Teddy answered. "A purpose. They've got some kind of processing facility at a summer camp in the woods."

Wren frowned. "A summer camp?"

"He said so. Cabins. An archery range. Tennis courts. A lake."

"Well that sounds like a good time. Are you sure he wasn't talking about summer camp kids?"

"He was terrified, Chris! I don't think they were playing pat-a-cake in those cabins, and he said most of the camp was abandoned. They weren't using it for standard camp activities."

Wren considered. "Any paper trail?"

"No meaningful records that he knows of. Nothing to track it down."

"Where?"

Teddy sucked air through his teeth.

"Where?" Wren repeated.

"He doesn't know."

"Doesn't know or won't say?"

"I'm certain he doesn't know."

"But he was there, right?"

"He said there were precautions. Blindfolds. He was a low-level guy, apparently, working security in the woods, never allowed inside the main hall. He heard things, gunshots, saw some bodies getting carried out, but he didn't know what they were doing inside."

"Does he at least know what state this was in?"

"He said north."

Wren sighed. "North? That could be Michigan, Wisconsin, Minnesota, even Canada for all we know. Nothing better than north?"

"That's all he knows."

"OK. How long ago was he there?"

"He says two years. But then he's also covered in needle tracks, so who knows what his idea of time is?"

"Let me talk to him."

Teddy shook his head. "Un-uh. I have him somewhere, locked up. Take me off the coin system for good and he's yours."

"You mean coin zero?"

"I mean off!" Teddy shouted. "Not watching me. Not controlling me, scoring me, anything. You see I'm holding a gun."

"It could be a banana," Wren said calmly. "I'm in your head now, Teddy, and I'll be there forever whether I'm dead or not, like the voice of Jiminy Cricket. Besides, if you really wanted to shoot me, you'd have done it properly the first time."

Now the gun trembled. "You're not in my head."

Wren just looked in his eyes. "Teddy, I haven't got time for this. You matter to me, but so do other people. I see potential in you, you know that. You were lost in stupid, cruel endeavors for years, and now you're not, and you feel empty.

I get it. Just look at this junk." He gestured at the mannequins. "You think this is what I hope for you? You're a caterpillar in a chrysalis right now, but the butterfly is coming. That day is coming, Teddy, I know it."

Teddy's eyes welled up and his voice cracked. "When, Chris? I feel like nothing all the time. There's nobody. There's nothing. None of it matters."

Wren shook his head. This was why the coin system worked, because the people on it wanted and needed it to; the exact same kind of lost souls the Pyramid had once preyed on. "When you're ready. It's on you, Theodore. We talked about this." Wren placed a hand on Teddy's shoulder and gave him a consoling squeeze, then shifted gears. "But right now I've got to go. Will you take me to the guy?"

Teddy just hung his head.

"OK. I'll go find him myself."

Wren strode to the door, ignoring the gun, and opened it. Cheryl was standing right outside.

"He's not shot you," she said, sounding disappointed.

"Maybe next time. Are my clothes ready?"

She frowned. "How fast do you think my washing machine is? They're still on spin."

Wren slid past her. "I'll wear them wet."

He went down the stairs with Cheryl at his back. "You can't open the machine mid-cycle," she said helpfully. "It has a lock."

"Then I'll just wear my towel."

He passed down the hallway, opened the front door and stepped out into the light. Teddy was shouting after him.

"You shouldn't do this to him," Cheryl called, as Wren stalked over the lawn to his van.

"He's a grown man. I asked for help and he pulled a gun. He's doing it to himself."

He sat in the van and started the engine. The hot leather

seats scalded his bare thighs. He started to back the van out, then stopped and rolled the window down.

"Did your cop get me the CCTV?"

"He's going to," Cheryl said. "He said by midday. I gave him your email, he'll send it to you."

"Good," Wren said. "Thank you, Cheryl. That's coin four when it comes through."

Cheryl couldn't hide her small, smug smile.

Wren released the brake, then Teddy appeared in the doorway. The gun was gone.

"I'll tell you," he called. "Just wait. I'll take you to the guy."

Wren sat for a moment. Teddy looked sad as he shambled over to the open window.

"Two choices in life," Wren said, looking into Teddy's eyes. "You grow or you implode. I know things are going to get better for you, Theodore. It just takes time."

Teddy looked pained. "So do I lose coins for this?"

Wren snorted. "A gun in my face? I think that's about par for the course by now, don't you? Keep your coins. Let's go see a guy about a summer camp."

24

TANDREWS

Teddy's contact was at the 'crypt', a country estate he kept as a memento from his glory days. It had more land, more walls and a properly stylized dungeon in the basement.

Teddy loaned Wren some clothes, then he and Cheryl took off in their hulking Grand Cherokee. Wren followed in the van, hair and beard drying in the rough breeze through the open windows.

Chicago soon bled away like a bad dream. The outskirts melded into outlying towns and golf courses. Wren didn't expect to come back now; the city had given up its secrets, and he was ready to move on.

He called Director Humphreys.

There were three rings then Humphrey's deep, resonating voice came on the other end.

"Chicago, Wren?"

Wren smiled. "That was fast tracking. And I'm leaving Chicago."

"Stop running, Christopher. Have you seen the news? You're everywhere. There's a half-million bounty on your head and it's growing every day. I've got teams coming for you already. What the hell are you doing out there, Wren?"

"I'm hunting the bad guys, just like you, except I'm on target. Ready for an information exchange?"

Humphreys sounded ready to blow up. "Turn yourself in, Christopher. That's the only exchange I'm interested in."

"Then I'll go first," Wren said, taking a deep breath. "In the warehouse I found a slip of paper, a receipt. I tracked it to Chicago, where it turns out our killers have been abducting the homeless for at least eleven months, maybe as far back as two years. I've got a lead on one of their trucks and I'm tracking it currently. I've also got another lead on a possible old member of the group. You should look into nationwide reports of homeless encampments missing. In one instance it looks like these guys grabbed maybe two hundred people right off the street, with no witnesses."

There was silence for a moment. Wren wondered how many intelligence agency heads were now listening in on this call, to the number one most wanted man in America.

"This is elaborate even by your standards, Wren. You want us to poll the homeless? You know what a dead-end that will be. It's a time sink."

"Not a time sink. I'm not telling you to hit the streets and count them. I'm saying run a search for reports in police systems. There must be reports, if the numbers are what I'm seeing. They're just vanishing. I didn't have that access, so I went around to local churches and asked about their soup kitchens. Attendance has been dropping massively, and I don't think that's because they all suddenly found housing."

There was silence again.

"Humphreys. I've just given you everything I have. Give me something."

"You mean tell you if we're closing in on you?"

Wren shook his head. "You were in Price PD, right? You

saw the cop at the back door, where he'd let the shooters in? You saw the size of that warehouse too. Somebody must've bought off the whole county to shuttle people through without anyone knowing. I'm telling you where those people come from, and it's Chicago. I can give you a name, Mason. He was a military vet, had scars all around his head, and I'm sure you can find his record in one search of the NPRC. They snatched him eleven months ago. Wendy was his girl. Now give me something in return."

The silence stretched out.

"I heard about what happened with your family," Humphreys said. "Shame."

"It's hardly a secret."

"I said it though, didn't I? You're no family man."

"What's your point, Gerald?"

"Only this. Our psychiatrists think you're having a breakdown. They say the pain of your childhood, all the lies about this 'Foundation' cult, it came to a head when-"

"It's not a cult," Wren said again. "It's a support group. People come, go, join, leave, whatever they want. And my childhood's off-limits. I'm talking about this case."

"It's all one case, agent Wren. You're experiencing a psychotic break due to the loss of your family, and you're sowing chaos in your wake. Maybe you even believe the things you're saying to me, when actually it's you all along, repeating the madness your father inflicted on the country." He sucked in a low, deep breath. "We never knew how damaged you were. Prodigy, they called you. But you were broken from the start. That's our fault too, to give you so much authority. Now you've left me with no other choice. I'm bringing in James Tandrews."

That name hit Wren like a punch in the belly, bringing him out in a cold sweat. James Tandrews was the man who'd found Wren wandering in the desert, right after the Pyramid burned. He was an FBI agent, Gold Team leader on the Pyramid cult dynamics teams, and he'd decided to personally foster Wren at eleven years old.

In the following six years, Tandrews had made Wren who he was, quite literally. He'd given him the chance to choose his own name, after the Pyramid had only given him a number.

"I'm not talking to Tandrews now," Wren said.

"He's right here with us. What did you think we were doing all this time? We're profilers too, we've got teams dedicated to breaking you and your 'Foundation'. They all say James Tandrews is the key, so I'm going to put him on the line. Maybe then you'll listen."

Wren imagined the button clicking and the old guy leaning into a microphone. This was going to hurt like hell, and he couldn't afford that now. Tandrews had been nothing but good to him, but after the horrors, cages and experiments in pain of the Pyramid, Wren hadn't known how to accept his kindness.

At first, he'd barely spoken at all. He'd been more like a mute animal than a boy at the onset of his teenage years. But Tandrews had dealt with people brainwashed by charismatic leaders before, he'd seen the effect it had on children and he played it right with Wren at every stage.

He'd given him his space, introduced him slowly to the real, wider world, while keeping in touch with the primal wildness Wren had learned in the Arizona desert. Together in the dark forests of Maine they would go camping and hunting for weeks at a time. Barely speaking. Slowly learning to trust, as Tandrews taught Wren how to face down a buck, how to topple it with an arrow from a homemade bow, how to skin it, gut it and cook it.

In those early years, Wren had kept himself apart from

other young people, at first for fear of what they'd do to him, then later for fear of what he'd do to them.

But as the years passed, Wren's emotional wounds scarred over. Tandrews tried to talk about the Pyramid a few times, but Wren couldn't. The past was just too dark to face, bringing him out in screaming terrors that roused him in the middle of the night. So they didn't talk about it. They just moved on. At fifteen Wren went to high school and became the top-ranking student of his year. He even headed up the football team.

It was easy. After surviving the Pyramid, other young people were simple. It wasn't that he manipulated them, but he was able to steer both his course and theirs. He worked hard to show them the best he could be, while bringing out the best in them too. It made him an exemplary leader through a conscious choice to be different from his birth father.

He became a normal teenager. He went to the movies. Had a girlfriend. At seventeen there was trust between him and Tandrews. Prom was coming. Graduation. Then Tandrews took the next step, a logical step as Wren was moving into adulthood and thinking about college, and offered to bond them together through formal adoption. It would override the fostering agreement and the emancipation papers Wren had been granted at sixteen, legally registering him as an adult in the eyes of a county court judge.

Wren agreed, and the adoption papers came in. Wren had nodded along through it all, not fully understanding what it meant for him until the night before the signing ceremony, and the same old fear hit like it hadn't in years.

A terror so thick and dark he could barely breathe descended across him, like he was back in the blackness of his father's cages, back in the desert town with all those people burning alive, with the Apex whispering in his ear about what was real and what wasn't, and how he could best serve the Pyramid.

He'd fled through an open window and never looked back. All night he walked, until he hit a turning point and realized what he was going to have to do; what he'd been preparing for, really, ever since Tandrews had found him.

He had to face the world and all its horrors head on.

Through the course of that one night, all thoughts of prom, graduation and his girlfriend were forgotten. He abandoned the idea of college. He walked straight into a Marine recruitment office in some shabby mall two towns over, handed his emancipation papers over to the guy at the desk and asked to sign up.

He sent a postcard to Tandrews from right outside, a thank you letter because he couldn't force himself to make a call, then threw himself into training. First he was in the Marines, then the special operations Force Reconnaissance group. In later years, the way he'd treated Tandrews haunted him with a bitter shame that was almost worse than the horrors of the Pyramid.

He started sending more postcards. He shared his news, as much as he could. Several times he tried to call him, to properly thank him or apologize, but always he pulled back. It was too hard to trust someone that much, not after what he'd been through, so he'd just kept on going.

Tandrews replied. Wren told him when he got married, and about the birth of his children. He even sent photos. Tandrews sent the occasional picture back. He never asked to meet. He never tried to call.

Wren had been meaning to go see him. Right after quitting the CIA, after he'd gone home to his family, he'd planned to take them all out to Maine so the kids could meet their grandfather. He'd even been excited about it.

But not now. He couldn't deal with it in the middle of this.

There was an intake of breath down the line; Tandrews warming up to speak. Any second now his voice would come through, warm and kind, a decent man who'd done his very best.

"I'm sorry," Wren said. "I'm sorry you got dragged into this. I'll call you when it's over, I promise."

He killed the call before anything could come back.

Abruptly he was alone in the van, though the air felt thick with swirling ghosts. He hadn't spoken to his adoptive father for eighteen years. He held the wheel with his elbows and pried the phone apart, strangling an incoming call. Silence reigned, but he heard voices anyway. His wife. Tandrews. Humphreys.

The Pyramid babies in their cages, screaming through the night.

His breathing rasped and it grew harder to think straight, making it difficult to keep Teddy and Cheryl in sight in their Jeep. He hit a pothole and almost lost control, heart racing too hard, breath coming fast.

He pulled over onto the shoulder as the past swamped him. He couldn't afford to do this now, and pushed back. He'd pushed all this darkness down once before, and he could do it again.

After a minute or two the black cloud lifted, shoved aside by a fresh upswell of rage. He was angry at Humphreys for pulling that stunt. He was angry at himself for walking into it. Most of all, he was angry at the people shipping innocents north to be slaughtered in some sick forest summer camp.

There was only one thing to do with anger, though, a lesson Tandrews had taught him a long time ago: burn it for fuel. The burner cell was already in pieces in his hands, so he threw the housing out of the left window, the battery out of the right then pushed the gas pedal down.

25

SACRIFICE

I n twenty minutes Wren veered off the highway and sped through leafy suburbs lined with palatial houses until Teddy's country estate appeared before him. It had tall iron gates flanked by heavy stone walls, a crushed coral drive flanked by cedars and stairs leading up to stately double doors enclosed within Roman columns.

The Grand Cherokee was already there in the large carport, but there was no sign of Teddy and Cheryl. The black cloud returned, bringing with it a sudden dread.

Wren skidded the van to a halt and shoved the door open, left the engine idling and strode up the stairs. He pushed through the double doors into a lofty marble entrance hall.

"Teddy!" he yelled, his voice echoing. "Cheryl!"

No answer came.

He hadn't been here since Teddy's party days, but he remembered the route to the crypt. The door in the kitchen hung open and Wren ran down a spiral stone staircase until the basement spread before him.

It looked like the set of a horror movie, with a gothic vaulted ceiling looming over a long, stone-paved nave which ended in a dramatic, ornate altar. Faux torches burned with dim orange light in sconces, and Wren ran between them, past shallow alcoves where reproduction devices of torture lurked in shadow: a tall iron maiden with its inner bed of spikes glinting; a rack and pinion with ropes and rollers for stretching bodies until they snapped; a large iron wheel with leather straps for arms and legs upon which a victim's limbs would be shattered.

"Teddy!" he shouted. "Cheryl."

Then he saw Teddy, on his knees in the furthest alcove. He was looking back at Wren with an odd expression on his face. Cheryl was there too, but she wasn't kneeling. She was lying on the floor in a pool of blood.

Then a man emerged from the shadows by Teddy, whipping a pistol in. The grip struck Teddy in the side of the head and his body jerked to the side. Wren focused on the man; he was dressed all in black like the killers from the warehouse, and he was a giant, at least 6' 6" with blond hair, blue eyes and a steely gaze leveled at Wren.

"You're him," the man said, and pointed his pistol.

Wren dived left without thinking, rolling over the dark stones to come up in one of the torture alcoves as shots cracked off the stones behind him. He pulled the Rorbaugh and powered right back out of the alcove, firing rapidly.

Gunpowder blasted and bullets ricocheted off the stone walls, but the shooter had already ducked behind the altar. The Rorbaugh clicked dry but there was no time to reload; Wren circled the altar, and slammed his shoulder into the guy's chest.

They fell together, the shooter's back cracking off the altar then the floor, while Wren's momentum carried him slapping across the stones. He came to a stop beside Cheryl and her eyes tracked him. Then the shooter's gun fired again, the bullet ripped by Wren's head and he spun to grapple the guy's wrist, yanking hard.

The guy yanked back and the pistol's grip slammed into Wren's left shoulder, discharging another shot that sent a shock wave into his ear. Another shot followed and Wren twisted and pulled. The gun skittered away over the stone, then a big fist came in and an arm swung around Wren's neck. He bucked before the headlock could close, the back of his head caught the guy's chin and he twisted free.

They both climbed to their feet and stared at each other.

"Who are you people?" Wren asked, panting.

"We're justice," the man said, then pulled a large Bowie knife from a sheath down his thigh and lunged. The knife stabbed out three times at a wicked pace, matched by three fast stamps forward. Wren backed up fast, sustaining one nick on his left forearm.

The guy came in again, but this time Wren was ready; he danced back for two strikes then deflected the third with his left forearm, spinning into a whiplash right backhand across the man's face.

He rocked sideways, blue eyes flaring in surprise.

"Justice for what?" Wren asked, and shot a push kick into the guy's solar plexus before the words were all out. The guy staggered back and lashed out with the knife, forcing Wren to step back.

He needed a way past the blade. The shooter charged in, and this time Wren flung the Rorbaugh at his face. It smacked off his cheek, making him fumble the last step. That was just enough for Wren to grab his wrist and elbow, thrust with his hips and drag the the big man into an arcing judo throw.

He swept up, over and slammed down hard on his left side. The knife clattered free.

Wren shoved him belly-down before he could get his footing, dropped onto his back like it was a saddle then locked an arm around his throat and wrenched backward. The guy thrashed to get free but Wren bent his whole weight into it.

Something creaked in the man's neck, and Wren rode the edge until he passed unconscious. Wren let his body flop down beside Cheryl's body, sucking in hard breaths. He still had zip-ties from the warehouse in his pocket, and hog-tied the man swiftly, then moved to Cheryl.

"It'll be OK," he said, and located a knife wound in her lower back. He stripped his shirt and packed it against the wound, guiding her hand to hold it in position. Her pulse was firm but her breathing was shallow. "Just stay still and hold that."

Next, he inspected Teddy's head; the blow seemed to have crumpled his temple, though the impact injury was barely bleeding. Most likely he had a subdural hematoma; all the blood pooling beneath the skull and putting pressure on his brain. He had a weak pulse and was completely loose, with limbs like a dead man. There was nothing Wren could do for him here; he needed urgent surgery.

He brought up one of his burner phones and dialed 911.

"911, how may I direct your call?"

"I have shots fired at this address, two victims down, one with a subdural hematoma and the gunman in custody. Send SWAT and an air ambulance."

A second passed as keys clacked. "I have your address, Sir. Are you currently in danger?"

"Good question," Wren said, and looked up. He only saw the one man, but hadn't cleared the house. If more were coming, it would be soon. "Let's find out."

He ran the length of the basement, only noticing the man tucked into the far right alcove at the last moment. He was sat in a chair and wrapped with a single chain, and he didn't look good. He looked like he'd been tortured, with blood caking his face where several teeth had been pulled out.

Wren stepped in and checked his pulse, then saw the bullet hole in his skull and the matter spread on the wall behind him. Suppositions spun through his mind. This all-in-black assassin had been waiting here. But how?

The answer came as he spun back to look at Teddy. He'd claimed to have access to unique darknet groups on the Internet, out of which he'd extracted this man. But what if these killers had been watching those groups?

He returned to the assassin and rolled him onto his side. The man's eyes were open now, but swirling as he sucked for air. Wren spoke in a gruff bark.

"Who sent you? Tell me anything. Tell me something. I could put you on a coin."

The man just gasped. Wren figured he'd mostly crushed his windpipe, but he should be able to speak a little.

"Where are you based? What are you doing with the homeless? Where are Mason and Wendy?"

The guy tried to say something. Wren leaned in.

"You're a ..." he began.

Wren leaned in closer.

"Dead ... man."

He breathed out then didn't breathe in again.

26

CHOICE

Wren searched the man's pockets and found car keys and a phone, which he took, along with the man's weapon, a Beretta M9. As he thumbed the phone's screen awake, it abruptly rang. No number was listed.

He answered it after the second ring. "Yeah?"

"Is it done?" came a rich, confident baritone. It was the kind of voice you expected to hear headlining a self-help seminar: in control, intelligent, throbbing with confidence. "Do you have him?"

"I have him," Wren said.

"Was he alone?"

Wren's mind raced. Could this man be talking about him? His name and photograph had been all over the news, but it seemed quite a jump to link his actions in Utah to a random darknet chat thread in Chicago.

"He was alone."

"Send photographic confirmation now."

Wren paused for a second.

"Send it now, Sergeant."

Sergeant?

"Sending," Wren said, then laid down, switched the phone to selfie mode, shut his eyes like he was unconscious and took the photo. It was a gamble now whatever he did, but maybe he could extract some intel before this self-help creep figured it out.

He sent the photo, and a chime played through the speakers as the image landed on the far side. Wren waited for the gambit to pay off or fail.

"He's unconscious?" came the voice, confirming Wren's suspicion. "Is he restrained?"

"Yes to both. Where should I take him?"

A second passed. "Don't worry about that. The cleanup squad will be there in minutes. Just ensure he remains immobile."

Wren cursed under his breath. The cleanup squad? "Yes, Sir. And Sir?"

"What is it?"

"He did a real number on me. If we're moving him, even restrained, we'll need enough members on the team to put him down. How many are there?"

Another moment passed. Maybe Wren had pushed it too far.

"You know how many members are on a team, Sergeant. The same there always are."

Wren tried one more time. "I may have punctured one of his lungs. He's not breathing right. Are we taking him somewhere with medical expertise, Sir?"

The phone line hung silent for a moment, then the voice came back, altered this time. "It's you, isn't it? Wren."

Now they were wasting time.

"Your sergeant's dead," he said, "and your cleanup team will be dead too, in a few minutes. I've just got one question before I come hunt you down next. Justice for what?"

The deep voice began to laugh.

"Justice for what?" Wren repeated. "It's what your sergeant said with his final breath. What justice are you serving by killing innocent homeless people at some forest summer camp?"

"Summer camp?" The laughter continued. "You really don't know anything, do you, Christopher? Who we are. What we want. I can't wait to see the look in your eyes when-"

"Google me," Wren interrupted. "Take a good look at my eyes, because next time we speak you won't see me coming."

He disconnected the line.

He needed to move right now.

These people had already taken out an entire police department. Wren had to assume they could do that again here, and he wasn't arrogant enough to think he could fend them off alone. Even if the SWAT team arrived in time, would they fare any better?

He dropped to one knee by Cheryl. She was short but solid, easily one-sixty pounds. He could carry her in a fireman's lift, but there was no way he could carry Teddy too. The big man was as heavy as Wren. He had to choose who went first.

He scooped up Cheryl and ran: along the crypt, up the spiral stairs and into the kitchen. A glance out the windows showed no sign of any squad. He exited through the entrance hall and down the steps to his waiting van.

"You're going to be fine," he called to Cheryl as he pulled the passenger-side door open. Slotting her in was difficult, as he didn't want to compound her injuries, but he managed to get her in position with the seatbelt holding her upright.

He ducked out and started back toward the double doors to collect Teddy, but a sound from the end of the drive stopped him. He spun and saw a large black SUV tearing up the gravel toward him, sending stone chips to either side like surf.

It wasn't SWAT. Three men were already leaning out of the windows pointing rifles in his direction. He looked at Cheryl in the van; suddenly that ten yards seemed an uncrossable divide.

Rifle fire burst out abruptly, raking a line through the gravel near Wren's feet. He never left anyone behind and didn't want to start right now, but saw no other option.

He ran.

The van took the brunt of the incoming fusillade as Wren slammed back through the double doors into the grand house, mind working rapidly. He had another set of keys in his pocket from the assassin, which meant his car had to be nearby.

Wren made a beeline down a glamorous black hallway toward the back of the house. He sprinted through an open dining room with an overlarge mahogany table laid out with cutlery and crockery for ten, then kicked through a set of gray French doors to the rear patio.

There on the gravel sat a low black sedan, a BMW 3 Series. Wren sped down, opened it and dropped into the driver's seat, shoving aside a box of hollow-point ammo for the M9 and a slim red booklet with the title 'The Order of the Saints' on the front.

The keys slotted into the ignition, a twist brought the engine to life and Wren slammed the gas. In seconds he'd spun and was accelerating toward the corner of the house when the SUV shot around the side.

They pulled to the side. Wren didn't, slamming straight into the SUV's left headlight. The BMW crunched almost to a dead stop while the SUV ricocheted off to the right. Bullets fired and splashed the sedan's windows but only spidered cracks into what had to be bulletproof glass.

Wren hit the gas and tore off down the side. In his rearview mirrors the SUV gave chase. The van whipped by on his right, Cheryl tracking him with her eyes, but he couldn't do anything for her now.

Slugs spattered the back window. He slammed on the brakes as he drew up to the gate, sending coral spray up ahead, then shoved the door open and leaned out low as the BMW rolled forward. He braced the Beretta with both hands, targeted the SUV's front right tire and emptied the magazine.

The tire blew and the SUV jerked to the side, too fast to brake away its momentum now, on gravel too treacherous to offer any friction. It caromed toward the solid rock wall and hit with a huge crunch.

The BMW cruised gently through the gate. Wren pulled the handbrake and climbed out, grabbing shells from the ammo box and feeding them into the M9's magazine smoothly. He leaned around the wall to see the SUV had a crumpled hood, smoke spewing from under the warped metal. Figures poured out.

Wren fired. One went down with a headshot. One took a bullet in the thigh and fell.

Wren advanced along the wall, firing and reloading. They were disoriented and blinded by the smoke, staggering and wheeling and shooting blindly. Wren kept firing until they were all down.

Seven men, it looked like. He reached the SUV and looked inside just as the hood caught fire. There was nobody left alive. Wren ran, and thirty seconds later the truck exploded.

Wren made it back to the door of the mansion, headed back to the crypt to retrieve Teddy, when a second SUV shot around from the back of the mansion. His eyes bugged. He hadn't seen them come in. He'd had no idea.

He dropped to one knee and executed the same maneuver, targeting the front right tire. It blew out, but there was no rock wall for the truck to slam into this time, and it skidded across the gravel then rocked to a stop.

Wren was already halfway across the drive toward the BMW, mind flailing for a way out of this with Teddy and Cheryl in tow, but he couldn't think of one. Men poured from the damaged truck, rifles raised, and Wren fired the last of his magazine at them as he ran, just enough to keep their heads down.

Then he was through the gate and back in the BMW, facing a choice he'd never failed before. Bullets hammered the rear window, had to be several streams of automatic fire at once. He wouldn't even be able to get out of the car now. He'd just die.

He cursed, put the car in gear and ripped away down the tree-lined drive, leaving Teddy and Cheryl behind.

27

THE ORDER

The killer's phone rang in the passenger seat.

Wren considered answering it as he raced along small roads toward the freeway. Maybe there was something he could glean from a further conversation with the jumped-up self-help guru in charge of this operation, but then he'd also be handing them a way to track him.

He opened the window and tossed out the phone then raced on in silence.

His mind whirred. For them to track him down from a random search by a Foundation member in Chicago was impressive. For them to levy an armed response in such a short time, two trucks' worth of heavily armed and well-trained operators, was astounding.

An exit road popped ahead and Wren accelerated onto I-94 heading north. He took the BMW up to ninety miles an hour and leaned in, weaving between vehicles like he had somewhere to go or somewhere to be, when really he was just running.

Every fiber in his body felt like it was vibrating. He'd abandoned Teddy and Cheryl and he couldn't stand it. He had to get them back, but the scale of this thing was just getting bigger and bigger, and still there was no sign of what they were really doing, or why...

He needed to stop and think. He checked the clock; thirty minutes had passed already, so he pulled off at the next rest area.

Sitting in the broad parking lot, his hands shook. He pushed open the door, stepped out and started pacing. He'd lost team members before but none quite like this. He saw Teddy yanking sideways again as the pistol grip crashed into his head, his whole body dragged after it. Wren had just got done promising him a brighter future.

He saw Cheryl again slumped in the van, bleeding through the makeshift bandage, her dull eyes tracking him. He remembered her small smile at the thought of reaching coin four. For all their moral failures in the past, these two were everything he ran the Foundation for.

He'd involved them and now he'd lost them, and that was unforgivable. He had to make it right, had to quit reacting and start acting.

After two more minutes of pacing to get control of his breathing, he ducked back into the BMW and scooped out his phone. There was no message from Cheryl's Chicago PD cop yet, though, and no CCTV footage or ALPR tracking data, which meant he still had nothing to go on.

He blinked hard and rubbed his eyes. The comedown from adrenaline was making him sluggish. He stuffed the M9 in his back waistband, filled his pockets with shells and was about to drive off once more when he remembered something else.

He looked at the passenger seat but it wasn't there. Had it fallen out? He didn't think so, and slipped one hand down the side by the door. His fingers touched paper, and he gripped it and pulled it out.

The booklet.

THE ORDER OF THE SAINTS, it read across the front.

He scooped it up. There was a simple design beneath the title, a stylized biplane leaving a trail of spray behind it, like a crop duster. Wren recognized that image; it came from the conclusion of the Turner Diaries, an extremist science fiction tale published in 1978 and set in 1999. It told the story of how a revolutionary organization called 'the Order' violently overthrew the government of the United States. The book ended with a crop-duster plane carrying a nuclear weapon to destroy the Pentagon.

Wren shuddered in his seat. The Order of the Saints. Something else came back to him, which seemed to sync up with what Teddy had said about a summer camp; both seemed to reference a second fictional forerunner titled the 'Camp of the Saints'. It was another novel set in an extremist science fiction world, describing the death of Western civilization after a vast wave of outrageously violent immigrants invaded the first world nations.

Wren opened the booklet, read a little of the first page then skimmed through the rest rapidly. It was twenty-five pages all told, packed in with a tight font with no further illustrations, no back or front matter and no author name, likely run off a home press.

It didn't take him long to recognize it as cult recruiting material on an epic scale, designed to attract people already half-radicalized against their own government.

If there was anything Wren was an expert on after his childhood in the Pyramid, it was cults.

He stepped out of the BMW, fed the keys back through the open window then laid the booklet atop the roof and started taking photographs of each page.

He uploaded the photos along with a brief summary of what had just happened at Teddy's mansion, referencing his call to 911 for the location, then typed a final message and sent it to Humphreys' direct line.

DUST THIS CAR FOR PRINTS. THE MAN WHO DROVE IT IS DEAD ALONG WITH SEVEN OTHERS IN THE ORDER OF THE SAINTS. HERE'S YOUR CULT.

Then he tucked the booklet into his back pocket and headed across the lot toward the mall. He needed coffee, waffles and bacon to clear his head, then he was going to dig deep into this cult's BS and start getting ahead.

28

THE SAINTS

W ren ordered an all-day breakfast with bottomless coffee from a Waffle House, then sat in a window seat eating, drinking and reading.

The Order of the Saints booklet was outrageous. On one level it was the same kind of cult dogma he'd read a thousand times before. From Charles Manson's rantings to the annals of Waco and the Jonestown 'teachings', it was all just the same thing: damaged people trying to control other damaged people. Often these texts ended in apocalyptic visions, when their leaders reached the limit of their creative vision. The only satisfying climax they could imagine was a fiery end.

Wren read it all the way through once, mopping up maple syrup with a second round of waffles that were both crusty and soft at the same time, matched by a second helping of crispy bacon rashers topped with sunny-side-up eggs.

When he finally looked up, hunger satisfied but mind frazzled, he felt like he could see atomic explosions bursting across the horizon.

The work was crammed with detail, conspiracy theory and symbolism; so much so that Wren was struggling to process it. There were references to Masonic law, to a secret pact enshrined by the Founders and concealed in the painting in the Capitol dome, to America's role in helping Hitler escape Germany, to fluoride in water and chemtrail control systems and the fake moon landing and JFK and the hidden truth that birds weren't real.

It went on and on, and all of it was bent to support a prophecy about America's vile future, if the people did not rise up alongside a man named 'Alpha' and take back control.

It was obviously bullshit, but spewed with such authoritative detail and hammered home with such repetition that trying to parse it was overwhelming, and Wren couldn't glean a single hint about specific plots, locations or people.

That was the point, of course.

He sighed and ran a hand through his hair.

Cults like the Saints weren't interested in giving their followers hard facts to analyze for themselves. They didn't want them to think. They wanted them baffled, stunned and overawed, ready to hand their bodies and minds over to the will of the leader.

The 'Alpha'.

Wren was an excellent pattern analyst, able to spot hidden details in the most obscure datasets possible, but he couldn't make any sense of this.

He needed help, and had just the person in mind.

Dr. Greylah Ferat was a lecturer at Yale whose classes Wren had audited, back when he wasn't sure what direction to take after several years in Force Recon. Across the duration of one term, Ferat had blown Wren's mind with her Abnormal Psychology course; the ways the human mind could be manipulated through simple neurolinguistic tricks and emotional exploits. It reminded Wren of his father's brainwashing techniques back in the Pyramid.

At the end of term, Ferat had invited several standout

students out for a celebratory meal. Wren had gone, interested to learn more about the woman, but by the end it was Dr. Ferat asking Wren the questions.

No one had told her that Wren was the sole known survivor of the Pyramid, but she'd somehow figured it out. She launched a barrage of questions, using every technique in her mind control book with fluidity and grace, all designed to earn Wren's trust and compliance. She was writing a book on the Pyramid, and offered to cut Wren in on the royalties if he shared his first-hand account. It was sure to be a mainstream bestseller, she claimed, certain to catapult her to head the college's Psychology Department.

It was then, perhaps more than at any other time, that Wren realized how well daily survival in the Pyramid had prepared him for a life of undercover black ops. Dr. Ferat was an incredibly charismatic manipulator, but nothing she said or did came close to the power or danger presented by his father.

She was disappointed when Wren rejected her idea for the book, but intrigued when he offered a different kind of partnership: a role in structuring Wren's Foundation, back then just getting started with only twelve members.

None of it would ever be written in a book, Wren made her promise, but together they would plumb depths and tackle heights in abnormal psychology that no one had ever attempted before.

Dr. Ferat had jumped at the chance.

Now Wren sent her the same photos he'd sent to Humphreys.

29

DR. FERAT

T wo hours later, a drained Oreo milkshake and Wren's fifth coffee rested either side of the now-heavily annotated Order of the Saints booklet. For two more hours he'd worked on it searching for some kind of clue, but he'd found nothing further of use.

He tapped his pen against his teeth and gazed out at the parking lot. Across the way FBI agents were swooping on the BMW. There was a squad of them around it, setting up a forensics tent and sealing off the area. On some level, Wren felt like he should be worried they might find him, but he wasn't.

They'd go for the CCTV, but Wren had parked carefully in a blind spot then taken care with his route to the Waffle House. Humphreys would never expect to corner him here.

He looked back down at the booklet, covered in cross-references, highlights and scribbled theories. It looked like gibberish.

Finally, his phone rang.

"Doctor?" he answered.

"Christopher," came the powerful alto of Dr. Ferat, a

voice befitting a Shakespearean actor on stage, which belied her thinning, frail frame.

The last time Wren had seen her was two years earlier on the Yale campus, with Ferat standing in the rain with a fifteen-year coin in her hand, looking proud. Fifteen years she'd spent helping to build something phenomenal, taking the Foundation from twelve members to over a hundred. She'd also made Head of her Yale Department years earlier, off the strength of her own impressive research, much of it fueled by revelations stemming from the Foundation.

"What have you got?" Wren asked.

Ferat cleared her throat. "I've scanned the whole of it, that idolatrous screed, and Christopher, I found it very troublesome material."

That was no surprise. "Tell me."

"I know you're familiar with the author's reference points, 'The Camp of the Saints' and 'The Turner Diaries'? The author, this 'Alpha', seems to be trying to use them to underpin their own ideas, but it's obscured by a dense range of conspiracy theories. It would seem the Alpha's version of 'The Order' believes the current state of our nation is untenable, and the only effective remedy is use of force."

Wren took a breath. "Which people are they targeting?"

"Based on this work, their primary target is the government, but also anyone in a position of power. The Alpha clearly despises all figures of authority, though one particular threat stands out."

"Go on."

"An interesting reference is made to one part of the Turner Diaries, where rebel forces take control of nuclear weapons in Vandenberg Air Force Base, California, and start launching them at their enemies on the East Coast."

Wren's eyes widened. "Nuclear? Where did I miss that reference?"

"It was obscure, a reference to Major General Phillip St. George Cooke."

"I don't follow."

"I'm not surprised, Christopher. Major General Cooke was a Union General in the Civil War, known as the 'father of the modern cavalry'. An army base was named after him in Santa Barbara County, California, in the 50s; a base that was later expanded and renamed as Vandenberg."

Wren's jaw dropped slightly. It was a tenuous link, but conspiracy theorists loves tenuous links. "So you think Vandenberg's a target for the Saints? You really think they might go for the nuclear weapons?"

Ferat took a breath. "It's certainly possible. The booklet could support that interpretation. Do you believe it's feasible?"

Wren's mind raced back over all his analyses. "I don't know. Maybe? This organization, these 'Saints', they're incredibly effective. They're clean and professional. Maybe they could, but they'd need backup. A military base is nothing like a rural police department."

"Could they get that support? Where would it come from?"

"I don't know. Groups like the Vikings, maybe? There are easily a hundred groups in the United States like them, pushing for violence against the government. They're largely all fantasists, though, without the will or the means to execute on that vision, but they might help." He paused, sorting his thoughts. "The Saints used the Vikings well, then cleaned them up when they were no longer necessary. Maybe they could pull that trick again. Maybe they really could breach Vandenberg."

"That is troubling," Ferat said.

"No kidding."

"It is just one possible reading of the text, though,

Christopher. There are alternatives, perhaps alternatives that are more logical. If these Saints truly despise the powerful and are seeking nuclear weapons, then why are they abducting the unhoused? These must be the least powerful people in the country."

That surprised Wren. "Good point."

"We need to weigh the evidence on balance, based on their actions as well their words. Do you have any idea how many people these Saints have taken from America's streets?"

"Nothing concrete, but likely in the thousands. The evidence in Chicago suggested multiple strikes over the last year."

"And what of other cities?"

Wren paused. "What other cities?"

"All of them. Any of them. I don't believe an organization on the scale we're discussing would only target a single city, do you?"

Wren opened his mouth then closed it. He had no good answer. He'd been so busy with narrowing the hunt that he hadn't thought about widening it, but now fresh ramifications spun through his mind. What if Ferat was right, and the Saints weren't just taking the homeless in the thousands, but in the tens of thousands?

"Christopher?"

"Sorry, I'm thinking. Maybe you're right. Why else would they snatch people in Chicago but keep a warehouse in the Utah desert? It suggests an incredible network, maybe warehouses in every state, every major city targeted with trafficking routes criss-crossing the country, and..." he trailed off, mind buzzing. "Why? Why so many?"

"That's the other major alternative, Christopher. There are hints in this booklet where blame is ascribed, and Hitler's name is mentioned three times. Many people forget that Hitler did not only persecute and slaughter the Jewish race, but also gypsies, homeless people, the disabled, anyone he considered to be a drag on his Fatherland. These Saints may also be taking inspiration from his holocaust."

Wren gritted his teeth. "You think they're executing the homeless?"

"It's possible. The booklet would support that."

"How does that link in with their hatred of authority?"

"As far as I can tell, they only hate the authority of others. Once they get authority themselves, mass culls are likely."

Wren cursed.

"Indeed."

"You're talking about an American genocide, Greylah. Could you glean any details? I need practical places, people, dates."

Ferat took a heavy breath."Beyond Vandenberg? There may be other concealed references, but I'll need time to look into them. For now, you mentioned those hundred extremist groups? I'd reconsider them. They may be part of the 'how'. From what I can gather, especially in the section on page seventeen discussing 'uniting the weft of lost tribes', this 'Order' has been knitting disparate organizations together for years. The Vikings are a prime example, along with various unnamed religious sects, politically extreme militias and dark Internet hate groups across the country. None are named explicitly, but they can be inferred."

Wren heaved a heavy breath. "OK. So it's either a race for nuclear weapons to start World War III, or it's a genocide against the unhoused. Neither's good."

"I agree, and those are just two interpretations. There are countless more possible, including all this being their preparation for the coming Rapture, the resurgence of Lilith's children, an uprising either from the hollow Earth or a city on the moon, and many more."

"That's batshit crazy."

"Crazy is dangerous, Christopher, as you know. It's easy to persuade people to act in ways that seem crazy to 'normal' people. Think of Timothy McVeigh, Anders Breivik, even 9/11 and ISIS. Think of the Hutu massacre of the Tutsis, where an entire nation was persuaded to kill their neighbors. A million died before sanity returned."

Wren swallowed hard. He'd studied all those cases extensively. "I need a location, Doctor. Vandenberg's a target, great, but I need their headquarters."

"I can't give you that, only that I believe these Saints are now everywhere. I believe they are hiding in plain sight, waiting for a signal to activate. They must be stopped."

Wren had nothing more to say. He knew that. "Thank you, Dr. I'll be in touch."

"My pleasure, Christopher. If I uncover anything else, I will contact you. Good luck."

30

ALPR

Wren rested his head in his hands. He had no leads, only the potential target of Vandenberg. He was no closer to understanding the real motive driving the Saints than before. He checked his phone, but nothing on the CCTV footage had come in yet.

Time was ticking.

He gazed out of the window at the FBI agents. They'd erected their forensics tent around the BMW now and were bustling around it.

They had the manpower. Humphreys could get the CCTV and analyze it in moments, if he chose to. He could coordinate a national-level response with the FBI, NSA, DHS and all the other intelligence agencies, rolling up extremist groups one after another, if only he believed Wren wasn't responsible.

Wren stood up. He could think of one way to refocus Humphreys, and that was to take himself off the board.

He picked up the booklet and headed for the door.

He owed it to Teddy and Cheryl. Humphreys might dump him in a black site, where he wouldn't see his wife or kids for some time, maybe ever again, but stopping this threat to the homeland mattered more.

Wren left the Waffle House and walked toward the FBI agents.

Then his phone rang.

One of the FBI agents looked in his direction. Wren turned swiftly and answered the phone. "Wren."

"I've got some CCTV for you," came a brusque male voice with a Chicago accent.

Wren started back toward the Waffle House at once. There was a shout from behind but he ignored it.

"Two semi trucks," Wren said, shifting gears rapidly. "Did you find them?"

"Yeah, pretty much the only freight passing through between the times you requested," the cop said. "Like a convoy. So, you want the license plates?"

Wren's heart began to race. Cheryl had come through for him. "I want the ALPR. Where they went. Do you have that?"

"Sure I do. But you gotta tell that bitch Cheryl to take me off her blackmail list."

"Done. Where did the trucks go?"

"I'm serious. She plays this trick one more time and I'm coming around to put a hole in her head, do you understand? I know where she lives."

"I'll be sure to relay that, now where did the trucks go?"

The guy sighed and shuffled papers in the background. "OK. So, I tracked them on ALPR until signal loss. They went north-west from Chicago on I-90 to, uh, Tomah, Wisconsin. From there they went north on 94 to Eau Claire." He paused for a breath. "I thought I lost them there, but then I picked them up on State 53 all the way up at Duluth, Minnesota, where I lost them again, but I kept looking, because Cheryl is such a hot bitch."

Wren walked faster. More shouts popped behind him. He needed a vehicle now, and fast. "Where?"

"You in some kind of rush or something?"

"Only the fate of the free world. Where?"

The guy snorted. "Fine, be a schmuck. I kept looking until I found what had to be the only ALPR-linked crosswalk cam northeast of Duluth, on local road 61 in a little town called Two Harbors. Does that sound about right?"

Wren brought up Google maps on his phone, zooming in on Two Harbors, Minnesota. It was a tiny outcropping of buildings clustered low on the northwest shore of Lake Superior.

"And that's the last sighting you had?"

"I said so, didn't I? After that you're onto backroads and into the Stone Age, like plate recognition doesn't exist. Yokels, you know. Now, tell-"

"I'll tell Cheryl," Wren repeated and ended the call.

Two Harbors. That was something he could work with; north like Teddy's contact had said, straight into a heavily forested area that had to be packed with summer camps. He ran a quick search and found dozens within a fifty-mile radius, all accessible via backroads.

More shouts were following now, so he ducked down low and broke into a run.

The shouting grew urgent, but there was nothing they could do. The parking lot was huge, and with his head bobbed down he'd just become a needle in the haystack. He cut left then right, weaving away from the BMW and the Waffle House, running until he'd reached the far corner of the lot, where he found a 2004 Jeep Wrangler Unlimited in muted mustard tones.

He bobbed up long enough to break the passenger side window, pop the locks and brush the glass aside, then he slid in. He tore the steering column housing away, ripped a few wires and jump-started the engine.

Looking up, he saw there were no agents anywhere near. They'd likely requisition CCTV of the lot and track him, but that would take time. Until then, Wren would be ahead. They'd struggle with ALPR just like the Chicago cop had, especially when he got into the rural areas. On the plus side, he'd lead them right up to the Saints, if he could find them.

Two Harbors looked to be a good spot. Seven hours drive, give or take. He wrote a swift email detailing the threat as he and Ferat envisioned it, coming from a range of extremist groups that might have thrown in with the Saints, along with a warning to watch Vandenberg Air Base, then he sent it to Humphreys from an anonymous email address.

With that done, he rolled calmly out of the lot and merged onto I-94, heading north.

31

FOREST

F or four hours Wren pushed northwest on I-90, leaving the suburban edge of Chicago and plowing through long green tracts of soybeans and corn and past the stink of countless hog farms.

His mind turned and turned. He thought about what was happening to Teddy and Cheryl, and whether they'd even survived. He thought about his family and when he might get to see them next.

Mostly, he thought about the Saints.

After four hours, after crossing into Wisconsin and skirting Madison, he stopped at a rest area just shy of Eau Claire. He grabbed a couple of burgers and a coffee at a diner then brought up Google maps on his phone.

A heavy gray downpour began outside.

Wren focused on the map. The area within a thirty mile radius of Two Harbors was heavily forested, sliced by only a handful of roads. He ran the same search for a summer camp and watched as dozens populated throughout amongst the trees.

Too many.

He needed to narrow that down, and took a long glug of

coffee, thinking back to what Teddy had said. This camp had cabins, an archery range, tennis courts and a lake.

Wren swiftly narrowed the possibilities down to camps beside lakes; only five in his search radius. He zoomed in and studied each of them while slurping on coffee, and found four that had cabins as opposed to tents, three that had visible archery ranges, two that had tennis courts and only one that had all three.

Camp Alden on Alden Lake.

Google supplied a number which Wren called. It went straight to a message.

"This line has been placed out of service. Your communication cannot be processed."

Wren zoomed as close in as the app would allow. There were a dozen small cabins radiating around a central hall, accessed by a dirt track running up from a single-lane road. There were no vehicles that he could see, no flag at the top of the pole, and both the tennis courts and the archery range were overgrown.

Abandoned.

This had to be it. His heart rate thrummed faster. He studied the roads leading up to it.

Would the Saints be waiting for him? It seemed possible. He scanned for a covert route in.

There was the main dirt track into the camp and two roads that passed nearby. One looked to be an old lumber route, dead-ending by a smaller unnamed lake, while the other continued to join a larger road twenty miles north. Wren dropped four pins on the map to represent choke points, places the Saints would likely lie in wait.

He scanned wider until he found a long line of grass cutting through the forest, passing within two miles of the camp. Zoomed out, he saw that it spread more than a hundred miles in either direction, but with no power lines or rail tracks in sight. Likely it was a disused freight line from a century earlier, bringing coal down from Canada, with the pilings now overgrown and the iron rails reclaimed.

Wren finished his burgers and returned to the Jeep, checking the console. It had 4-wheel drive. He had his way in; travel the old line from five miles out, stop two miles from the camp then trek the rest of the way on foot.

He memorized the route then set out.

It was dark by the time he passed Duluth, looking out over Lake Superior's dark, vast expanse. At Two Harbors he bore west, switching off his beams and driving by moonlight, until soon enough he reached the old railway line. It stretched dead-straight through the forest, a gulley between the trees, part-filled with low brush and saplings.

His heart pounded in his chest. He hit the 4-wheel drive button, then rolled the Jeep down onto the old rail line.

The dense undergrowth rasped against the vehicle's underside. Through the open windows Wren breathed in the scent of crushed sap, navigating by the broad band of stars in the northern sky; the W-shaped zags of Cassiopeia, the great K of Taurus, Lyra shaped like an urn.

It felt like a return to an older, wilder past. The sky brightened as Wren's eyes adjusted, casting the gulley in a haunting, silvery relief. It took him back to his early hunts with Tandrews in the backwoods of Maine. It was those times that had brought him back from the memory of all those burning bodies. Out there Tandrews had let him choose his own name.

"There's power in a name," Tandrews had said, sitting across from him over a fire with venison steak hissing on the spit. "It's how you take your space in the world."

Christopher Wren, the British architect who'd built the greatest structures of his era, had been a wondrous discovery.

After spending his childhood watching his father tear things down, he'd decided to take the opposite approach.

Miles ticked by on the odometer. Soon Wren squeezed the brakes and the Jeep slowed. He killed the engine then sat perfectly still, listening to the forest.

Life was everywhere around him: bats swooping and screeching; opossum and bobcats rustling; birds calling mournful nighttime dirges; an owl hooting and cicadas scratching. It wasn't the same forest that he'd known, wasn't even within a thousand miles of Maine, but it felt like home.

Wren stepped out of the truck and started forward. Soon trees enveloped him, and he recognized them by their rough bark and scent: Jack Pine, Black Spruce, Tamarack. He knew instinctively the footing around each of them, the particular gnarled fingers their roots turned through the earth.

His pace increased, rising to a jog. His muscles felt loose and limber. Soon a familiar scent carried on the air, getting stronger with every step forward.

Smoke.

It hung stale and thin through the trees like a mist. Maybe the Saints had already burned the camp down. Maybe he'd find nothing at all. Maybe they were still here.

Only one way to find out.

32

CAMP

Wren came upon the camp from the southwest, where the long finger of lake Alden shone like mercury under a clear, cloudless sky. He approached the water's edge and picked out a sinking dock at the northern side some two hundred yards away. Beyond that lay a clearing and the edge of a building; the main camp hall. No sign of any Saints, but if they were proficient operators, there wouldn't be.

He advanced until he crossed a trail. It was overgrown and crunchy with years of composting leaves. A light wind blew, rustling the branches overhead.

Wren kept on until the trees gave way to a low bank of ferns. The main hall was a log cabin structure, less damaged than he'd anticipated. Char marks of deep, silvery soot ran up its sides and the roof was missing in places, but all the walls still stood. Beneath two large windows lay heaps of wreckage, as if the building had vomited its contents onto the soil. A long ventilation duct poked up in the midst of broken chairs and charred wooden desktops like some strange periscope. Here and there sections still smoldered, releasing thin tendrils of smoke.

Wren crept through the ferns. They'd set the camp on fire, but a rain had fallen soon after, putting it out.

Maybe there was still something to find.

The center of the camp was empty. Wren looked across the fire circle, from the cabins on the right to the lake on the left, and saw no one. They could be hiding, but that didn't matter. He had to do this now.

He stalked along the shadowed front of the building and stepped into darkness through the open door.

The interior deadened the sound from outside instantly, and revealed a dark, narrow lobby coated in ash. The walls were scorched through in places, revealing dark, large rooms to either side.

Wren strode deeper, sweating now, throat constricting with the pungent smoke. The floor creaked and shifted. Above the door to the left was a fire-scarred sign that read 'Office'.

He stepped through into a black, hollow space, lit by moonlight through many holes in the ceiling. The Saints must have dumped a barrel of gas in here to cause this much damage despite the rain.

The floor was littered with ashy metal desk frames and chairs, with all of the wood and padding material burned away. Cinders crunched underfoot, releasing a sour musty ash. His toe struck an obstruction, and in the darkness he knelt down to feel its contours. Some kind of metal eyelet embedded in the wood. He worked two fingers through the hole and gave a yank, but it was screwed in tight.

He patted the floor around it. The hardwood boarding was pocked with dozens of furrows, each no deeper than a single knuckle and no longer than his index finger.

Odd.

Wren looked up and tried to envisage the 'Office' as it

might have been a day earlier. At the head would be the manager's desk, with buddy-desks leading along the length of the hall and a central aisle down the middle.

He padded down that aisle, occasionally reaching to either side and running his fingers through the damp ash to find more eyelets and more furrows. In a pool of moonlight he saw blotchy stains like spilled ink.

By the head of the room his breathing came rougher as the smoke and ash gathered in his lungs. He knew what he'd find by the skeleton of the manager's larger desk frame: a single eyelet below the chair with more furrows and stains around it.

Wren's head spun as he looked back over the ravaged room. It reminded him of something, but he couldn't be sure what.

He went back to the lobby to the doorway on the right. Here the sign on the wall was unclear, but he could guess at the missing letters.

'School'.

The room beyond was burned just like the office, though here the metal desk and chair frames were smaller, suited for children, and many remained laid out in rows. At the front a blackboard leaned drunkenly against the wall, warped by the heat.

There were more eyelets beneath every desk, along with furrows and stains, offering answers Wren didn't want to find. He felt dizzier still, standing in the middle of that abandoned space.

Teddy's contact had talked about shots fired and bodies being carried out. He thought of the homeless snatched from Chicago and brought here to die.

How many people had died here?

Wren had a pretty good idea about their procedure now.

He imagined the school desks filled with Masons and Wendys, yanking at chains secured to the eyelets until their wrists bled. Bullets were fired into their bodies at point-blank range, running furrows into the wood and leaving iron-rich bloodstains that the fire baked in.

A massacre every time. A whole room at a time.

But why? Why bother with the chairs and tables, the 'Office' and the 'School' labels?

Then an answer hit him, growing from that feeling of familiarity, and he had to steady himself against the wall. He'd done scenarios much like these many times throughout his Force Recon training. There were whole fake schools, churches, office buildings and homes set up in the Marine training grounds, populated with both innocents and targets, played by actors. In their training raids he'd used paint balls or beanbag guns so nobody was actually hurt.

Not here.

He imagined himself walking into this, a new recruit in the army of the Order of the Saints, faced with chairs full of screaming, desperate victims. Tasked with starting a massacre across the nation, this would be his moment of truth. Success here would harden him as a killer, making him the kind of person able to kill anyone who got in his way without a second thought.

The homeless were just live-fire fodder in the training of an army of active shooters.

He felt sick, but it added up.

Everything in the booklet pointed toward an endgame like this.

He caught himself on one knee as the dizziness spread.

This was it all began, churning out a stream of mentally broken active shooters, ready to wreak devastation in offices and school across the country. Innocents were going to die.

Wren's mind reeled. How many camps were there like this across the country? How many graduates? How many dead?

There was a sound from outside. Wren straightened at once.

Someone was coming.

33

LAKE

Wren ran and dived for the open window just as the raucous bark of rifle fire chewed up the night. He flew through the frame and for a moment was airborne and falling, glimpsing the glint of silver moonlight on the finger lake, then he hit the periscope vent on his left shoulder.

The metal crumpled, dropping him into the heap of ashy wreckage. Wild bullets raked the cabin wall around him, muzzle flashes blinking from afar.

Wren rolled and ran.

Bullets whipped nearby as he raced into the ferns then the forest, zagging an unpredictable path that set his thighs burning in seconds. He glimpsed more muzzle flashes through the underbrush; from across the lake, from the depths of the forest, from beyond the circle of benches around the fire.

The Saints were everywhere, tightening like a noose.

Wren hit the track and swerved right toward the lake, riding a blast of adrenaline that drove him on harder, until the side of his left thigh took a hit like a red hot poker slicing through the skin.

He gasped, stumbled and almost fell, shifting trajectory to stay upright. His left leg barely took his weight on the next step, and his mind spun fast calculations as he lurched over knotty roots. It had to be a flesh wound only, a glancing blow; a dead shot in the hamstring would have put him on the ground bleeding out right now, femur crushed to powder.

Still, it wasn't good. Red tinged his vision as he staggered to the waterline; adrenal wrath bulling through the pain of every step. He was not just another innocent victim to be ushered to the slaughter, though. He too had been born in blood, a thousand burned alive in the Pyramid's streets, and since then he'd killed hundreds of evil men.

These wannabe school shooters didn't know the wasp they'd bottled. Rounds barked out ahead and Wren emptied his M9 into the bodies of two lurching shadows. They fell and Wren hurtled on toward a man at the waterline, who was now swinging his rifle like a club. Wren ducked the blow and sent the M9's barrel in an uppercut thrust into the man's chin, driving the muzzle up through the base of his jaw.

The weapon lodged, the man dropped back and Wren dived. There was an instant only to suck in a deep breath, then the cold lake water splashed around him. Powerful strokes raked him deeper, his hands grabbing clumps of slimy pondweed in the lake's base, navigating by feel as his lungs rapidly began to burn.

Thirty seconds passed fast, and the urge to suck in brackish pond water heaved within his chest. A minute went by, and now silver lights danced behind his eyes as he swept his arms in a broad, churning stroke. A minute thirty? He had to be close to the middle of the lake now. His left leg throbbed and the panicked drive to breathe became unendurable.

Silver was everywhere. Close to blacking out, Wren rolled onto his back and let his lips break the surface of the water, gasping in breath. No bullets came. He had to be out in the middle of the lake, hopefully invisible.

He allowed ten breaths, each deeper than the last. Through the thin sheen of water he tracked the constellations above and re-oriented his body, bearing for Cassiopeia above the northern tail of the lake.

He had to hope he could get out, stagger clear, and make it back to the Jeep.

He had to get the message out. Humphreys had to know the scale and spread of the Saints' diseased extremism.

He submerged again and swam ahead, surfacing a minute or so later at the north bank. He slithering out of the water with his fists tight in the weeds, keeping his head low and barely breathing. A voice called nearby, but no rifle fire followed.

The dark forest opened and beckoned him in. Rising to his feet, limping and bleeding, he ran.

34

ONE BAR

A few minutes passed then a wave of dizziness brought Wren to his knees.

He reached for his left thigh and felt the torn jeans and wound; a deep slice across the side of his quadriceps muscle. The bone underneath was solid, the muscle not too badly compromised, but he was losing a lot of blood.

He pulled off the wet black hoodie, wrapped it around his thigh and knotted it tightly over the wound.

Voices came from behind. Flashlights flickered through the trees, and he pushed himself back to his feet. His options were narrowing with every passing second. If they hadn't found his trail yet, they soon would, dragging one leg behind him, scratching up a path through the carpet of pine needles.

His fingers dug numbly into his pocket, prizing out the burner phone. Lights sparkled over his shoulder as he pushed the power button. The screen scrambled to life in a rainbow of waterlogged colors, and Wren almost laughed.

Always he'd prided himself on his strength, the umbrella of protection and rock of certainty he offered to those in his Foundation, but he'd never lied to himself about how dependent he truly was. He'd survived the Pyramid, but without Tandrews' help he might have become a very different man; maybe desperate like Eustace, twisted like Teddy and Cheryl. The coin system gave him the same thing it gave his members, an anchor in a world that had never really wanted him.

The truth was, he needed their help just as much as they needed him.

He squeezed the phone's screen, trying to throttle a last spark of life out of it, and somehow that worked. The kaleidoscope of colors narrowed down to a usable band of screen. He huddled it close to his chest to hide its light and checked his reception.

One bar of signal.

With stiff fingers he tapped in Humphreys' direct number. Long seconds passed and voices came closer in the dark, then there was a click but no answer.

"Humphreys?" he whispered.

"I'm here, Wren," came Humphreys' baritone. He sounded weary. "We're tired of this game. It won't be me answering the next time. I'll be the one slapping cuffs on you and escorting you into the darkness. You're never coming back up after this."

It took Wren a moment to catch up with what Humphreys was saying. "What?"

"The Order of the Saints? It doesn't exist, Wren. The only group we know of with substantial membership and a potentially nuclear objective is your own. You're gloating or maybe you've actually cracked. There were no bodies at the mansion, and there was nothing in that BMW but your own prints and phone. Theodore Smithely III and Cheryl Derringer, the people you mentioned? They are missing, but as far as we can see they're connected to nothing, except perhaps your investigation into the Ripper Crew copycats. Is that how you recruited your 'Foundation', Wren? Piggybacking for vulnerable people on FBI investigations? It's disgusting."

Wren couldn't parse all that. Something about nuclear objectives? "I've been shot," he managed. "You have my location? Maybe a mile north of Alden Lake, near the abandoned Alden summer camp that the Order of the Saints were using, seven miles west of Two Harbors, Minnesota. Do you copy that, Humphreys?"

Now Humphreys sounded confused. "Yes, I copy that. But what do you mean, you've been shot?"

"I'm hunting the Order. Or they're hunting me." He barely stopped a high note of laughter edging through. "I've seen what they were doing here, Humphreys. Taking homeless people and using them as live-fire training. They had one hall set up like a school, the other like an office, with the victims chained down when they let the shooters in. They're training their people to kill without hesitation."

Humphreys said nothing. Perhaps the signal had gone.

"Did you hear that? It's the preparation for a mass wave of killings, Gerald. Like in the booklet I sent you. They're priming the pump. They're-" he trailed off, losing his sense of the sentence in the dark of the forest, until the final revelation came. "They're trying to start a civil war, one active shooter at a time. Like the Hutus killed the Tutsis. It's coming. I've got a-"

He stopped as a flashlight briefly shone in front of him, splashing through the trees and away. Had it seen him? He stumbled on. There was something else playing on his mind now, but couldn't quite grasp it.

"Whatever happens now," he pushed on, "it isn't me doing this, Humphreys. It's the Saints, and they're everywhere. You have to stop them."

Another pause, then Humphreys came back. "Are you in danger?"

Wren felt giddy. The voices were closing in. "If you could send an evac helicopter to my location right now, that would be a big help. I'd appreciate it."

"I can arrange that. What else can we do, Chris? If it really isn't you, where should we be looking?"

Wren laughed, and more flashlights danced around him. He dropped to his knees then laid flat on the pine needles. He'd be harder to see that way, buying a few more seconds.

"I don't know." He racked his mind. There was something more there, but he couldn't be sure. Something Humphreys had said, or Dr. Ferat, or... "Vandenberg!" he hissed sharply, drawing flashlight beams in his direction. "If it's a small-arms civil war, they're not going for the nukes. Maybe it's their west-coast headquarters. Are there any extremist groups out there?"

"In Vandenberg? I'll check that. And Chris-"

The phone died in his hands.

Wren tried to get up but his limbs barely moved. It felt like he was surfing a gray wave of unconsciousness. He'd lost too much blood, and-

Was that the sound of a helicopter coming down?

He looked up through the thick canopy of trees and picked out a narrow river of stars winding across the sky. He'd seen these same skies as a child when he hadn't known a thing; not who he was, not what he was heading toward, not what he was running from.

Did he know any better now?

Flashlights slashed closer. A voice shouted.

"He's here!"

Boots stamped over. Wren watched the first of them come in as his mind drifted back over the last four weeks.

"Loralei?" he asked, gazing up into the light. "Is that you?"

Strong hands reached down, scooped him up and carried him through the darkness, to where his family would be waiting, to Loralei, Jake and Quinn. Then a hand closed around his throat and squeezed, ushering him through the black door into nothing.

35

BLACK SITE

Wren rose to consciousness in a metal chair with Loralei's name on his lips. It came out a croak, but of course she wasn't there.

Now he was naked and cold in a white cell maybe fifteen feet square, surrounded by mirrors, bright light and the pounding bass of repetitive trance music. He jerked to get free, but his wrists and ankles were strapped down with tight leather buckles.

His injured left leg was wrapped in bandages, and there were strips of gauze taped to various wounds on his chest and arms. Beneath that, there was an eyelet cemented into the cold tile floor.

He almost laughed. He'd finally made it into the Order of the Saints.

Cold reality settled over him.

He knew what they were capable of now. Images from Camp Alden flashed in his head: eyelets, stains and bullet furrows. He imagined Mason and Wendy being forced through that brutal system.

Now he was in it. They were almost certainly going to torture him.

He'd been tortured before, enough to know that everybody broke in time. The only way to survive was to turn the tables, but to do that you needed information.

Wren gazed into the mirrored glass.

He knew some things. Camp Alden. Their manifesto. Vandenberg. Maybe, if he used that information at the right time, he could leverage open a gap that would flip the whole infernal Order over.

It started right here: a white room, clearly a specialized space designed for interrogations. There'd been nothing like it in the Utah warehouse or at Camp Alden. Most likely the Saints had only one or two such facilities across the whole organization.

This was their headquarters. Judging by the redness of fresh scratches on his chest, they hadn't traveled far from Camp Alden, a few hours at most.

Chicago was seven hours away, and therefore unlikely. That left only one major city within range: Minneapolis.

A strong bluff to start.

The cold seeped deeper and he shuddered. The volume of the music ramped up, then the door opened and intense white light flooded in, momentarily blinding him as two figures came through.

It was about the worst thing he'd feared.

Teddy.

He stumbled in naked and gagged with his hands bound behind him, alive but barely. His skin was ashen, with a blood-soaked bandage around his head and his left eye swollen shut. His right eye rolled uncontrollably.

Wren was stunned to see him conscious and walking, let alone alive.

A woman came in beside him, tall and beautiful with pale skin, green eyes and blond hair. She wore a tight-fitting navy suit that accentuated her figure, and there was a neat oblong scar on her throat that looked to have come from a custom branding iron.

Wren only had eyes for Teddy. "Theodore, it's Chris. I'm right here. You're going to be OK."

Teddy's rolling eye halted for a moment, almost focusing on Wren, then two guards shoved him roughly to his knees. They wore tactical black suits and their faces were marked by more oblong brand scars; maybe evidence of some kind of cult rite.

"Get your hands off him," Wren snarled, unable to hold back the anger, but the guards ignored him. They zip-tied Teddy's bound wrists to an eyelet in the floor, then the woman gave a signal and they left.

Teddy's head bowed forward.

"Theodore," Wren called, and Teddy tried to lift his head to look, but the woman stepped in, gripped him by the hair and held his head pointing down.

"My name is Sinclair," she said in a laconic, Ivy-league voice. "I'm going to ask you some questions and you're going to answer."

The pounding music stopped abruptly, leaving a silence broken by Teddy's labored breathing. Wren switched his gaze to her, biting back the fury. Getting emotional now wouldn't help anyone. This was a display of power, and as if to reinforce that the woman slid a knife from a holster at her waist.

"Hurt him and I'll kill you," Wren rasped. "There'll be no mercy for you or any Saint."

Her lips spread into a smile. "Too late. I've already hurt him. I've been doing it for hours. I can hurt him more, if that helps."

She shook Teddy's head by the hair. He made no sound, too far gone to protest, but droplets of sweat mixed with blood sprayed across the white floor, forming pinkish blots.

"I won't help you if he dies," Wren said. "He needs a hospital."

"Of course he does. But we don't always get what we need, do we, Pequeño 3?"

Wren blinked. He couldn't quite believe she'd just said that.

Pequeño 3.

It was the name he'd been known by in the Pyramid. It meant 'little one 3' in Spanish, and not even James Tandrews had known it. Nobody knew it. He hadn't heard it spoken aloud for twenty-five years.

"How do you know that name?"

Sinclair's smile spread. "We know all about you, Christopher Wren. The CIA's wild child, 'Saint Justice' himself. Bane of terrorists worldwide. Survivor of America's worst death cult, the Pyramid."

Wren stared back. She was baiting him and it was working. "What do you know about the Pyramid?"

"More than you, I expect," she said dismissively. "And about your Foundation, too. We know he's one of yours." She gave Teddy's head another rough shake. "We found a three-year coin in his pocket. It's an interesting system, simplistic maybe, but one we might adapt in the future. Easier than brands."

She stroked her fingers down the scar on her throat.

"If he dies, there'll be no coin system for you or your organization. I'll see every one of your Saints burn in hell, just like the Pyramid."

Sinclair's smile faded. "Really? That's a threat with no incentive, Pequeño. You're supposed to be a master of human drives, but twice now you've only offered punishment. Where's my reward to let him go?"

Her smile was gone but Wren saw the amusement in her

177

eyes. She wasn't worried at all. That was either well-earned confidence or complacency. He had to make it the latter.

"I'll join you."

She laughed. "You'll join us?"

"The CIA and the FBI hate me. They're hunting me right now. The enemy of my enemy is my friend. It won't mean anything to betray them, and I can help you."

She gave Teddy's head another light shake. "I think you'd have to adopt a creed to betray it, wouldn't you? Don't you agree, Theodore?"

Teddy groaned.

She nodded, pleased with his obedience. "We both know you're a lawless vigilante, Pequeño, working for the CIA by convenience alone. That's the story of your life, isn't it? After the Pyramid, you wanted to kill people, and who could blame you? The CIA just gave you permission to do it." She took a step closer, dragging Teddy's head over. "But it is true, we could use a man like that. A killer who knows his place. You could be a substantial resource to us." Her eyes narrowed. "But would you know your place?"

"I'll fit right in," Wren said. "Bring in the Alpha. I'll kiss the ring."

She laughed again. "And how do you know I'm not the Alpha?"

Wren didn't answer that. It was apparent in her bearing. He'd seen many cult leaders in his time, and they all dominated a room by strength of their vision. Sinclair had presence and authority, but her eyes lacked the light of true madness.

"It's got to be the Alpha."

A flicker of annoyance crossed her face, but she quickly tamped it down. "Perhaps that can happen. But let's start small. Tell me, why have you been hunting us?"

Wren weighed lying and dismissed it. The details were

too easy to check. "No special reason. You're right about me. Your Vikings stole my truck, and that was my excuse. I just started killing and then I couldn't stop."

Sinclair shoved Teddy's head lower, forcing a grunt from him, and took a step closer to Wren. "You killed a lot of men for a truck."

"It was mine. They shouldn't have taken it."

She leaned in then, so close that Wren could almost reach her with a headbutt, until she placed the blade lightly on his chest. "That's good, Pequeño. Pride. Honor. We know all about that. We know how the CIA fired you, because of your pride. You're a ronin now, aren't you? A masterless samurai, floating on an ocean of people who don't care about what you've done for them. Your sacrifices. You're lost."

"It does suck," Wren allowed.

"That's because America is a myth. It isn't real. It's a story we tell ourselves, but it lets exploitation in through the back door. We won't see them as they stab us in the back."

Wren looked into her green eyes. "I hear that, sister. Preach."

She leaned closer still, so close that Wren could reach up and strip out her throat with his teeth, if it weren't for the knife between them. "I would love to believe you, Pequeño 3. You're an intelligent man. A man skilled in manipulation. Maybe, with enough brands to overwrite your past, the Order might genuinely admit you. A fresh Saint for the war to come."

"Bring me the papers, I'll sign them right now."

Sinclair leaned all the way in, pressing her hot chest against his. The scent of her grew overpowering, perfume and sweat and the iron tang of Teddy's blood. Terror brought out the primitive sex pheromones; arousal was a state tied up with so many other emotions. It was a torturer's trick that could make even the most seasoned operators spill.

"Can you read my brand?" she whispered.

She tilted her chin up in another show of power. Wren craned to see, picking out the capital letters burned into her otherwise flawless throat.

SIC SEMPER TYRANNIS

"Thus always to tyrants," he translated. "What John Wilkes Booth shouted after shooting Lincoln."

Sinclair smiled, bringing her lips within inches of his own, her eyes so close he felt the heat of her cheeks. "You should like that. Your father was a tyrant, was he not?"

"He was a madman with charisma. I'm sure your Alpha has a good reason for what he's doing. Why he's training an army to spark civil war."

She laughed. "Fishing, are you? Everything you need to know, I already told you. That is the Saints. We protect real Americans. The little guy. You can help with that."

She smiled, almost like she was challenging him to call her out, but Wren was committed now to playing his role in the script she'd laid out. "How?"

"Start small," she said, and pulled away slightly. "Tell us who's coming for us. Tell us what they know so far. From there, we'll see."

Wren studied her. This was the power he had, even if it was small. This was what they needed from him. "Let me speak with the Alpha. I'll tell him everything."

"You won't tell me?" She sounded hurt.

"It has to be the Alpha."

Sinclair pulled all the way back. "Very well."

She raised the knife high then swung it down hard, before Wren could say anything. The metal grip struck Teddy on the back of the head, jolting him forward. His right eye rolled up in his head and he sagged forward unnaturally, unconscious and only held up by his wrists attached to the eyelet.

Wren was sickened.

Sinclair looked at him, and slit the zip-tie tethering Teddy's wrists to the eyelet without looking away. He slapped forward, face cracking on the hard white floor.

"Maybe he'll live," she said casually, like she'd done nothing at all, "maybe he'll die. It's in your hands."

She strode from the room.

Wren was left alone with Teddy, facedown on the floor, bleeding from the head and barely breathing.

36

PYRAMID

The room grew colder and the music grew louder. The lights began to flash in unpredictable, maddening patterns. Teddy lay still on the floor, his chest only rising and falling in tiny pants, unresponsive to Wren calling his name.

Wren had to think, but the cold and the noise were all-consuming. He closed his eyes and worked to regulate his breathing and enter a meditative state. Steadily he brought his heart rate down and calmed the shivering, until the pounding beat and flashing lights seemed very far away.

There had to be a way to play this. A way through for him, a way to save Teddy. He had only one point of leverage: what he knew about Humphrey's investigation. He had to save that until the moment was just right, when it could make a difference.

He barely noticed when the flashing lights and music stopped.

The first punch took him square on the forehead. He opened his eyes and did his best to roll with the second blow as it cracked into his jaw.

A large, golden-skinned man stood by the door, watching

with a curious expression. He wore a white button-down shirt open at the neck, dark slacks and wingtip black shoes. Every inch of him was perfectly coiffed, with a rakish side-part in his dense blond hair, a slender nose, strange blue eyes and a square jaw. His skin was a deep, burnished bronze, and he carried no visible branding iron scar. He had to be early thirties, still carrying the effortless vigor of youth in thick arms and a broad chest.

The man punching Wren was younger, and there was something familiar about him. His face was a mass of scar tissue from SIC SEMPER TYRANNIS brands, peaking in a crown of thorny white knots in the skin around his scalp. Wren's eyes widened.

Could it be?

Another punch came in that flipped his head back. The golden-skinned man took a step forward.

"It will go poorly for you now," he said in a rich, confident baritone. Wren recognized it from the call he'd answered in Teddy's mansion, the kind of voice belonging to a self-help guru. "We'll take you apart, like we've done many times before. It's a process. You understand."

Wren hawked and spat blood, struggling not to gasp for breath. "I understand you."

"Do you?" The man sounded curious. "Tell me."

Wren's mind thrummed. This man had the look of the cult leader, and the best cult executions began at the top. Time to gamble. "I know you're from here. Minneapolis. It's a poor choice for a headquarters: too far north, too few cities to snatch from and nothing to the west but the sprawling Dakotas. You'd have been better off choosing Chicago or Indianapolis for your base. Too damn cold. But you didn't, because this is home."

The man's odd blue eyes flickered for a moment. A hit.

"Guesswork," he said. "And wrong."

"Not wrong," Wren sped on. "I've got you all mapped out. Your lieutenant Sinclair wanted to know about my Foundation? They're coming as we speak, rolling your organization up, along with the FBI and all the King's horses. You should run while you can, maybe emigrate to Canada. We're close to the border up here. But we do have extradition." He sucked air through his teeth. "Tough break. They'll follow you there. I'll follow too."

The golden man gave a nod, and the man with the scars hit Wren hard in the gut. He coasted for seconds on the edge of choking.

"Empty threats," the golden man said. "Parlor tricks. I know you're not operating under FBI direction or with FBI information. They're hunting you, not me. Your director of special operations, Gerald Humphreys, has had an inter-agency alert out on you for three weeks, ever since you went AWOL after your 'resignation' in New York. They don't know where you are or where we are. They are blind. And as for your Foundation?" He gestured to Teddy by his feet. "I think it's been neutered."

Now Wren smiled, getting control of his breathing. "So you Googled me after all."

"I went beyond Google for this, Pequeño 3. What a record you have."

Wren grimaced. There was that name again; a name nobody should know. "I'll bet it's nothing compared to yours. 'Lead a civil war' will certainly make for an interesting entry on your prison resume."

"Who said I'm leading the war?" the man asked, but there was amusement in his eyes now, and that confirmed it for Wren. All cult leaders got high on power. Even if it wasn't what they'd sought at the start, they soon became addicted to it.

"I say you are." Wren flashed on the name of the author of

the booklet. "You're the Alpha, exercising control over life and death. The brands are just one sign of that. I see them on your boy here, I guess he resisted?" He nodded at the mutilated boxer. "Even Sinclair had one. I notice you don't, though."

"Not on my face."

Wren laughed mockingly. "That's solidarity. You wanted to feel the pain but without the drawbacks. Difficult to find gainful employment with a face brand."

The Alpha's expression smoothed out, showing no pleasure now. That was better. That was a defensive position, which gave Wren the advantage. "In truth you're just another junkie," he pressed, "like all the cult leaders who went before you. More power, more adulation, more love." He spat another mouthful of blood. "Are you having sex with them all yet?" He looked at the boxer and nodded toward the 'Alpha'. "Is he? It'll come. And the civil war? You can't gratify a junkie better than that. People dying on your command is one hell of a trip, and people killing in your name has gotta be the greatest thrill possible for a nutcase like you."

The Alpha's face remained flat and unimpressed. "Honestly, I expected better."

"So swallow this," Wren pressed on. "You never thought it would grow this large, but things got out of control and you couldn't back down. There's no plan, so let's talk about what happens after your war. Say you overthrow the government and rewrite the Constitution. You get your glowing picture in every schoolhouse, post office, police station. Next comes indoctrination, gulags for protesters, re-education and a war of global expansion. Is that about right?"

This time the Alpha didn't respond. He had a great poker face, making him impossible to cold read. "It's a well-worn track," Wren said. "But at some point, you start to lose the people, and you won't be able to bear it. You'll break out the poison Kool Aid, like in Jonestown." He smiled. "It always goes that way in the end. Junkies can't help themselves. Once you've killed your first million, how can you settle for less? You need the obedience, you need the proof of selfless love, and there's no better proof than mass suicide." He took a breath. "Seems you know I was with the Pyramid, so you know I'm speaking from experience. My suggestion is, why not jump straight to the big finale, with you at the front of the line?"

The Alpha's jaw set tight. "Pop psychology. I could go to a fortune teller in the street and get much the same. Surely the Pyramid taught you better?"

Wren snorted. There he went with the Pyramid again. "So you asked around, figured out something about my past."

The Alpha leaned in, back on the attack now. "I didn't need to go far, Christopher. Imagine my surprise when the news reported it was you hunting down the Vikings. I already had the inside line."

Wren frowned. "Bullshit. There is no inside line to the Pyramid. There were no survivors; they all burned themselves alive with home-brew napalm. The town's a wreck; there's nothing left."

Except perhaps that wasn't completely true. There'd been one body never fully accounted for...

The Alpha grinned. "Not bullshit. I have grand news, Christopher. Your father survived the Pyramid. I've sent word that you're here. He is very interested; I can tell you that."

"You're lying," Wren spat, though his heart rate was already spiking. "He's dead."

The grin faded from the Alpha's face, and he grew ominously sincere. "You think so? You think I don't know you, Pequeño 3? You think I don't know things he did to you, and the things he made you do? And how else would I know that, other than direct from his lips?" He paused, blue eyes digging into Wren. "Where does that put your profile of me now?"

It left Wren reeling. Inside he came unmoored.

That name existed in no record Wren had ever found. He'd spent considerable time and effort destroying all records on the Pyramid. So did that mean...

The Alpha's eyes gleamed. Wren could feel he was losing the exchange. It didn't matter that no questions had been asked, that he'd spilled nothing of value; he'd just spilled everything with his silence. It showed his weakness, the key to who he was. This man knew him better than he knew himself.

"It appears I've given you something to think about. Let's see if we can't drum that in."

The Alpha turned to leave, and the boxer's next blow hit Wren in the belly again, blowing the air out of his lungs.

37

BEATING

The beating came and went in stages: a disorienting slap across the ear, a punch to the sternum, a kick to the thigh. The young man with the scars moved around Wren constantly, looking for weakness.

Just when Wren thought he had the tempo of it, that tempo changed, sometimes interspersed with long minutes of agonizing tension. Wren tried to push thoughts of the Pyramid and his father to one side, studying the young man when he could.

Oblong brand marks had ruined his fair face. They all said the same thing. SIC SEMPER TYRANNIS. Through stamping the message in, they transformed the man. More blows came, but Wren barely noticed. The words stinging inside his head were far worse.

Pequeño 3.

There'd been dozens of Pequeños in the Pyramid's heyday. In beat-down cabins in the desert wilds of Arizona, isolated from the world, they'd existed completely at his father's mercy.

Apex of the Pyramid. Leader of America's worst death

cult in history. He'd considered all his followers to be his personal possessions. If ever there'd been a tyrant, it was him.

Young Christopher Wren, then known as Pequeño 3, had been born into that tyrant's brutal domain and raised to believe in the reality of a hell that was coming for all their souls, alongside his brothers and sisters and the Pyramid one thousand.

With each punch and slap more memories shook loose. They'd all done terrible things at the Apex's command, in fear of hell: dunking disobedient followers in the boiling vats; digging pits in the desert to test the belief of the faithful; building cages that served as gibbets for those who failed to appease the Apex's whims...

Another hit dragged Wren back into the moment. It wasn't the strength of the blow, this time, but something else. If anything, it was the weakness.

The hits were coming softer. He blinked back sweat, blood and memories to focus on the young man with the scars. He was stalking and staring at Wren with such intense eyes from that wreck of a face.

So why pull his punches? He didn't look tired, wasn't even short of breath. Something else was going on behind those furious eyes.

Time to play his trick card.

"Mason?" Wren said.

The next punch came with some sting behind it.

Wren righted himself. That seemed like confirmation. Felipe back in the Chicago convenience store had described Mason as a simple man lit only by love for his girl, Wendy.

Now there was the light of a different purpose in his eyes, much like the madness of the Pyramid faithful.

Another hit came, harder still, and Wren tried to picture what he'd been through; enough to make a loyal Marine flip on his creed and his country, escape his cannon fodder fate in the active shooter training at Camp Alden and become a top-tier Saint himself. Maybe the facial scars went some way to explain it, but not enough. That kind of torture could break even a Marine, but to twist his loyalty so completely?

Wren didn't think so. If he was the Alpha he'd have used something else, and it didn't take him long to land on it.

"Where's Wendy?" he asked.

The effect was immediate. Mason froze. It answered the question and raised a dozen more.

"She's here, isn't she?" Wren tried. "They've got her chained up somewhere. They're blackmailing you."

Another hit came then, spinning Wren's head and splashing stars across his vision, maybe the hardest yet. Wren couldn't take too many more of those. He blinked and refocused. Mason's eyes were furious, but was that because he'd guessed right, or because he hadn't?

"Not chained up," Wren offered, reading Mason's eyes. "But she was here, wasn't she? Is she even alive?"

Another hard hit came, and Wren glimpsed the shape of it. The live-fire exercises. How he'd do it, if he wanted not only to break a Marine, but to shift his whole system of loyalty and belief. Shared guilt formed some of the strongest, darkest bonds.

"You killed her."

Mason shook once, like a ghost had run icy fingers up his spine, and there it was. To really break a man, you had to make him complicit.

Wren's mind spun. There was an urban myth about Hitler's SS, about how they were given a puppy to raise which they then had to kill to prove their loyalty. It wasn't true, but the psychology behind it was real. Make someone kill for a belief, and they were yours. After that, they'd do everything they could to make that belief real, because if it wasn't real, then they were actually an evil person and nothing they'd done could be justified. It became self-protection.

Wren gamed it out. The Saints would have framed it all wrong. Brainwashed Mason, tortured him, kept working on him until he was thinking along dark new lines of loyalty that made him believe his only choice was to kill Wendy.

They would have made her into a traitor and him into a hero.

That could break a Marine all the way. The dozens of SIC SEMPER TYRANNIS brands proved it. Mason had resisted them for as long as he could.

So Wendy was dead.

"They made you do it," Wren said. "Brainwashed you. And you killed her."

Now Mason unloaded a flurry of blows. Wren rolled them easily, the fury too predictable. Mason kept on until he was panting hard.

"You don't know me," he said at last, the words coming slow and thick, then he stamped out before Wren could say anything more.

Wren was left alone. Blood drooled through his lips. His own battered face mocked him in the mirror, throwing back his failures echoed in the names of his children tattooed on his chest, not so unlike the brands covering Mason's face.

What wouldn't Wren do in their name?

38

CHERYL

W ren floated on a tide of pain, noise, light and exhaustion. He couldn't tell how many hours had passed, but it felt like a lot. Maybe half a day?

The trickle of blood from Teddy's head had stopped, but his chest was still rising and falling almost imperceptibly. Wren talked to him, hoping that his words might somehow get through and keep Teddy alive just a little longer.

At some point the door opened.

The Alpha, Sinclair, Mason and one other person came in. Wren saw her face and grimaced. Things could always get worse.

Cheryl.

The last time he'd seen her she'd been propped up in the van outside the mansion, her eyes tracking him. Now she had a much fiercer gaze. Her black hair trailed across her sweat-soaked face, but somehow that only made her more fearsome to behold. She saw Teddy's body on the floor then nodded toward Wren.

"I'll sell this bastard out. Just tell me what you want, I'll cough it all up. Coin four my fat ass."

Wren couldn't help but smile. In the mirror it was near invisible, but Cheryl saw it. She was stubborn and would be a tough nut to crack.

Mason kicked out her knees, zip-tied her wrists into another eyelet beside Teddy's still body, then circled behind Wren. Their eyes connected briefly and something flashed between them, though Wren wasn't sure what. The Alpha took up position beside Teddy, watching everything, while Sinclair stood behind Cheryl with her knife drawn.

"It's time to talk, Christopher," the Alpha said, "or lose another member. I want to know-"

Wren stopped listening to the words and focused on the Alpha's tone and manner. Something was different. Even mired in blood and pain, he could feel it in the air. Something had happened to shift the calculus and make them bring Cheryl into play.

Something big.

"The first raid came," he guessed, interrupting the Alpha.

The hit landed. The Alpha stopped talking and his eyes sharpened.

"The FBI hit one of your bases," Wren went on. "It's begun."

A second passed as the Alpha looked at Sinclair then back at Wren.

"More guesswork," he said, recovering quickly, but Wren had seen that moment of uncertainty. "P. T. Barnum would be proud. But you don't know anything."

"Then why ask any more questions?" Wren countered. His lips and tongue were numb, but his brain felt like it had been jump-started. "If I know nothing, why waste your time?"

The Alpha showed a brief glint of annoyance, then inclined his head, and Sinclair pressed her knife to the top of Cheryl's right ear.

"Bitch, you do not want to try cutting off my ear!" Cheryl snapped.

"Hurt her and I won't tell you where they're hitting next," Wren said.

"Will you tell me if I don't?" the Alpha asked. "I killed one of your men already, and still you haven't said a worthwhile thing."

Wren didn't want to correct him that Teddy wasn't quite dead yet. A better gambit was to try and force a wedge between him and Sinclair. "Sinclair killed him," he said.

"You're parsing a nothing. Sinclair is an extension of my will. Whomever she kills, they were killed by me."

Wren snorted. Here was another opening. Cult leaders were ridiculous figures if you dared to point it out. Their self-importance was a ball of hot gas. "And the brands, are they an extension too? Is that why you don't have any on your own face, because Mason's face is an extension of your own?"

Another chink of annoyance shone through, not least because Wren knew Mason's name. The Alpha would have to assume Mason had told him, and that helped tear a gulf. He responded by nodding to Sinclair, who began to saw the knife down through the cartilage of Cheryl's ear.

Cheryl sucked in a sharp breath.

It was time for Wren to use the last leverage he had.

"Vandenberg," he said.

The cutting stopped at once. Sinclair gasped and looked up as blood streamed onto Cheryl's shoulder. The Alpha's gaze bored into him and his face turned pale.

"How do you know that?" he demanded.

Wren stared back at him. Humphreys must have found something out there, an extremist militia or a religious sect or another group like Ferat had suggested, and struck. Only now, after the raid had come and the Saints were spooked, did it give Wren any authority, and put the rightful fear of Uncle Sam into the Alpha.

"I told you earlier, they're rolling you up," Wren said, feigning total confidence. "It's a pattern at my direction, because I've got a Foundation mole in your Saints, loyal to me." Sinclair gasped again as she bought the bluff wholesale, and Wren focused on her. "You asked why I'm hunting you? What you don't know is I've been hunting you for months. Why do you think I started in Utah? So I could take as much as possible at the edge of your network before I came for your headquarters directly. Do you really think you're safe here?"

All of that struck hard, but Wren knew it wouldn't be enough.

"You're good," the Alpha said, recovering. "I'll grant that. But a mole in the Saints? That's a lie. Our people are loyal. I know that you stumbled upon the Vikings by chance. Everything you've said so far has come from guesswork, cold reading or a close study of the booklet you stole. They're all lucky guesses."

He turned to Sinclair and nodded. Sinclair finished the stroke, lopping off Cheryl's ear. She shrieked. Blood streamed out and Cheryl vomited to the side.

"How about now?" the Alpha said, as Sinclair moved to the next ear. "Any more guesses or are you ready to start talking?"

Wren needed another location, one big enough to break the Alpha wide open.

Sinclair sawed and Wren spun a map of the States in his head, trying to imagine the Order's network as it grew out of Minneapolis. He drew a rough line west through Price, Utah to Vandenberg, Santa Barbara County, a line that passed through South Dakota, Wyoming, Utah, Nevada and California.

Dr. Ferat had said the Saints were knitting together existing extremist groups, and in Utah that had proven true with the Vikings; they'd used them to grease the wheels of local law enforcement and keep the Saints invisible. It must've been the same in Vandenberg, though Wren didn't know any extremist groups out there.

But that was OK.

He had Utah and California already, which left South Dakota, Wyoming and Nevada. He strained to overlay more groups from his memory of the last multilateral confab, and swiftly ruled out Nevada and South Dakota. Las Vegas was a hub for crazies; there were too many groups for him to pick just one, and South Dakota was too sparsely populated for him to recall even a single extremist group.

That left Wyoming.

Cheryl cried out.

Wren burrowed into his internal register of extremist groups in the Cowboy State, and one popped up: Prairie Dawn. They were an anarchist sect based across several compounds on the high plains. As far as he remembered, they were loosely focused around both Sioux Falls in the east and Rapid City in the west.

Cheryl screamed.

Wren recalled reports of murdered government workers in the vicinity of Sioux Falls, lynched and left to be found, but no convictions yet. That suggested Sioux Falls, but it was so close to Minneapolis that Wren doubted its usefulness.

Either way, it was a gamble.

"Rapid City, Wyoming," Wren said.

The Alpha visibly jerked. Sinclair gasped and let go of the blade, stuck now in Cheryl's ear.

Direct hit.

"They're coming," Wren drove on, punching the guess for all he was worth. "Prairie Dawn are up now, then it'll be you.

The whole of your Order is poised to break wide open. I can guide you on an escape route where the FBI won't be looking, but you can't hurt my people anymore. You let them go."

The Alpha stared, his jaw now clamped, his mind doubtless racing as fast as Wren's. Sinclair looked to her boss then back to Wren. If they bought this, then it would seem like the whole Order hung by a thread.

"He's got to be guessing," Sinclair attempted, but the words fell flat. She didn't believe it.

Neither did the Alpha. The easy bravado in his stance was gone, and Wren saw the end of the Order playing out in his eyes. The best cult executions started at the top, after all. Break the leader and you broke the spell. Wren took a chance and craned his neck back as far as he could, so he could just see Mason.

He only had a second. He could have said anything, whispered any message.

He simply winked.

Then he swung back and pressed on. "You'll never see them coming. They'll mass in plain clothes and bring you down in synchrony. They're probably coming here this minute. Ask your sources in intelligence; hefty logistics are being put into play." He was freewheeling now, feeling the room bend before him and leaning in. "Believe it or not, they value me. You know I have my own Foundation, over a hundred operators around the States and the world? What you won't know is how much the government wants them. Honestly, that's their big goal here. Your little civil war hardly matters. They're after my network."

He could see the words registering in the Alpha's head. It didn't matter that they were all bullshit, inflated with forced arrogance and bad logic. The Alpha was having a moment of weakness, doubting the security of his own Order, which made him vulnerable to bad ideas, especially those thrown out from a fellow alpha male.

"When the FBI rolls up," Wren kept going, "it'll be to rescue me. You they'll execute on the spot. Your Saints around the nation will roll belly up and flake out on their targets. When the rubber hits the road, your live-fire exercises won't mean a thing in the face of an armed response. Because let's be honest, when you go fishing for domestic terrorists and train them on victims who can't fire back, you're not getting America's finest." He turned again to Mason. "No offense."

At last the spell broke.

"It's a wonderful story," the Alpha said, his face finally calming. "And you tell it so well. But a story's all it is. Everything you've said could've come-"

"So kill me," Wren interrupted. "If it's just a story, kill Cheryl. See how far that gets you, when I'm your only shot out of this. You'll have no collateral, nothing to trade when your flea-speck 'war' goes down the tubes. Take it from me, 'Alpha', you're going to want us when the end comes. Even Hitler had his newlywed in the bunker at the end."

Wren focused his gaze on Sinclair and sped up, planting seeds as fast as he could. "Imagine those last feverish moments, with Herr Adolf freaking out like your boy's doing right now, hugging his dear Eva to his chest and trying to decide if he shoots her first or himself." He let a beat pass. "I know death cults, ma'am. My father killed a thousand people as an 'extension of his will'; he gave the order and they died, and where was he? Body never found, just like it'll be for this idiot. A dollar takes ten he's already got his second life planned. No face brand? That makes it easy. He'll start all over again while you're forever marked. You're nothing special, and he never really committed."

The Alpha was seething now, the veneer of calm he'd just

summoned stripped away. He took a step closer, pulled Sinclair's pistol from her belt and trained it on Wren. "I question your commitment," he hissed.

Wren laughed. "I'm all the way in, pal. I'll die for my people. Will you?"

The barrel held rock steady, but Wren felt the Order of the Saints crack as the Alpha's bronze face rippled with flashes of emotion.

"You talk a great deal, Pequeño. I am fascinated what your father will make of it. Apex of the Pyramid. Did I mention that he's coming?" His eyes flared wide. "A truly great man. I'm sure he'll be pleased to have the last surviving Pyramid member delivered to him on a plate. His own misbegotten son. I'm looking forward to it."

Now it was Wren's turn to be stunned. It had to be a bluff. The Apex hadn't been seen since the Pyramid burned. All accounts said he had died with his cult.

But maybe...

The Alpha smiled brightly, raised the gun and strode out.

39

BREAK

They were left in silence. Seconds passed. Sinclair stared at Wren.

"Get this knife out of my ear," Cheryl said into the silence, "you bitch."

Sinclair took a step, thought for a moment, then removed the blade. Cheryl yelped. Wren pulled his thoughts away from his father and back to the moment.

"Go after him," he said to Sinclair. "Before he kills all your collateral."

Sinclair's eyes focused on him. She seemed confused and angry. "What are you talking about?"

She was asking him for direction now, and that was good. The Alpha probably should have killed both her and Mason already, to prevent the virus of doubt spreading. That was his mistake.

"You saw that light in his eyes," Wren said. "He believes me. I'd wager he's about to activate all your Saint terror cells right now. The civil war begins today." He narrowed his gaze, pushing the bluff further. "I don't think it'll take off, though, Sinclair. There's not going to be a war. The FBI knows about you. Some of the Saints may slip through and chalk up some kills, sure, but I'm thinking ninety percent of them will get shot down." He pulled the number out of thin air, aiming to overwhelm her. "That leaves a couple hundred Saints; maybe they kill a handful of people each? It's not enough, not when the authorities get their narrative out before you. Your uprising won't appear like a grassroots thing anymore. The country will stand against you and smother your revolution in the crib. The element of surprise was the only thing you had going. Now that's gone."

Sinclair's eyes widened. On some level she believed him. Wren's bluff had gotten through to her just like with the Alpha.

"It can't fail," she said, not really to him but to the air. "It's too important. This matters."

Wren just laughed. She twitched, as if only now realizing who she was speaking to. Half of what he'd said had just gone into her head unfiltered, and now she was trying to figure out where she stood. Her hand went to her waist, but the gun was gone; taken by the Alpha. It took her a moment to remember the bloody knife in her hand, and she pointed it toward him.

"I should kill you."

Wren met her gaze dead-on. "Mason, what would the Alpha want?"

Sinclair looked at Mason, then back to Wren. "Why are you asking him? He works for me."

"He works for the Alpha," Wren corrected. "An extension of his will, right? And it seems like the Alpha wants to make a present of me for my father. Are you going to stand in the way of that?"

She was angry. She was uncertain. She held the knife out like a gun, as if all it would take was a gentle squeeze and it would shoot through Wren's skull.

"I know him. I know what's right for him."

Wren nodded, putting the pieces together. "I'm getting

that picture. You built the Saints as a partnership, right? One question, though. Where's your title? He's Alpha, so what are you, Beta? Maybe you were equal once, but that's not been true for some time, has it?" He paused a beat. "You do know what humans usually put a brand on, right? Animals, Sinclair. Property. You're like a cow to him, but still you think you're equals?"

She said nothing.

'They call that brainwashing. My man Mason here knows what I'm talking about, don't you, Mason?"

Again Sinclair looked to Mason, then back to Wren.

"Quite seriously," he went on "if you think I'm bluffing and your boyfriend shouldn't trigger the Order right now, then you should go stop him. If you think he should trigger it, shouldn't you be there by his side, helping him do it right?"

She stared, then straightened up and stabbed the knife toward Mason.

"Watch this liar. Gag him if you have to. It's all poison."

Then she left, leaving them in temporary silence.

"This is so messed up," Cheryl said, weaving woozily. Blood trickled down both sides of her neck, and she gazed into the mirror at her own reflection. "Like, extreme body modification."

"We'll fix it, Cheryl," he said. "They can reattach your ear."

"They shouldn't need to," she slurred. "This is your fault."

"I'm really sorry. I never imagined you'd get involved like this."

She cursed at him. He looked at Mason in the mirror.

"Can you help her please?"

Mason didn't move. He just stood there like he had throughout, as if he'd dropped into a catatonic trance. Maybe that was one effect of the brain damage from his war injury.

Cheryl weaved in place. "This is some real nonsense," she mumbled.

"Mason!" Wren said sharply, and that woke him up. "Please help Cheryl. Nobody ordered her dead. That means she shouldn't die, don't you agree?" He allowed a second for that to sink in. "The Alpha will hold you responsible if she does. Plus, I know you want to help her. The Army didn't teach you to be a sadist."

Mason blinked, then stepped hesitantly forward until he was standing next to Cheryl. He seemed lost. "What should I-"

"Bandage her ears," Wren said gently. "Use your jacket. It's OK. You know how to do this. You've had the training."

Mason began, ripping his jacket and bandaging Cheryl's head. Occasionally he looked to Wren then away swiftly, as if stung.

"I can't see," Cheryl grumbled, and Mason mumbled a soft apology and shifted the angle of the bandage. "Better."

"Now let her go," said Wren.

Mason turned to him.

"I don't mean out of the room," Wren went on. "I don't expect that. The Alpha is going to trade us, remember, when the civil war fails? No, I mean untie her wrists. That's an unnatural position, and it's cutting off her blood flow. She might die from that alone. You've done this much to follow the Alpha's wishes and keep her alive. Go the whole way."

It took Mason a moment longer, but he took out a knife and went to cut Cheryl free, then stopped. He turned and looked at Wren square on, with the light back on in his eyes.

"There you are," said Wren. "Good to see you."

"I don't do what you say," Mason said. "It's the other way around."

Wren nodded. "Precisely. So tell me what you want. Ask me."

"Ask what?"

"What you've wanted to ask since you were pulling those punches. How I know about Wendy."

That sparked the same anger; a clear desire to rush over and punch Wren again for even saying her name. "You guessed," he managed to say. "Like the Alpha said."

"Her name? How would I, I'm not a telepath. Try again."

Mason chewed on his lip. "Maybe I told you. Sometimes I forget things that I said."

"Ding ding, no. Third time lucky?"

Mason stared. "I don't know. How?"

"I found your note. In the warehouse in Utah. I'm sure you didn't know where you were at the time. After they snatched you from Chicago, under the West Pershing bridge. After they took Wendy." Mason flinched. "Her name was written on a receipt for flowers, in blood. You screwed it up and put it in a socket in the floor and I found it. Those days must have been hard, almost a year ago now."

"I don't remember," Mason said reflexively, but Wren could see that he did.

"I went to Chicago looking for you, Mason. I found where you lived under that bridge. I talked to the man in the convenience store who bought you the flowers, Felipe? He was worried about you; said he called the police several times to find you. I went to the church where Wendy volunteered and I found your trail. They told me about her; how kind she was to others. How kind she was to you. She must have been a special woman."

Mason's eyes shone. It didn't matter that half of it was lies and the Revival Faith outreach director had never even met Wendy.

"She sounds wonderful," Wren pressed, charging right up to the edge. "So where is she?"

The first tear fled down Mason's cheek. It worked a path through the crevices and ridges of his many scars.

It was always the same when a committed cult member finally saw the light. In place of so much certainty, all that remained was pain; pain at being fooled, at committing atrocities for a lie, at wanting to belong so much. It broke many people, and there was no one who could help; you were alone with what you'd done. Wren knew all about that, and saw Mason was almost over the edge.

"She's here," he whispered.

"Alive?"

Mason nodded almost imperceptibly, and Wren read between the lines.

"But not free like you, right?" Mason said nothing but Wren could feel it now. "Maybe chained up? Maybe they're holding her for you."

Mason said nothing, but his eyes swam with tears.

"Do they let you see her sometimes, Mason? Maybe when you're good, when you please the Alpha? Like you're both animals. But Mason, you're not. She's not. Neither of you deserve this."

Mason was shaking now, trying to throw off the shackles in his mind. Wren didn't want to think about how they'd clamped those shackles in place.

"If she's here, then we have to free her, Mason. Right now she's in grave danger. If I'm right, the Alpha is about to kill every person in this building, just like he killed everyone at Price PD, at the warehouse, at Camp Alden."

Now the tears broke down Mason's cheeks. The pain was coming. Nothing would help Mason when the dam broke.

"The Alpha said-"

"The Alpha is a liar. He ripped both of you from under that bridge, Mason! You were innocent. He burned a dozen brands into your face, he locked Wendy up and made her your 'reward', then he put a gun in your hands and turned you against the world, but you didn't deserve any of it! Look at me, Mason."

Mason glanced up, away, then back at Wren.

"You don't deserve this. Wendy doesn't and Cheryl doesn't, but you can fix that."

Mason thick hands went to his head. "I don't know. I can't think."

"Then ask one of your handlers. Any moment someone's going to come through that door. It might be the Alpha or Sinclair or a Saint sent to kill us all. You saw that in his eyes too, didn't you? He was on the edge of turning this room into another live-fire exercise. He has to be stopped, Mason, and you're the only one that can do it. Only you can save Wendy."

Mason stared. He looked lost, a child in the body of a full-grown Marine, but slowly, steadily, he drew his gun.

All eyes turned to the door.

40

BROKEN

I n moments the sound of distant shots carried from beyond, starting slow and intermittent then bunching together like a string of firecrackers.

"What's that?" Mason asked.

"Depends," Wren said, "who's left in the building?"

Mason stared at him, his brow working hard as thoughts rippled under the scarred surface. He reached a decision with a tight nod. "My strike team. Hounds of the Saints. Forty elite soldiers, all ex-special forces." He paused a moment. "Wendy and some others, in the basement. And the Core. They're inner circle. They run the computers."

Wren grunted. "How many in the Core?"

"I don't know. Thirty?"

"That's thirty-three gunfire reports so far," Wren said. The shooting had stopped. "Best guess, your Alpha just took the first step to cleanse this place, starting with the Core. Thirty-three for thirty tells me they let him, execution-style. This is his MO. Everyone here who knows who he is will die."

Mason glared. "You're twisting it. You want me to think I'm next."

Wren softened his expression. Sympathy could do so

much with a person starved of it. "Mason, it's not me making you think that."

Moments later footsteps stamped closer outside. The door slammed open and Sinclair strode in. She was sprayed with blood. She'd retrieved her pistol and aimed it now at Wren, until a click came from her left.

She turned and saw Mason training his gun at her heart. A few seconds passed.

"What the hell are you doing, soldier?" she demanded.

"Who've you been shooting?" Mason countered.

She glanced at Wren then back again. "What has this liar been saying to you?"

"We talked about Wendy. He said you should let her go."

Sinclair threw back her head and laughed. "Let her go? Mason, you moron! Are you really defying the Alpha for a woman? Do you know how ungrateful that is?" She let that hang for a moment. "Do you know how much I did for you? I saved you from the street. I gave you a home, a place to belong, an important role in our new Order, and here at the edge of all our dreams you're turning on us over some useless dreg bitch?"

Mason inched the gun closer. "Don't call her a bitch."

She laughed again, then she fired.

Mason's chest absorbed the first slug with a flat, meat-smacking thump, but he was already moving, and her second shot only skimmed his side. His first shot entered her shoulder and tore out through her back, his second entered her stomach as he fell, at which point her third powdered through his thigh.

They both dropped.

"Oh my," Cheryl murmured as the gunfire echoed around the room.

Sinclair slumped awkwardly on her knees and chest, her trigger finger twitching slackly by her side, though the gun had fallen away. Her bright eyes darted side to side as if looking for a way out. Mason gasped and rolled onto his back on the white floor. The sound of their gurgling breaths filled the room.

"Let us go, Mason," Wren pressed.

Mason's head lolled toward the sound. He was pale already. His lips framed words and his eyes throbbed with some aching need.

"Let us go!"

"Why didn't you-" Mason began, speaking in barely a croak. "Why didn't you come get me earlier?"

He slumped back, his breathing growing shallower.

"I'm sorry," Wren said, "but I'm here now. I can still save Wendy. I can save so many people, if you'll just cut me free."

Mason rolled and started to army crawl. His eyes were alight again, but this time with something Wren recognized. It wasn't the madness of a cult follower anymore. This was hope.

Mason made it to Wren's chair and Wren urged him on. He managed to pull his knife, and in the seconds before his eyes rolled back in his head and he sagged to the floor, he cut Wren's hands free.

Wren snatched up the knife and did the rest. He sprang to his feet. His left leg barely held him and his right was stiff from sitting for hours, but adrenaline kept him moving.

From the floor he scooped up both Mason and Sinclair's pistols, a pair of black Glock 19s. He couldn't use them both, so he rapidly disassembled one and tossed the pieces to the corners, then he used the knife to cut Cheryl free.

"About ... time," she wheezed.

"You'll be fine, help's coming," Wren said, fishing in Sinclair's pocket for a phone.

"Already said that ... once," Cheryl murmured.

"I am sorry about your ear. I'm sorry about Teddy. He might make it too."

Then he dug in Sinclair's pocket and found her phone, an old flip-style burner Nokia. He dialed Humphreys' direct line, brought up the Glock and kicked open the door.

41

JIB-JAB

The corridor outside was empty, with plain white walls and floor marked by bloody palm and foot prints. Cold vinyl stung Wren's bare feet but he followed the blood trail, scanning ahead and behind for sign of any remaining Saints.

The phone rang then connected as Wren turned a corner.

"Yes," came a voice on the other end.

"Christopher Wren for Director Humphreys," he said, "codeword clockjaguar3, he'll take it direct."

"Yes." There was a beep. In the gap Wren brought up the phone's GPS app, then Humphreys' voice came through.

"Wren, we've been waiting, where the hell are you?"

He'd never thought he'd feel so happy to hear the Director's voice. "I'm in Minneapolis, Gerald. I was shot, captured, tortured and now I'm free, but the Saints' civil war just began. Multiple shots have already been fired here; dozens are likely dead, I'm currently clearing the compound."

"What compound? Where?"

"One second." The GPS app localized to a commercial looking complex, and Wren zoomed in. "Looks like, northwest of the city, near St. Michael, a complex marked as 'Jib-Jab'. Send armed response and ambulances immediately; two grossly injured females and two males in a room on the-" he reached a window and peered out, seeing rinsed-out blue skies with the sun a low crescent on the horizon to the left, orienting himself. "South-east corner, third floor."

There was a parking lot below, but only one or two vehicles were in it.

"What are we walking into here, Christopher?" Humphreys demanded. "Do you have evidence for any of this?"

"Yeah," Wren said, and flipped the phone, activated the camera and began a livestream that showed himself as he walked along the blood-streaked corridor. "Looks like the local force has gone, a forty-strong elite strike team called the Hounds of the Saints. I need to find them."

"Perhaps I can help. I'll order satellite wind-back over your location, CCTV access too. We might find them, but-"

"That's not all," Wren interrupted. "That's just the start. You need to mobilize the whole country, Humphreys. Evacuate every government office, town hall, school and wherever else federal workers might be. The Saints are activating; I don't know how many, but I'm guessing thousands of active shooters, both solo and in cells." He almost fell down a flight of steps, barely catching himself on the handrail.

"Christopher-" Humphreys said, but Wren cut him off.

"You need to get the President on the airwaves right now, addressing a national emergency so people are forewarned. This is a nationwide attack with extensive planning. They want it to look like a grassroots uprising, so we cannot allow that notion to spread. This is a coordinated attack by domestic terrorists. You need to get that immunization in."

A moment passed as Humphreys processed that. "OK. I've already dispatched emergency units to your location. We found the camp where you left the phone, Christopher, but it was completely burned out. You said it was a training site for this 'active shooter' army?"

"Exactly. The whole country, Humphreys, right now."

"And if this is a distraction from whatever attack you've been planning?"

Wren barked a laugh. "I'm not planning anything! Look at me, Humphreys, is this a good look to run a war?"

"Possibly. It could be an elaborate ruse."

Wren laughed more. "Elaborate, yeah. I resigned to be with my family then decided to start a civil war in thirty days. Very impressive, right?" He turned a corner and passed down another flight of stairs to a heavy-looking black double door. There were red boot prints stamped brightly around the entrance. He raised the Glock. "I thought I'd be free, but I was wrong. My wife figured it all out anyway and took the kids. Maybe I'm not a family man, like you said. Now watch this."

He shoulder-barged the black doors and they gave way, leading him through into a slaughterhouse.

Sinclair hadn't been lying.

Bodies were everywhere, slumped at three ranks of desks arrayed like a flight control deck before a large central screen. There were around thirty of them, like Mason had said, and all were dead. They'd been executed with shots to the head up close, now tipped over their keyboards or lying on the floor by the wheeled legs of their ergonomic office chairs, blood slashed across their monitors.

Wren took it all in. There were no eyelets or chains to hold them in place here, because they hadn't been needed. This was an execution they'd accepted, just like the Pyramid, and his gorge rose.

Humphreys cursed.

"Yeah," said Wren.

The large screen at the front showed what seemed to be a list of some fifty text messages and emails, along with phone numbers and emails. Each one said, 'GO!', followed by an address.

Government offices. Schools.

Targets.

A second passed and the screen refreshed with another fifty, then another fifty.

"Start with these," Wren said, pointing the phone to stream footage of the screen. On individual monitors he found more lists: all had fresh batches of targets going out to fresh operatives. "It's happening now."

He shoved one of the Core bodies out of its seat and dropped down at a keyboard. The phone squawked in his hand and Wren leaned it against a monitor so Humphreys could capture the big screen.

Then he laid his hands on the keys and took the operating system to its root command line. Wren was no hacker, but he'd been on enough undercover missions to know a few backdoors.

'Alpha' was his first command line search, but it returned nothing. He tried 'attack' then 'Sinclair' but still nothing came. He hot-keyed through to a file directory and scanned the hierarchy, then noticed that the contents were self-deleting.

He slammed ctrl-alt-delete, hoping to disrupt another bid by the Alpha to burn his trail, but it did nothing. Wren settled for ripping the cables out of the back of the monitor and the tower computer it was connected to.

Maybe some evidence would survive for later analysis.

He stood and surveyed the room. Already monitors were switching themselves off as the self-erase code completed its work, followed by the main screen, leaving the room lit only by the red glow of its EXIT signs.

Wren cursed.

The phone squawked and he picked it up.

"It's not enough, Chris." Humphreys said. "There's too many."

42

PROFILE

"I couldn't get anything off the computers," Wren said, rising to his feet in the ruddy dark.

"If this is what you say it is," Humphreys pressed, "a nationwide attack by thousands of armed terrorists, we're woefully unprepared. We need more."

Wren jogged back to the doors, mind racing. His legs were loosening up, now, as the muscles warmed. "I'm thinking."

"Well do it faster!"

By the door lay a big man, looked to be about Wren's size, dressed in jeans, a check shirt and brown leather boots. Wren swiftly stripped him and pulled his clothes on, tucking the Glock into his waistband and shoving out through the door into the bright, bloody corridor.

The phone grumbled again and Wren swapped it to speaker mode. "This comes down to the Alpha, Humphreys," he said, figuring out his route forward. "Head of the snake. If I can take him out, I think the Saints will start to crumble."

"So where is he?"

Wren ran through another set of double doors, the floor marked by fading bloody footsteps, and along a corridor running down the side of the parking lot. Now he heard emergency sirens drawing closer. "I don't know. Did you get anything on satellite?"

"That compound you're on is in a blind spot. No satellite overpasses it."

Wren gritted his teeth. There was no way that was an accident. "So we need another way. Hang on."

Ahead lay a security gate. He vaulted over it, circled a bank of elevators then found himself in a large lobby marked as the nexus of Jib-Jab. From its bright, colorful logo stamped onto the walls it looked to be some kind of Internet shopping firm. Not a bad cover operation, he figured as he ran through; space for a large standing stock of weapons in a concealed location on the verge of the city, with constant incoming and outgoing deliveries, a big motor pool, many freelancers rolling in and out every day, and a whirlwind of financial transactions, many of them invisible to state auditors due to their international status.

The lot's few cars lay ahead, but where was he going?

"Wren?"

"The Alpha," Wren said, pushing through a glass revolving door and out into the light. "All this is personal for him, I'm sure of it, and the same will go for his first target. It'll matter, it'll be personal." He strode toward the nearest vehicle, an electric blue Porsche, with his mind racing. "If we can figure out who he is, what motivates him, maybe we can predict that target."

"I'm listening."

"Start with demographics," Wren said. "He's male, 6' 3", 220 pounds, approx 38 to 42 in age, Caucasian but with a deep tan, likely fake, blue eyes and blond hair and likely no criminal record."

"Got it. BOLOS are going out, searches of NCIC and Nlets databases also. What else?"

"His choice of headquarters," Wren went on, framing words as the thoughts came to him. "Minneapolis is an unnatural choice to run a nationwide terror network. He's got to be a city native, it means something to him, so the target is here, in the city."

"That narrows it," Humphreys said, with the sound of keys clacking behind him. "What else?"

Wren racked his mind, arriving at the Porsche. "The summer camp, Camp Alden. Why choose that, out in the middle of nowhere? I'm thinking he went there either as a kid or a counselor, summers of," he did a quick calculation, "1980 to 1986."

Wren put the grip of the Glock through the Porsche's window, opened the door, swept the glass then slid in.

"We need more, Chris."

Wren hot-wired the car, thinking hard. What else could he add? The Alpha was megalomaniacal, but that in itself was no use. Lots of crazies hid their delusions of grandeur perfectly. He needed something harder, and returned to the Alpha's appearance.

It was unusual. He didn't have any visible branding, but something had been off about him. That deep tan was part of it, bordering on a golden sheen, but it wasn't only that. His eyes were strange too; maybe wearing contacts? His nose seemed too slim for his face. He was clearly vain, like most cult leaders, but unlike most of them the Alpha actually looked the part.

"I think he's had plastic surgery," Wren said, taking a leap into the dark. "Maybe to his nose, jawline and cheekbones. He may have muscle implants, too."

"Muscle implants? How sure are you, Wren?"

"Uh, fifty percent."

"Fifty percent on it all?"

"Something like that."

"OK, well, we can check that. All plastic surgeons in the country register their work for this reason. Anything else?"

The Porsche growled to life, and Wren raked his mind back over the conversations he'd had with the Alpha, homing tighter until a final piece clicked into place. Wren realized he'd been pushing it aside because it made no sense, something the Alpha had said in a throwaway boast about the Pyramid, but it had to mean something.

The Alpha claimed he'd read everything on the federal record.

But Wren had spent twenty-five years fighting to expunge all federal records on his childhood cult. There was only one place in the world to access the records that remained, one single room which kept a meticulous record of all attendees, but allowed no material out.

"The reading room at the Library of Congress," he said. "He must've been there. He knew things about the Pyramid that no one else does. That's the only way."

"Library of Congress, OK. That's good, Chris. I'll get those records immediately."

"It's going to be downtown," Wren said, "somewhere showy, somewhere he can visibly lead."

"I'm putting teams on it now."

Wren hit the gas. The Porsche's wheels bit the blacktop and he tore past an incoming stream of SWAT vans, police cars and ambulances, headed for the heart of Minneapolis.

43

CANDIDATES

W ren raced southeast well over the speed limit, weaving through midday traffic and heading for downtown. The broad Highway 10 ushered him through flat suburbs with the green floodplain of the Mississippi River swinging in and out on his right.

Exits whipped by but he stayed on the 10 like a bullet. What was the price of failure here? His head felt filled with fuzz. It was only one more attack amongst thousands, but if it was successful, it would serve as inspiration to every Saint out there.

They'd push harder, fight further, kill more.

Wren had to cut off their head.

The 10 swerved to become the 47 headed downtown; Wren was almost to the city center and he still had no destination. The phone rang and he snatched it up, tapping for speaker.

"Talk to me."

"Christopher," came Humphreys voice, "we don't have anything."

Wren slammed the gas pedal harder, nearly ramming into the back of a silver Lexus.

"Not possible. He's got to be in the record somewhere. Explain."

"Maybe he's in there, but we can't find him," Humphreys said. "There's no single cross-correlation across the data points you shared. It'll take time to sift through all the possible candidates. Isn't there anything else we can use to narrow the list down?"

Wren smacked the wheel and the horn blared. A guy in a red Toyota gave him the finger but Wren sped by in seconds, closing in on downtown and about to butt into a winding tail of traffic.

He pulled right across three lanes and shot onto the off-ramp for the city circular. "You're saying they found candidates but no standout."

"Exactly."

"How many candidates?"

"Who attended that summer camp across those years? Thousands. Who match that demographic? Hundreds. Who might have had plastic surgery? Hard to say, but fewer. Who also went to the Library of Congress? None, Christopher."

Wren cursed.

"Have you got photos? Send them to this phone."

"Sending."

The phone chimed and Wren braked to a stop on the narrow shoulder. The file was a simple Excel table, populated with names, photographs, addresses and markers corresponding to Wren's profile. He scrolled rapidly through three hundred odd cells, narrowed by the demographic data, focusing on the photographs first. It felt like drinking from a fire hose of tall, caucasian men but the Alpha wasn't amongst them.

"He's not here."

"That's what I'm saying."

"We're missing something."

"The attacks have begun, Christopher. We're already stretched thin. They're hitting everywhere. We need this now."

"I'll call you back," Wren said, and killed the call.

He squeezed his eyes tightly shut and pressed his palms hard against his eyelids, sparking silver flashes.

There had to be something else, something he'd missed.

Thousands of candidates, but not one who'd attended the Library of Congress. Hundreds who matched the demographic and attended Camp Alden, but none who looked like the Alpha. Wren felt his brain jamming. There was no other lead, so where did that leave him?

He scrolled swiftly through the photographs again, enlarging the screen to see them better. White male after white male raced by. All were far paler than the Alpha, but then he had that golden glow like he'd been deep-fried in bronzer. Wren tried to see past that to the shape of his eyes, imagining contact lenses to change the color of his irises, and past the different shades of hair, because hair could be bleached or dyed, past the shape of his nose and his lips, because all of those could be changed too, until-

The record skipped in Wren's head. He reversed back in his thoughts and ran over it one more time. Could it be? Maybe it was something but he couldn't be sure. He ran it forward once more.

Eyes could be changed. Hair could be changed. Noses, ears, chins, cheeks, lips, all those could be changed. So couldn't you also change...

He jerked upright in the seat.

That was it. It had to be. It explained the Library of Congress, it explained the three hundred non-matching photographs. The Alpha had never even been listed because he'd been ruled out from the start.

222

Wren slammed the gas and kicked the car back out into traffic, bringing the phone up with Humphreys' number already ringing.

44

ALTERATION

"He's not Caucasian!" Wren shouted into the phone as he weaved through traffic.

"What?" Humphreys responded.

"The Alpha, I don't think he's Caucasian. His eyes might've changed, his nose, his hair, everything, so why not his skin too? I saw him and thought he had to be a white guy with a heavy tan, but bronzer that thick could cover anything. He could be black, brown, purple underneath, whatever. Include the non-Caucasians and run the data again!"

"One moment."

The Porsche tore around the outskirts of Minneapolis, and now Wren could see the work of the Saints spreading. There were numerous threads of smoke rising upward from the downtown area, signaling what could only be arson or explosions.

"Minneapolis is burning, Humphreys."

"I know that, Wren. Every city is coming under fire, but none more so than there. The emergency lines are swamped and we've got National Guard coming in, but they're not going to mobilize in time."

"Where's my list?"

"The team's cross-referencing."

"I just need one guy!"

"It's coming. Any min-"

An explosion burst to Wren's right. One moment there'd been a van driving nearby, the next there was only a ball of flame. The Porsche took the blast wave and shrapnel hailed off the metal work and cracked the glass. The wheel skidded but Wren held firm, whipping through a sudden cloud of smoke and regaining control.

His heart pounded. Smoke pumped upward in the rearview mirror from the blazing shell of a vehicle, and cars were crashing and skidding everywhere. Ahead an SUV lost control and fishtailed; Wren braked and barely threaded the needle between it and the median, shooting into empty space.

"What was that?" Humphreys shouted.

"I think a Saint just blew himself up in his van."

Humphreys cursed.

"Have you got him?"

"It's coming through." A few seconds passed, then Humphreys' tone changed. "Chris, you might be right! There's one man that fits all the criteria, but he was ruled out from the start."

Wren's mouth went dry. "Why was he ruled out?"

"Because he's, well..." Humphreys hesitated. "I can't quite be sure, but it looks like he's black."

"Send him to me."

"I'm gathering the package. Sending."

Wren whipped over to the shoulder once more and braked the Porsche, bringing up the phone. His hands suddenly felt hot and clumsy. In seconds an email arrived from Humphreys and he tapped through to the attachment, opened it then found himself gazing into the Alpha's eyes.

It was him. His name was Richard Acker.

Wren scrolled on with mounting disbelief as Acker's life

track unraveled like a social media stream in fast forward. He was everything Wren was searching for, yet different at the same time. He was rooted in Minneapolis, but not in the way Wren had imagined. He had received plastic surgery, but not the kind Wren had expected. He had attended the summer camp off Two Harbors, but not in any recognizable way. He had been even to the Library of Congress, but under an assumed name and with a different face, before plastic surgery changed it forever.

The pieces spun together. Wren returned to the opening photograph of Acker and just stared. In it he was maybe eighteen, wearing graduation robes with a forced smile. The forehead was the same. The broad shoulders, the build, the set of the eyes, even the chin and some aspect to the cheekbones were recognizable, but everything else was different.

Richard Acker was indeed black.

Or at least his skin was, in blotchy sections, like it had been clumsily stained a dark cherrywood. Wren peered closer. Wispy blond hair straggled down over brown eyes and a face with the hawkish nose and thin lips of a Caucasian male, but with that blotchy dark skin.

Records of surgical alteration followed in an avalanche, from trips to Thailand, Vietnam, Singapore; all medical tourism to get skin bleaching treatments that were illegal in the US, along with numerous attempts at beautification; cheekbone enhancement, nose-bump reduction, chin contouring.

Further photos cataloged the transformation as Richard Acker changed himself from a black-and-white-skinned man with desperation in his eyes to a golden-skinned surgical creation. There were hair implants to thicken his scalp to a lustrous mane and muscle implants in his arms, back and thighs. He'd undergone a technique called 'distraction osteogenesis', which involved repeated breaking and resetting of the leg bones to increase height by up to six inches.

Wren would have laughed if it weren't so horrifically sad. Last of all, the blotches on Acker's face came into sharp focus as he read his childhood diagnosis: N1 neurofibromatosis, causing scoliosis, skin lumps, hearing loss and café-au-lait spots.

That shook Wren. Café-au-lait were birthmarks that grew and expanded over time; a skin condition where pale skin turned dark and blotchy. There was an accompanying picture of Acker as a child, maybe five years old and mostly white-skinned, with only four café-au-lait blotches on his face, small round blots no darker than spilled tea.

But they'd spread.

Wren sped through further photos recording Acker's transformation, as those spots spread and darkened across his cheeks, nose and forehead until his entire face was an uneven blur of black.

"We were never going to find him," Wren muttered.

"The Library of Congress recorded his visit before all of these changes," Humphreys said. "He was a different man."

Wren brought that image up. In the ID log taken at the Library, Acker looked like a black man with some vitiligo, not a white man with extreme café-au-lait marks. "It's incredible."

"It is. It also made his life a misery."

"How so?"

"It seems he was abandoned at birth by drug-addicted parents, leading to a very troubled adolescence in the municipal system of foster homes."

Wren scrolled ahead to that section of Acker's life, while Humphreys continued to summarize. "His unusual skin saw him ostracized and bullied by the other children. Accusations of child abuse against his various foster parents were leveled but no action was taken, except to shuttle him on to the next set. As he hit his mid-teens he began acting out violently, leading to several stints in youth detention."

Wren scanned those records. There were many photographs of assorted injuries the young Acker had received during that time, including huge bruises, broken bones and lost teeth.

"He was a fighter."

"He had to fight back," Humphreys went on. "But it seems he got sick of fighting other orphans and went online, seeking a deeper revenge."

"Against authority?" Wren asked.

"Yes. We have his earliest Internet record, where he starts posting on numerous anti-government sites. He advocates sabotage of the foster care system, and you know how it is in those kinds of groups; the more violent and extreme you are, the more likes you get."

Wren found the posts and glanced through them. There was mention of branding irons and cleansing fire. "This is him, no doubt."

"Skip forward a few years and those smaller groups are no longer enough for him."

"He's self-radicalized," Wren said.

"Exactly. He widens his target to the whole federal government, to bigger sites where his bloodthirsty threats get him more and more attention."

Wren knew just what this young Richard Acker wanted. He could see it burning in his eyes in every photograph.

"What about the abuse? Did he ever get justice through official channels?"

"It was never substantiated," Humphreys answered. "But I believe his account. There are holes in the foster care system you could drive a truck through, and he would've been an extremely easy target. His changing skin made him isolated, weak and easy to exploit by sick adults. He had no friends, no advocates, no one to take his side."

Wren's knuckles tightened. In another situation he'd be fighting on the same side as Richard Acker. He'd felt the call to revenge every day of his life since the Pyramid fell; a shapeless fury that needed to be fed.

If it weren't for James Tandrews he might have become every bit as vengeful as this Richard Acker. He would have sought any means possible to make somebody pay, and he wouldn't have cared how many innocents he hurt.

Tandrews had just steered that rage in a better direction. The Foundation had helped. Maybe it could help Acker, too.

"He moved onto the dark Internet," Humphreys went on, his keyboard clicking as he worked through the briefing. "The conspiracy theory believers loved his rage and his passion and he grew to become their hero. With their support he started the Saints, developing it into an organization with hundreds of devoted members, but he didn't get off the Internet and take it into the real world for several years, at least not until-"

"Sinclair," Wren whispered, finally seeing the connection.

"Precisely. It looks like she set him up with the reconstructive plastic surgeons."

"In Thailand," Humphreys said. "All the correctives plus a whole range of skin-bleaching treatments that are illegal here."

Wren found the photos showing the process and tracked Acker from a white man with wide black spots to an unevenly pale man with burned-looking reddish patches.

"No wonder he wears a lot of bronzer," he breathed.

"Poor bastard," Humphreys said.

Wren stared. Traffic slashed by. The civil war was happening, but now he had a better sense of what Acker's main goal was. Revenge. He wanted to inflict pain on the federal government for the crimes he'd suffered when he was too small to fight back.

And that was the key. The pieces fell into position. The most personal shots in the Alpha's great civil war would be fired against his earliest tormentors. Wren whipped back through the file until he found the detail he was looking for.

There it was.

He knew where Acker would be.

45

BISHOP HENRY WHIPPLE

Wren cranked the Porsche into gear and took off, hitting a hundred miles an hour plus in ten seconds flat.

"The Bishop Henry Whipple federal building," Wren shouted over the roar of the engine. "That's where Acker's going, along with his elite Hounds. It's where the Minneapolis Fostering Authority's based, the place that let him be abused for years as a child. I need-"

"If it's a federal building then we already sent forces there," Humphreys interrupted. "As for sending more, I can try, but all FBI field agents along with police, fire, ambulance and the incoming National Guard are all engaged securing hospitals, schools and other government offices. If the Henry Whipple Building is lost, it means Acker already broke through. There's no one else to send."

"So tell the people," Wren barked, making a hard right heading south. Ahead a thick black pall of smoke was already rising over the Mississippi delta like a shadow on the sky; grisly confirmation of a mass fire. "Citizens, militias, the Boy Scouts and Girl Guides, whatever it takes, Humphreys. The building's already on fire!"

"It's not the only place on fire, Christopher," Humphreys answered. "The country's in uproar. I'm coordinating with a dozen agencies already, and there's not a free team in a hundred miles that can tackle an army of forty fanatics!"

Wren cursed. He wished he'd seen it coming earlier. "There's got to be a thousand people in that building, Humphreys."

"So get them out! You're the only one in the vicinity, Wren. Figure it out."

The line went dead. Wren dropped the phone and focused on the road ahead. Humphreys wasn't wrong; he had a nation to help secure. A thousand lives in Minneapolis mattered, but there were thousands of lives everywhere at risk.

Acker was the head, though. Kill the head and the body would die.

Wren pushed the pedal down harder, heading directly for the smoky cloud. The off-ramp was coming and he sped onto the bridge over the Mississippi. The Whipple Building emerged through the smoke as he shot out over the water, a large standalone office block shaped in two tiers; a broad one-story lower level with a narrower tower rising another eight stories up from the center, encircled by a broad parking lot.

The ground-level floor was an inferno already. Orange tongues of fire burst through the windows and licked toward the second story, gushing smoke in a thick charcoal column. Wren could just about pick out the Hounds of the Saints, circled around the ground floor in their black strike suits, firing automatic rifles toward the roof.

Hundreds of people were clustered up there, wreathed in smoke.

All access was cut off.

Wren calculated. There was no easy way through the Hounds, and no way at all through the ground-floor fire. He was going to have to make his own route in.

He scanned his mirrors, saw what he was looking for then accelerated hard, shifting lanes to sweep in front of a large semi truck. Its trailer had metal sides and looked to be a refrigerated unit, which should help.

Wren slammed on the horn and tapped the brakes. The semi responded quickly, swinging over to the next lane to avoid hitting him and answering with its own roaring horn. Wren pulled left just ahead of it, staying in front with his horn blaring and one arm out the window signaling to stop.

The semi braked.

At a dead stop in the middle lane, Wren climbed out into traffic, holding one hand authoritatively up at the driver, an older woman in a jean jacket and red cap. She looked down at him in surprise, a bloodied, staggering man on the Interstate, as he climbed up to her door and spoke through the window.

"I need this truck for a federal emergency, ma'am. You see the burning building over there? I'm going to rescue those people and I need your truck to do it. No one else is coming for them."

She stared a moment longer, then clicked the lock release. "Get in."

He opened the door and slid in. "I need you to get out, ma'am."

She sneered at him. "You think you can drive this beast?" She had a loose Boston accent and tight lines around her mouth, pushing sixty. There were pictures of kids on her sun flaps; tow-haired grandchildren with her sharp eyes. "I saw you in that tin can. You won't even get across the median."

Wren lined up arguments and dismissed them. Everyone was a soldier now. The radio played in the background detailing breaking reports on shootings across the country.

"I'm a patriot," the woman said, and punched the gas without waiting for his approval. The semi started forward with a jolt.

"We need to breach a line of elite marksmen and hit the government building," Wren said. "Dead-on, without getting shot up."

She snorted. "Been dying to hit that place. My alimony's a bitch."

Wren laughed.

"Lacy Demille," the woman said, extending a hand to him as the semi thundered around the curve of the Interstate. Wren took her calloused hand and shook.

"Christopher Wren."

"Like the architect. What are the chances we get killed in this, Chris?"

Vehicles screamed by on either side, their horns jammed down hard as Lacy picked up speed. The exit for the Federal Building was half a mile away.

"High," he said. "Or the fire will get us."

"We're good for fire. Gas tank is under the trailer and I'm full of iced meat; you picked the right truck to hit a burning building with."

Wren laughed again. "I'm selective."

"Shouldn't have picked that toy car then. You've got a gun?"

"Sure, have you?"

"Under your seat," she said.

Wren reached down and hunted under the seat, pulling out an old, well-oiled Colt .45.

"Personal protection at nights is a son of a whore," Lacy said, and winked.

Wren ejected the magazine and checked the breech: all smooth. He slid it back into place and cranked the slide to push a bullet into position. Properly maintained. He tucked it into the glove box.

"Take it, but try to stay out of the firefight until I'm back, ma'am. The men we're dealing with are hardened killers."

She frowned. "Don't call me ma'am, I ain't your school mistress. It's Lacy. And until you're back, where are you going?"

"To the top of that building. Now, can I climb back into the trailer from here?" he asked, checking on the Glock stowed in his waistband.

Lacy laughed. "Are you crazy, into a refrigerated unit? Of course not."

"Of course not." Wren grinned back. This felt more like it. "Don't corner too hard while I'm out there, OK?"

"What?"

He pushed open the door and pointed off to the side. "You're going to drive me right up to the roof of that building. Just imagine I'm surfing and you're the wave. Hunker low as we come in, aim for the least burned-up section then get out of the cab and run. The smoke should cover you."

She stared at him.

"Thank you, Lacy," he said, then pulled himself out of the cab and up onto the roof, using the wing mirror as a foothold. The wind whipped at him and the air stank of exhausted gasoline and smoke. Off to the left lay a panoramic view of the Whipple Building, angry fires climbing higher through its shroud of smoke.

"Hang on!" Lacy called from below, and Wren just managed to snatch hold of the trailer's metal rim as the cab swung sharply right. The trailer's momentum yanked against the truck's coupling, metal screaming high before obeying Lacy's command, cornering onto the exit road at an outlandish speed.

46

HELTER-SKELTER

L acy's truck raced helter-skelter around the exit road, shot out on a short bridge over a tributary stream the Mississippi then crashed hard into another screaming turn on the far bank. Smoke hung thick in the air.

Wren's left leg throbbed but held, and he stood tall on the cab scanning their approach. Acker's Hounds encircled the Henry Whipple Building about fifty yards apart; several of them tracked the semi with their rifle muzzles as it rocketed into the last hundred yards.

The Whipple lay directly ahead, its bottom floor ablaze while the upper eight were veiled in smoke. As the semi sped into the parking lot and toward the Hounds' line, Wren spotted a long trench dug out around the building's base.

He cursed and threw himself flat to the cab's roof, ducking his head in through the window.

"Swerve left, Lacy, now!"

Lacy raked the wheel left. Wren was sent tumbling as the truck cornered hard, brakes screeching and metal shearing. His body slid off the cab roof and into open air, but his right hand clamped onto the edge. He fell through the air like a closing hinge to slap against the cab's door, smacking the wind out of him.

For a second he hung there, legs dangling above the front wheel, then the truck fishtailed right onto the access road around the parking lot. Wren used the shift in impetus to drag his feet up onto the running boards.

"I thought we was gonna ram it?" Lacy shouted through the window.

Wren snatched a breath. "Security moat," he managed, "they started digging them after Oklahoma City. I didn't think-"

"Didn't think? How we gonna hit the building now?"

Wren's mind raced. The moat was maybe five feet deep, a shallow incline filled with large shale rocks, but there was no way a semi could traverse it. That was the whole point. He scanned the building's layout as a nearby Hound sprayed the semi's side with automatic gunfire. Lacy flinched automatically. There were only moments left until they were out of the lot and back onto the highway on-ramp.

Then he saw it.

"There, northwest corner," he shouted, making the bet based on the curve of the road, "there'll be delivery access."

"What?" Lacy shouted back. "I don't see anything but them idiots with guns."

"It'll be there. There'll be a bar gate strong enough to stop anything short of a tank, but we'll get through. Trust me." He winked and hauled himself back up onto the cab.

A long block of low outbuildings flew by then Lacy cornered hard to the right, and finally Wren saw it up ahead: access to a service courtyard in back of the building, screened by the lowered arm of a reinforced security gate.

He stamped on the cab's ceiling and shouted. "Hit it, Lacy!"

The truck sped up, crumpling the fenders of parked cars

and smashing a path over a low separating verge of bushes. At the building's fringe the trailer released a massive crack as it went over the brick curb, splitting one of the axles. An instant later they slammed down at the edge of the narrow courtyard and crashed into the secure arm.

It thumped into the truck's grille then buckled with a metallic shriek, leaving the semi to race straight ahead to the raging building.

"Brake!" Wren shouted.

Smoke wrapped the roof ahead like a dark cocoon, making the edge impossible to pick out. Wren leaped to the top of the trailer as the tires locked and burned rubber below. Two seconds later the cab dead-ended into the wall with an almighty crash, launching Wren into the air.

He flew through smoke for what felt like seconds, trying to judge the landing until his right leg caught on the roof. He managed a single step at full-sprint then his left leg gave out and he folded into a barrel roll. His hips, elbows, shoulders and knees battered off the slick felt roof until finally he came to a halt on his side.

Wren grunted against the pain and lurched to his feet. The heat of the fires below had melted the tarpaper surface, and now black rubbery streaks clung to his clothes. Smoke was everywhere, vomited from the gathering blaze.

Wren ran toward the second tier of eight stories. Gunfire carried from behind, answered by the pop and whine of the fire ahead. He picked a spot twenty yards over from the worst of the smoke, then drew Sinclair's Glock and shot out the window, releasing a blast wave of heat. He kicked through the shards of glass and dropped down into a long office of desks, chairs and cubicle dividers obscured by leaping orange flames.

His skin burst out in sweat in the sweltering air. Suddenly it hurt to breathe, with each gasp carrying too little oxygen.

His eyes watered and he could barely see. A fine rain of sprinkler water played down from the nozzles above, but not nearly enough to extinguish the fire. He held his shirt to his mouth with one hand and ran deeper between desks and trailers of flame, heading toward the central core.

After twenty seconds he hit an open area: to the left there were banks of elevators opening and closing crazily, ahead on the leeward side a wall of fire shot up outside the windows, while to the right lay a door to the central stairwell.

He pushed through. The stairwell offered some relief from the heat, but drifts of black smoke were already pluming upwards. Wren squeezed his eyes half-shut, slammed the door behind him to slow the spread of the fire then started up the steps two at a time.

In seconds his injured left leg began to buckle but he kept on, working the railing hard to pull himself faster. Twenty-two steps he counted to the third floor with one switchback, the same to the fourth, the fifth, the sixth, the seventh then thirty-two to the eighth.

One hundred and forty two steps in all. Even in prime condition that would be crushing. Halfway up and he was running on willpower alone, soaked with sweat, both legs burning and lungs panting. By the seventh floor he was gasping so hard he saw silver motes floating in his vision. By the eighth he was a wreck, left leg shuddering uncontrollably, holding himself together with only adrenaline and rage.

People were screaming nearby. Wren clung to the railing and sucked in air, watching as smoke rolled like a river out of the stairwell and down a corridor. He followed to an emergency exit that led to the stairs to the roof.

47

ROAR

The roar of the fire only grew as Wren emerged onto the roof, sounding like a ravening beast ripping chunks out of the building's guts. Automatic rifle fire skittered off the roof's edge, masked by swirling updrafts of encircling smoke, flecked now with orange tongues of flame.

People lumbered in the hazy gray like lost souls in Purgatory, shouting and terrified, and Wren plunged into their midst. He passed tight throngs locked in heated arguments, people sobbing into their cell phones, some wailing with raw burns, others lying still or slumped coughing from the smoke, all blinking tear trails down their soot-stained cheeks.

Wren sought the center.

Panic and fear were a lethal cocktail. He needed to calm these people while also offering hope. One wrong step and he'd start a wild exodus that would drive them over the edge like lemmings, or bottleneck and asphyxiate them in the stairwell.

Survival required control, and control required authority, and authority required attention.

Just like the Pyramid on the final day.

Wren found the whirling center of the roof. A single shot fired from his Glock would get their attention, but it might also start a stampede.

Instead he assessed those nearest to him, swiftly selecting a slender man in his thirties wearing a pink shirt smeared with soot. His eyes were flickering and panicky, but that was better than dull and numb.

Wren strode closer, grasped him by the shoulders and looked dead into his eyes.

"You will live if you do what I say," he said, slowly and clearly. "Drop to one knee and listen. Do you understand?"

The man just stared, so Wren pressed on his shoulders and guided him to one knee. "Stay like that and you'll survive."

The man stayed. Wren moved on to the next, a young woman who was screaming and beating at her scorched skirt though the fire was long out. He held her wild arms and repeated the same trick, calming and quieting her.

She dropped to one knee and fell silent, staring at him as if he wasn't real. Now there were two. Wren pointed at a third person, a thickset man in his fifties who had watched it all.

He had a different bearing from the other two, maybe a manager, maybe FBI himself, and his eyes were full of doubt.

Wren drew the Glock and pointed to the roof.

The man dropped to one knee.

Wren nodded his approval and moved on, radiating outwards.

In minutes he had some twenty people kneeling silently, and from there the effect spread organically. The hubbub of motion and sound dropped sharply away, until in five minutes the rooftop was silent but for the churning of the fire.

"I'm FBI," Wren called over their heads in a deep, controlled voice, letting his words hang for a moment, encouraging their rational minds to switch back on. He needed them as thinking individuals for what would come, not a mindless mob. "My name is Christopher Wren. Some of you might have seen me ram the building in a semi on the northwest side. I got up here, which means there's a way out. We can-"

Abruptly one person rose and ran. Wren fired the Glock without thinking; the shot went over the man's shoulder and he flattened to the hot roof with a cry. A man running was a leader whom others would follow.

"I can lead you out," Wren went on, "but you need to follow my orders to the letter. The stairwell is filling with smoke so we'll be climbing down half-blind. Panic there and you'll kill everyone, and trust me, you really don't want a thousand deaths on your conscience." He left that long enough for them to imagine how it might feel. "So we go in single file. We go in a line. We use our brains and we'll all survive."

They stared at him with teary red eyes, hope mingling with desperation. He wasn't done yet though.

"Once we're out they'll be shooting at us. The northwest lot is narrow, they can get maybe ten of their shooters in there. They have automatic rifles and they're going to shoot at us, but remember, there's no retreat up here, is there? This is not about bravery, just necessity. With sheer mass of numbers we will bring the bastards down, I swear."

He gazed out over them. Nobody said a thing.

"In an orderly fashion," he said. "One hand on the shoulder of the person in front. Cover your mouth and nose with whatever you can to block the smoke. Follow me."

He took the hand of the first man, put it on his own right shoulder and strode back through the throng.

48

HEAD OF THE SNAKE

T he stairwell was choked with swirling smoke, limiting visibility and stinging Wren's eyes. He covered his mouth with his shirt then plunged in.

Heat billowed from below in waves. His feet found the edge of the steps and he started down. The railing was painfully hot to the touch, and soon the vertical chute filled with the sound of gasps, cries and clattering feet.

"It's OK," Wren called back gently, resisting the urge to charge down at full speed. "Slow and steady wins the race."

He counted the steps to the first switchback, felt the tug as the line behind him tightened, then counted the steps to the landing. As he passed the lit EXIT sign over the door to the seventh floor, a rush of heat rolled over him. The corridor beyond the fire doors had to be ablaze.

He sped up slightly, to the sixth floor then the fifth, until the smoke grew so thick his eyes were streaming constantly and he could barely see a thing.

"Close your eyes," he called back, "pass it along. Trust each other."

By the fourth floor he felt dizzy and light-headed, by the third his left leg gave out on every other step, but he clung to the steaming railing despite the pain and kept going until the final switchback deposited him on the second floor.

The cries from his entourage had been replaced by coughing now. He risked a glance through cracked eyelids but saw little other than the red glow of the EXIT sign. The heat was fearsome.

"We're there," he called back, then kicked through the door.

Light and air fresh rushed in. The building's core around the elevators and stairwell was yet to burn, though channels of flame were spreading closer from the hellscape of an office beyond. Now the walls, ceilings and floor were all roaring, making a long tunnel of fire to the windward window.

"Now we run," Wren called, and broke into a sprint.

His feet thudded on the burning vinyl, left leg barely holding his weight, acrid smoke filling his lungs. Flames rose to each side as computers, desks and personal effects fed the blaze. The heat was crushing, but there was a cooler breeze running over his cheeks too, as the fire sucked in fresh air through the window he'd shot open.

In moments he reached it and burst out onto the first-floor roof.

There was more smoke than before and the tarpaper roof instantly scalding through the soles of his shoes, but it was better than the interior of the building. Wren sucked in cool, smoky air and held his hands out to the people following behind.

Bodies shot through the window one after another and Wren caught them, slapping out small fires in their clothing as they passed. A woman's hair was scorched. A man's shirt was cinders, stuck to his chest and back.

A dozen passed by, then another, then Wren grabbed the first few people who'd escaped and positioned them as catchers by the window.

"Help them as they come out," he shouted, voice hoarse and too loud after the thunder of the fire, "then follow me."

He turned and ran, drawing his Glock. The grip was so hot it hurt his palm. Through the rising smoke and flames either side he picked out the black figures of the Hounds of the Saints in the lot below, still standing sentry around the building's moat.

At the edge Wren picked out the oblong block of the semi trailer and jumped, hitting the flexing metal of the trailer's roof with a hollow bong. The surface warped beneath him, and a rush of rifle fire rang out in response.

Wren dropped flat and shuffled to the trailer's edge, where he grabbed the rim and let his body tip over the side. Bullets thumped into the trailer's far side; it sounded like some punched through the metal and cracked into the cargo of frozen meat.

Wren dropped down to the blacktop and his wounded left leg collapsed beneath him, laying him out. He grunted and crawled to the shelter of a huge melting tire. There was no sign of Lacy anywhere. God willing, she'd gotten away before the Hounds had closed in.

Gunfire kept coming, striking sparks off the blacktop near his feet. Wren pressed his cheek to the cold ground and edged his right arm around the curve of the melting tire, squinting for a target. There were some twelve Hounds standing out in the open unleashing fire on the trailer, but they couldn't see Wren wrapped in smoke by the wheel.

Just then a metallic bang came from above, followed by others as the first of his escapees dropped from the roof.

Wren fired. One of the Hounds went down, shot in the chest, but the others kept up a steady rain of bullets. Wren sighted and fired again, taking one of them in the gut, another in the shoulder, one in the leg, then they swept their fire toward him behind the wheel, just as somebody dropped down beside him.

"Hold for now, charge on my signal," Wren said in a low voice, as bullets hammered the tire's heavy frame, then he rose to his feet and loped to the semi's cab, now half-buried in the wall and choked in thick black smoke.

Operating largely by feel, Wren clambered up into the cab and ducked low in the footwell, scrabbling for the gearstick. The engine was still grinding. He found the clutch, cranked the huge machine's gears into reverse, sent a swift prayer up to whoever was listening and pushed the gas.

The semi rumbled to life, extricating itself from the building and pulling away backward with a chorus of warning beeps. It removed the escape route from the roof, but Wren couldn't think about that now, as the remaining eight Hounds concentrated their fire on the trailer as it reversed toward them.

Bullets smashed atonally into the trailer's back and sides, some even rattled through the load of frozen meat to plink musically off the wall behind Wren's head. The speedometer crept up to five as the truck reached the edge of the smoke, then Wren cranked the stick to neutral and jumped out of the cab.

The Hounds kept firing at the trailer. Wren limped along behind the retreating cab, shielded within the black fumes gushing from the grille, until the truck rolled through the line of remaining Hounds.

Muzzle flashes popped to left and right. Wren picked them out and fired back, felling three before the truck's rear wheels mounted a sidewalk and it slowed. Wren picked off another Hound on his right then ran over to snatch his rifle. An AR-15, old faithful, with a bump stock for extra rounds and the conversion parts to make it full-auto fire.

Wren hefted the stock, slapped the slide and let rip against the remaining Hounds.

He took out three of them to the left before they knew what was happening, completely clearing the near side of the trailer.

"Come on!" he shouted back at the smoke, and into the breach came a crowd of escapees from the building. A woman in a power suit snatched up a rifle and fired.

Wren loped around the semi ahead of them, flanking the remaining few Hounds and opening up with the AR-15. Two dropped instantly, and the others turned and ran. Wren sped in pursuit, bringing both down just as they reached the thinning edge of the smoke.

Ahead lay the parking lot, and something Wren had not expected.

Vehicles were pouring in off the expressway, but not fire trucks or ambulances, squad cars or riot police; these were all civilian. A blue SUV, another semi, a white Ford panel van, a cluster of leather-clad bikers on Harleys and Triumphs, a Prius with a guy standing up through the sunroof. These were citizens, and they brandished handguns and hunting rifles with the muzzles flashing, targeting the Saints.

The bark of their gunfire clamored across the blacktop, encircling and outnumbering the Hounds, who took shelter amongst the parked vehicles and returned fire.

Wren's heart swelled at the sight, pumping fresh energy into his legs. People had come off the street and out of their homes in defense of their country, and that was a beautiful thing.

His rifle clicked empty and he dropped it, then put his hands up and jogged toward the lead civilian vehicle. It was a blue Toyota SUV, and it pulled up with twin rifles trained in his direction from the rear windows.

"People are coming down from the roof," he shouted, his

voice hoarse from the smoke. "Northwest side, pull up so they can jump down on your vehicle, then get them away from the fire Thank you."

The driver, a steely-faced man with a handlebar mustache, nodded sharply. "You're him, aren't you? The terrorist on TV."

"I'm not the terrorist," Wren said, pointing. "They are."

The guy stared a moment longer, then nodded again and drove directly toward the fire.

Wren sped out across the lot, surrounded now by parked cars gleaming in the afternoon sun. It was so different out here, as if the fire wasn't even happening. He rubbed grit from his eyes and spun, searching for Richard Acker. He pulled out his phone and brought up the Whipple Building's schematic.

The Fostering Authority was on the southeast corner. It seemed the best shot. He surveyed the ongoing firefight around him, reading the flows of civilian vehicles and Hounds.

All exits from the lot were blocked by incoming vehicles, which left no escape. Wren watched a distant pair of Hounds as they ran low between rows of cars. They were headed southeast.

That was all the confirmation Wren needed, and he took off at a sprint. Acker was still here, he felt sure of it. He wouldn't have been able to resist watching his old enemies burn.

Time to cut off the head of the snake.

49

WALK IN THE FIRE

Wren's breath came in rasping wheezes and each stride felt like a hot dagger in his injured thigh. He was singed, battered, bruised and lightheaded from smoke inhalation, but that wasn't going to stop him.

A squad of Hounds spotted him and ran to intercept, firing rapidly. Wren took cover behind a Tesla and fired over the hood until his bump magazine ran dry, taking out two, three, until several of the vehicles racing around the exterior road descended, taking out the remaining two. Wren raised a hand in thanks and ran on. The nearest driver blasted her horn.

Wren scanned the southern side of the building as he approached the defensive moat, but there was no sign of the Alpha. Unless he'd gone into the Mississippi and taken his chances with the current, though, he had to be here. This was the beginning and the end for him.

Wren turned back to the center of the building. Across the shallow moat, the glass entrance doors hung open now, cracked in a maelstrom of flame. Wren thought he saw movement and ran closer.

Then he saw him, a large golden man with a bloody face,

haloed by raging fires in the lobby behind him. He held a gun in his hand, pressed to the head of a terrified young woman held before him as a shield.

Richard Acker, with a hostage.

"Christopher!" Acker boomed. "Come die for me."

He pulled the gun from the hostage's head and fired; the bullet struck a vehicle to Wren's left, starting the alarm caterwauling.

Wren broke into a zig-zagging run. At fifty yards out, Acker would have to be an incredible marksman to hit him with a handgun given the adrenalized conditions, and Wren didn't believe he was.

Acker was a talker. He was all noise and fury; fake face, fake muscles, fake skin. He'd never seen combat, his only training had been slaughtering innocents chained to the ground, and with the inferno surging at his back and his team of Hounds in retreat, Wren figured every shot would miss.

But the same didn't go for the woman held before him.

Acker kept firing until at thirty yards out Wren dropped to one knee, butted the rifle against his shoulder and took aim. Then Acker returned the barrel of the gun to his hostage's head.

"You think you can save one more soul, Chris?" Acker called.

The woman was young, early twenties, with tear trails burning red down her blanched white cheeks.

"Call it two if we include you, Richard," Wren shouted back.

Acker laughed. "So take your crosshairs off my head."

"Let the girl go and I will." Wren had the training Acker lacked, the hard-earned ability to ride the swells of combat adrenaline and still make the shot, but there was still risk. Even a perfect headshot might not prevent a nerve twitch triggering Acker's weapon and blowing out the young woman's face.

"Then come a little closer and join us. We can all walk in the fire together."

Acker advanced out onto the bridge, forcing the woman to walk ahead. His face was a mask of blood welling from a wound in his forehead, while flames framed him on all sides.

Wren's finger rode the trigger hard, then he remembered his promise to Sinclair; to save Acker's life. If at all possible, he wanted to keep that promise. Better for this man to face judgment for his many crimes in a court of law, where all his victims could see true justice done.

"It's over, Richard," Wren called, and let the rifle barrel drop, advancing slowly and steadily toward the bridge, like he was approaching a wounded animal. "Time to come in. I'll see you're treated fairly."

"Fairly?" Acker boomed, the light of madness shining in his eyes. "Do you think anything in my life was fair, Christopher Wren? You'll put me on display in one of your courts, a monster for the masses to poke and prod. Better to die a martyr here as the spark that ignites America!"

Wren started up the steps, only ten yards away now. Acker was right; martyrdom was incredibly powerful. There would always be those to follow a man like him, no matter how misguided. To this day many people still lionized his father, Apex of the Pyramid.

Better by far to take Acker alive.

Wren slowly laid the rifle down at the top of the steps, raised both hands and kept advancing. Acker was a talker, after all. That had come through in everything he'd done: his darknet postings; his booklet manifesto; his endless yammering in the torture room at Jib Jab.

Wren was going to have to talk him down. "It won't be

like that, Richard," he said, closing the gap to eight yards. "I promise."

"You promise!" Acker retorted, holding his ground. "You're nothing, Christopher. You speak for no one, you don't know what they'll do to me, or what they did."

"I know what they did to you here," Wren nodded toward the building. "The fostering authority. I know how none of them protected you, how the ones assigned to care for you abused you. I know exactly what that was like, because my father was the same. He tortured us all."

Acker laughed, the sound ringing with a wild edge. "You think you know? You had brothers, sisters, a family. You had friends, the entire cult around you, and when they died, they died together. You don't think I would have loved that? You don't think I'd be willing to die for that?"

Wren frowned. There was a twisted logic to what Acker was saying, one he couldn't argue with so he didn't try. "Then you'd be dead, Richard."

"Better to be dead, then!"

Wren took another step. Acker pulled the gun from the hostage and fired at his feet. "Stop right there, Pequeño 3!"

Wren stopped momentarily, counting the paces. At seven yards he could close the gap in four big strides, maybe three seconds total. He just needed to jam Acker up for that long, and maybe he had just the thing: the fresh wound in Acker's forehead.

It looked familiar, the same rough shape as Mason's many face brands, but this was deeper still, as if the branding iron had been held in position too long, burning the letters into his skull.

SIC SEMPER TYRANNIS, it read.

"I see you finally got your brand," Wren said. "Do you feel like you belong now?"

Acker laughed and started moving backward, extending

the distance again. "Yes. You were right about me; I wasn't willing to sacrifice everything for the cause. I am now."

"What cause is that?" Wren pressed, tracking closer with Acker's every step back. "You're killing hundreds of innocents here, Richard. They didn't all abuse you."

"They covered it up!" Acker roared back at him, closing on the blazing entrance doors now. "They're all complicit. This bitch?" He shook the woman in his arms. "She's from fostering authority records. She knew! They all knew and they did nothing."

"She wasn't even born when they were abusing you," Wren countered. "She inherited a bad system. Does she really deserve to die for that, is that justice?"

"Justice? These people hurt me when I couldn't defend myself! I'd think you would understand, after all you've been through. We're brothers now, Christopher, though I've walked where you would not dare."

Wren pointed at the building. "I've walked in there, Richard. I got most of them out. I'll get her out too." He nodded at the woman. "Now it's just your soul to play for."

"My soul?" Acker snarled. "Would you put me on a coin, Christopher, add me to your Foundation of wannabe vampires and hackers, your bikers and broken souls, swap one cult for another?"

Acker stopped with his back almost touching the outer wall of fire, but Wren kept coming, closing the distance to six yards now.

"I would. It's exactly what the Foundation's for. You want to burn the guilty alive, I'll even light the match, but not like this. Not innocents too."

"None of them are innocent!" Acker raged. "Not them, not me and not you!"

Wren took another step. Five yards, now. Two strides and

he could grab the weapon, grab the girl, maybe save them both.

"I've committed crimes," Wren admitted. "I've killed a lot of people. I lied to my family. To my children. I survived the Pyramid, when a thousand didn't."

Acker's lips split in a grin. "Ah yes, the Pyramid. Your father is a very great man, Pequeño 3."

Four yards. "Not 'is', Richard, 'was'. He died twenty-five years ago."

Acker's grin spread. "Are you so sure? Maybe he's with your family right now. Maybe he's painting them with napalm and lighting a match."

Wren's heart skipped a beat. "You don't know what you're talking about. You're bluffing."

"What bluff, that I told him where they are? Look at my works, brother, am I a man who bluffs?"

Three yards. Wren was ready to charge and grab Acker, but abruptly he shoved the woman toward Wren and leaped backward, through the shattered frame of the doorway and into the shooting flames.

"I would've loved the Pyramid," he shouted over the fire's roar, as red and orange tongues lapped at his clothes. "I would've walked the streets as all those bodies burned and been grateful. Do you remember how that felt, Christopher?"

Wren caught the girl and moved past, squinting against the punishing heat of the fire. "I remember I escaped, Richard. I survived, and you can too."

He lunged deeper, reaching out, but Acker was too fast.

He skipped three steps deeper into the inferno, churning all around him. "Nobody escaped the Pyramid, Christopher Wren! Your father told me about how you killed them all."

Wren had to hold both hands up to shield his eyes from the fierce heat. "Killed who?"

"I know you were his favorite," Acker cried as the fires

licked up into his golden hair. "How you painted every one of the thousand with napalm and lit the match, and he was so proud. Do you remember how that felt?"

Sudden images flashed before Wren's eyes; fire everywhere both in the past and the present. He saw himself burning the gang members under the Chicago bridge, then something deeper; a long line of people stretching back into the desert, waiting for their turn to be anointed, with little Pequeño 3 holding the brush and dipping it into the acrid barrel of napalm.

He shook his head.

"Never happened," he boomed and plunged directly into the conflagration, but his hands closed on empty air.

Now the Alpha of the Saints stood in the center of the lobby, arms spread and engulfed in flames.

"Someday you'll see the beauty!" he cried as the fire consumed him. "Do you know these people put a mark on my record, brother, to show that I was weak? They passed me around like a thing. Where were you then?"

Wren sprang back as Acker's body became a yellow pillar of flame.

"Make sure they write songs about me," his voice screamed out of the hellscape. "Bigger than Manson!"

Then he was gone.

The fire swallowed him completely, licking up his bronzed head and into his golden hair, melting him like a pillar of wax.

Wren backed away with his eyes burning, past the girl and across the bridge until he almost fell at the edge of the steps.

Sweat drenched him. Both legs shook. Old ghosts danced in the flames where Richard Acker had disappeared; memories long buried.

He saw again his small hands holding the brush, and

painting the faces and chests of all his family, and touching the lighter to their skin again and again, all with his father watching proudly on.

Was that real?

Had he been the one to burn the Pyramid one thousand?

He grasped the railing and turned in a daze.

The lot swirled with vehicles. Smoke-blackened people streamed away from the building while others rushed over with water and bandages.

Acker was dead. It was over.

The phone chimed in his hand. Wren looked at it numbly: a message from Director Humphreys.

A NEWS HELICOPTER CAPTURED THAT, CHRISTOPHER. IT'S GOING OUT EVERYWHERE. ALREADY THE SAINTS ARE STARTING TO STAND DOWN.

It was good, he supposed. It was hard to think. He turned and saw the young woman standing above the moat, dizzy and clearly deep into shock.

Wren ran and caught her before she could fall into the moat.

"It's OK," he said, cradling her in his arms and jogging down the steps, into the lot and toward the crowds of surging civilians. "Everything's OK now, you're safe, I swear."

50

REAP IT

Wren came back to himself some time later, smeared with soot and blood, after the rescue was done and all the people cleared. He only had the vaguest memories of the last few hours; just that he'd worked through them all.

There'd been people still coming down through the stairwell for over an hour, despite the thickness of the smoke. There'd been people roaming the first floor looking for a way down, and Hounds with their weapons down, looking for someone to surrender to.

Wren had done everything he could. At times he found himself working CPR on bodies right alongside bikers in leather jackets and workers in hi-vis vests and businesspeople in smart suits. Soot and blood marked them all and made them all the same.

Now he stood by the side of the Mississippi, watching the waters flow by, still seeing afterimages from the flames. He didn't know what he was looking at, whether these were real or invented memories.

He didn't know.

His phone rang. He brought it up and grunted when he

saw the caller. It wasn't anyone he'd expected. He clicked answer. "Yeah."

"Chris? Is that you?"

It was Charlie, his father-in-law. He sounded gruff and angry.

"It's me," Wren said, cupping the receiver against the receding wail of ambulance sirens, carrying the last of the injured away.

"She asked me to call," Charlie said. "Loralei."

Wren grunted. He remembered something else Acker had said. "Is she OK? Are the kids OK?"

"They're fine. They're OK. They're watching the attacks over there, though. We all are; it's on every news channel. We saw the confrontation on the bridge with that madman." He paused, and a long moment passed. Wren pictured Charlie sitting in his armchair, in his home at the edge of London, England, living a totally different life. A sigh came down the line. "We saw you, Chris."

Wren said nothing. A tidal wave of relief was rushing through him, so strong it sent silver specks swamping his vision. In the crush of immediate action, he'd forgotten Acker's threat to his kids. He'd forgotten his family.

"The things that you did," Charlie went on before Wren could speak, "it speaks well of you, Chris. I can see your fingerprints all over this. I can see you fought it."

Wren understood the rest of what was coming from Charlie's tone. It wasn't happy. It was resigned. Why else had Loralei not called him herself?

"But she still won't let me see the kids?"

Silence hung for a long moment. "That's two different things, isn't it?" Charlie said. "On the one hand, she's proud. We all are. You've saved a lot of people today, haven't you? But after this, you'll be more of a target now than ever. For crazies, for enemies of your country, whoever. That means

Loralei and the kids are targets too, because of you, doesn't it? Nothing's changed, really. If anything, it just got worse."

Got worse. Wren didn't know what to say.

"Give it another month," Charlie said. "That's what she asks. That's what I'm asking. Things will calm down."

Wren thought about it. He thought about the images he'd seen in the flames. "No."

"No?"

"No. They're my kids, Charlie. Not yours. They don't belong to Loralei. They're mine too."

"Don't do that!" Charlie cautioned. "Unless you want this thing to get legal. You won't have a leg to stand on then, will you, after a decade-plus of lies?" He took a calming breath. "Like I said, just wait one more month, son. It's best for everyone."

Best for everyone.

Reap it.

Wren hung up, then slumped down by the river's side and watched the water roll by.

51

FAMILY MAN

Three days later, with his leg stitched and wrapped and his burns treated, Wren sat at Teddy's bedside at Abbot Northwestern Hospital.

Teddy was in a coma. His chart said it was medically induced, to allow his brain a chance to heal. His head was bandaged thoroughly, though stitch lines were just visible stretching down the sides of his scalp, from where they'd operated.

Wren took his hand. It was limp.

Tubes ran into his nose carrying liquid nutrients. A cannula fed into the crook of his left elbow carrying anesthesia from an automated drip bag. Another tube disappeared down his throat, keeping his lungs working. His pulse beeped on the monitor nearby. His cheeks were thinning already, losing some of his middle-age bulk.

"Is this what you meant," came a stark, angry voice behind him. "When you said he was a caterpillar in a chrysalis?"

Wren turned to face Cheryl. Her anhedonia condition kept her from feeling joyful emotions, but that did nothing to prevent angry emotions, and she was clearly furious now;

eyes tight and lips pinched in a snarl, red blooming through the black and blue bruises on her cheeks.

"I'm sorry for what happened," Wren said.

"Sorry," she repeated. Her head was circled with bandaging too. Wren had already checked; they'd been able to reattach both of her ears. "You already said that, didn't you? At Jib-Jab."

"It's true. I am. I never meant for you to be a target."

She snorted. "They told me you were here. The same place as us. They said I couldn't see you, though. There was a guard on your door."

Wren nodded, then turned back to look at Teddy. Wrapped up like that, he did look a little like a man in a chrysalis. The thought made him feel ill.

"I put myself on the map with all that. My family, too. I didn't think any of this would happen."

"Then you need to think harder," Cheryl snapped. "You're responsible for us. That's the whole point of the Foundation, right?"

Wren just watched Teddy as one machine inflated his lungs and another pushed blood around his body. After blows to the head like that, you never knew how much of the person you were going to get back, if any.

"That's right," he said softly. "Sort of. The Foundation's a scaffold. It helps people get stronger, then they take responsibility for themselves.

Moments passed. Then Cheryl's hand closed around his. She squeezed hard.

"Teddy's strong," she said. "Stronger than he ever thought. I think you were right. I think when he comes through this, he will be better. A butterfly from the chrysalis, right?"

Wren turned to her, standing by his side. The anger was

261

still there, but now it was blurring into hope. He'd rarely seen hope in Cheryl's eyes, and it moved him.

"I hope so."

"I hope so too," Cheryl repeated, and patted his hand. "Just be careful, OK? Be careful with us, Chris."

He nodded. She touched his cheek, then went to sit by Teddy's side. She took his hand and held on.

Wren left.

Within an hour he was behind the wheel of another rented Jeep Wrangler, driving on I-94 out of Minneapolis. His mind turned slowly as he drove, heading for the border with Wisconsin.

Memories drifted up with each hot pulse in the side of his thigh. Sometimes he was back in the flames with the Alpha, as the man called out his madness from the depths. The desperation in his eyes blurred with the stinging heat, and his last words echoed in Wren's ears...

At some point he turned on the radio and tuned through stations. All anyone was talking about was the Saints, even three days later. The current death toll stood at around three hundred people, scattered across the country. Many of them had been Saints themselves, as citizens rose up to protect their fellow Americans.

Many more Saints had been arrested before they could strike, and a mass trial before federal court was being posited. Wren followed the story distantly as he drove on, heading east and south toward Delaware.

Toward his kids.

That first day, he covered only a few hundred miles before pulling over at a motel. He ate well and slept better than he had in years, as if a burden had been lifted.

The next day he drove down into Indiana. As the hours passed, he watched the Foundation's darknet boards. His members were more active than ever in their coin groups, discussing the Order and the cleanup, their addictions and their progress up the levels. They shared stories about past failings and current temptations.

It filled him with pride.

On the third day, Dr. Ferat called. Wren was driving through Ohio when he answered.

"Doctor," he said.

"Christopher," Dr. Ferat said. "It's so good to hear your voice."

"And yours, Greylah. I owe you. Without your help, I wouldn't be here. Vandenberg saved me."

"Nonsense," said the doctor, but he could hear the pride in her voice. "It was my pleasure to help. Now, how are you?"

That was a tough question. There were lots of possible answers, none of which Wren was really sure about. "OK," he settled on. "A lot of thinking."

"About what?"

"Something Acker said before he walked into the fire."

"Yes?"

Wren gritted his teeth. Saying it made it real, but it was already becoming real in his head. "That I was a part of the final burning of the Pyramid. That I actually painted all the people with napalm and set them alight."

There was a long silence.

"And do you think he was telling the truth, Christopher? Do you remember doing any of that? You were only eleven years old."

Wren sighed. "I don't know. Maybe. I see flashes. Maybe they're memories. I definitely saw it happen, I know that, but did I hold the brush? Did I set them alight?" His knuckles tightened on the wheel. "I just don't know."

The silence stretched out. Wren heard Dr. Ferat breathing. He waited.

"False memories are possible," she said. "It's also possible you did what Acker said. Neither changes the man you are now. You were eleven, and your father was the most vicious and gifted manipulator in American history. You didn't stand a chance."

Wren grunted. Maybe that helped. Maybe it was an excuse.

"But if it is true, how did Acker know it?" the doctor went on. "I've searched every record on your history, and they all say you were the only survivor. There's no one who could've told him that."

Wren sucked in a slow breath. "He said it was my father. The Apex. He said he was alive, and even said he might come for my kids."

There was another long silence. "I found something, Christopher," she said eventually. "I'd discounted it, but it may be relevant, now. It was in Acker's digital records, salvaged from the Whipple Building."

Wren clenched his teeth. "What did you find?"

"There was a symbol drawn on Acker's profile. An infamous symbol used by sick men to signal a weak target."

Wren felt the world tunneling down. "He mentioned that, a symbol on his record. What was it?"

"It's called the the 'Blue Fairy'. Like the character from the Pinocchio tale? It's a symbol your father also used, apparently, during his Pyramid days. To mark out certain children."

That thrust Wren back into the past. He pulled the truck over and had to sit by the wayside and just breathe, staring out at blue skies as a cold sweat ran down his back.

Did he remember that? A blue fairy symbol chalked onto the bunks of his brothers and sisters. Maybe he did. Maybe he'd doodled it himself in the sands of Arizona, never really knowing what it meant.

"You're saying the Apex really was linked to Acker? That he might really be alive?"

"It's possible, Christopher." She took a heavy breath. "They managed to save Sinclair, and she's been talking to me. I volunteered as an expert in cult deprogramming. She says the scale of Acker's ideas were out of character. He was angry and vengeful, but not on a national level. Somebody or something radicalized him. Maybe it was your father."

Wren squeezed the wheel so hard it hurt. "Maybe."

"We only have the Blue Fairy as a clue, but there's a myth about that symbol on the dark Internet. Apparently, it represents a cabal of the world's richest, most depraved men. We can hunt them down."

"I can't," Wren said sharply. "You'll have to do it without me."

Ferat paused. "What? Christopher. You-"

"I owe it to my family. I'm out, Doctor. Of the CIA, the Foundation, whatever I have to do. My kids matter most. I have to-"

"Jake and Quinn," Ferat interrupted sharply. "Your children's names, correct?"

Wren had never told her anything about his kids. "How do you know that?"

"There were records embedded in Acker's files. Their names, ages, photographs of them, where they live." A beat passed. "They're somewhere in Delaware, staying in a duplex with your wife's new boyfriend, correct?" A pause. "I'm sorry, Christopher. It seems both your children have been marked with the Blue Fairy brand."

That hit Wren like a punch in the face. He'd do whatever it took to keep his kids safe.

"Tell me everything you've got," he said, and stepped on the gas.

THE NEXT CHRIS WREN THRILLER

NO MERCY

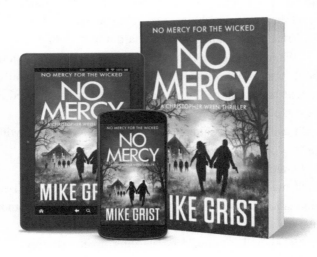

They came for his kids. There can be no mercy.
Black-ops legend Chris Wren has hunted the Blue Fairy for
months - a hacker group stalking innocents on the dark
Internet. Including his kids.
Now an anti-Blue Fairy activist is dead in Detroit, two more
have been abducted, and Wren alone knows what it means.
The monsters are crawling out into the light.
As a Blue Fairy army rises and a mass hacking attack
threatens to cripple the USA, only Wren and his brilliant
lieutenant Sally Rogers stand ready to enforce true justice:
No mercy for the wicked.

READ ON FOR AN EXCERPT.

THE FIRST GIRL ZERO THRILLER

GIRL ZERO

They sold her sister. Now they'll pay.
At 7 years old, the girl known only as 'Zero' was locked away
in an Idaho dungeon. Her torments didn't end for 9 years,
until she broke free and executed her captors.
But her vengeance couldn't end there.
When Zero was locked away, she had a little sister, Hope. She
never saw her again, but she's been searching ever since.
Now she may finally be getting close. There's a man
'breaking' girls with a hammer and nails. But something is
different this time. This man is tied to something bigger. This
man may be the key to setting Hope free…
Zero just has to break him first.
LIVE BY THE HAMMER, DIE BY THE NAIL.

AVAILABLE IN EBOOK, PAPERBACK & AUDIO

HAVE YOU READ EVERY CHRIS WREN THRILLER?

Saint Justice
They stole his truck. Big mistake.

No Mercy
Hackers came for his kids. There can be no mercy.

Make Them Pay
The latest reality TV show: execute the rich.

False Flag
They framed him for murder. He'll kill to clear his name.

Firestorm
Is the new President a traitor?

Enemy of the People
There's a target on Wren's back. Everyone's a hunter.

Backlash
He just wanted to go home. They got in the way...

Never Forgive
5 dead in Tokyo. His name's all over it.

War of Choice
Russia renditioned his friends. This means war.

Hammer of God
A US city annihilated. All bets are off.

HAVE YOU READ EVERY GIRL 0 THRILLER?

<u>Girl Zero</u>
They stole her little sister. Now they'll pay.

<u>Zero Day</u>
One little girl dead in Haiti. More will follow.

Kill Zero
The past isn't dead, but it can kill...

HAVE YOU READ THE LAST MAYOR THRILLERS?

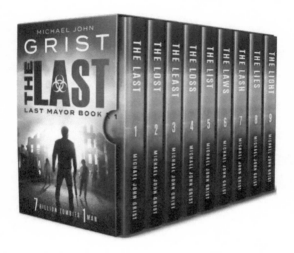

The Last Mayor series - Books 1-9

When the zombie apocalypse devastates the world overnight,
Amo is the last man left alive.

Or is he?

NO MERCY - CHAPTER 1

Christopher Wren laid out flat atop a snow-capped roof somewhere on the outskirts of Minsk, Belarus. Through the scope of his Barrett M82 sniper rifle, he watched a building three hundred yards.

The Blue Fairy was in his sights at last. He prayed this would be the raid that finally made his family safe.

In the tawny dusk light, the building looked like nothing special. Just another communist-era construction, a brutalist block of thin concrete slabs half held together with propaganda postings, like the gravestone for a dying ideology. Wren picked out scraps of communist-red clenched fist posters, overlaid atop Lenin's jutting arm and the old and gold hammer and sickle. Breaking their torn-wallpaper effect were a few tinted, metal-barred windows on each of the building's seven floors, with a single steel door at the bottom opening onto a snow-frosted sidewalk.

Wren switched to his Thor infrared scope. Heat-mapped, the building was alive with processing power. The outlines of hundreds of computer server racks across all seven stories blazed like a hellish scaffold, glowing brightest at the top. Thick data lines burned hot down the building's exterior, venting heat before they plunged through holes drilled to the sewers, each laundering vast quantities of dark Internet data out to the open digital ocean.

This had to be an important node in the Blue Fairy's international data trafficking operation. Wren had been hunting it for three months, ever since the men behind it had placed the crosshairs on his children's heads.

The Blue Fairy brand mark, symbol for all manners of depravity, had been attached to their names. Jake and Quinn, five and seven. He'd hoped to stop fighting and spend more time with them, but after that threat he'd mobilized like never before.

In the three months since the threat landed, he'd leveraged his Agent WithOut Portfolio status with the CIA to track the Fairy's trail ten times around the world already, coming up every time with smoke and mirrors.

The Blue Fairy was a myth. She flitted through the darknet's hidden trunk lines like a ghost, leaving only her stylized, child-like image as a calling card on forums and chat boards, a signal to the world's most depraved men.

Drugs. Sex. Weapons. Children.

Wren redoubled his attention to the building ahead.

Five bright orange figures were on guard on the ground floor near the entrance. A few stood scattered across the levels, two patrolled the roof, and three were seated on the seventh floor; their faint haloes outlined within the white-hot heat of the servers, searing through the thin walls.

These were the Blue Fairy's cyber traffickers, hard at work managing the ceaseless flow of criminal data; every byte another slice of human misery. It would be better to take them alive if he could, gather every possible shred of evidence, but the real prize was the building itself. The data flowing through its hundreds of servers, kept invisible by

Belarus' dictator-sanctioned haven status, should be enough to bring the Blue Fairy closer to heel.

"In position, Commander," came a voice in Wren's earpiece. This was his Interpol captain, name of Isa Rashidi, a 6' 5" ex-GRU Russian special forces soldier.

Wren swung the scope over and down to a dark alley at the building's side. Rashidi stood in front of the glowing yellow engine of their bullet-shaped UAZ-452 insertion van; a Russian Military Police vehicle that looked like a VW camper van. Plenty of them around in Belarus, easy to blend in. Around it stood Rashidi's five-strong Interpol IRT Incident Report Troop.

Rashidi was a man Wren trusted implicitly. He'd been instrumental in one of Wren's biggest black-ops stings on the Belarusian regime, toppling an underground railroad in trafficked humans. Wren pulled back from the scope to bare-eye the alley, but the troop were wholly invisible in their gray urban camo gear.

"You have eyes on the power line?" Wren asked, switching back to the scope.

"Da, Commander." Rashidi opened the rear doors of the van. "Under the chassis, beneath a grating. It looks like two-inch reinforced copper sheaths. We will burn the grate, then my team blow the lines on a ten-second fuse. All the lights will go out."

Not all the lights. Wren swept his gaze up to the seventh floor, where the lone dark block in the superheated space marked out the building's backup generator. Taking that out fell to Wren. He scanned up to the roof, where the guards patrolled. They didn't seem to have noticed a thing. Wren's overwatch team had already digitally looped their CCTV remotely. If only it was as simple a thing to hack their darknet.

"You're screened from above?"

"Da, under the UAZ. We are ready to cut the grating for access. Two blowtorches, two minutes."

Two minutes. Three months of prep.

"Cut it."

Wren caught the flare of the blowtorches igniting underneath the van. He checked again on the two men on the rooftop through the scope, but there was no response. No line of sight, with the van in the way. He shuffled his grip on the M82's stock, then checked his chamber; loaded with .50 caliber Browning Machine Gun rounds, able to make mincemeat of a wall even ten inches thick. With the rifle on semi-automatic, he could put a dozen shots from the box magazine through the wall in ten seconds flat.

He'd need them all. Turn the backup generator to slag, and no one else Wren trusted to make the shot. Miss it, or the traffickers if they ran, and the warning signal would go out. The darknet would know a hit was underway, and any trace of the Blue Fairy would flush from their servers as if they'd never been there at all.

Three months' worth of intelligence capture and asset risk lost in a flash.

"Explosives placed," came Rashidi's voice in Wren's headset. "Standing ready."

Wren took one last breath, looking out over the city. The faintest glow of a cold, dreary day died out in a rust-red line across the western horizon. Some four thousand miles further on, his kids would still be asleep in their Delaware duplex with no idea of the threat hanging over their heads.

A wind gusted, pulling Wren back to the moment. Maybe minus ten degrees out now, and seemed fresh snow was in the offing. He adjusted the scope's reticle to the wind, took a steadying breath. The air tasted of diesel fumes and raw onion, stinging down his lungs.

He wasn't a fan of Minsk.

"Blow it."

"Fuse is lit," answered Rashidi. Wren refocused his scope on the backup generator, nestled between two of the traffickers on the seventh floor. At the same time he watched with his off-eye as Rashidi led his IRT troops toward the building's front, readying a portable ram. Five seconds, three, then came the firework flash from under the van, the firecracker snap as the blast reached Wren, and he was firing.

The first shot burrowed dust from the wall dead-on, the second hit three inches over, the third tore a divot and the next five .50 cal slugs tunneled wider through crumbling concrete to rupture anything on the other side. Metal, plastic, wiring, bodies.

"Power's out on the ground floor," came Rashidi's voice in his ear, accompanied by the muted barks of rifle fire. "Two down so far. We're seeing heavy-gauge server stacks, computers are all dark."

Exactly as planned. Wren scanned the guys on the seventh floor. One of them was down and motionless already, might have caught a ricochet or shrapnel, another was balled-up under his desk, but then Wren caught a shadow of the third, running west toward the core server racks.

Either making a break to escape, or toward a kill switch to fry every computer on the grid. Every darknet hub he'd come across had a self-destruct plan of some kind: one pull to self-combust the servers, sending the evidence Wren needed up in digital smoke.

He couldn't take that chance, and fired three times through the wall. The guy's orange silhouette collapsed. Maybe going for the door, but equal chance he was going for a

He swung back to the two other guys, saw the one lying flat was now moving at a crawl. Wren put a shot through his chest to be sure. No loss. The balled-up one hadn't budged.

All the better to keep at least one alive. He could help them open Pandora's Box.

"Ground floor clear," Rashidi said in his earpiece. "Five hostiles down. We're heading up."

"Proceed with caution," Wren said, and reached out a hand to his loader, who dropped a fresh box of BMGs into it. Took three seconds to eject the old box and insert the new, then he swung the scope up to the roof.

The two guys there looked to be panicking, dithering at the edge. Their heat signatures came in crystal-clear compared to the diffused blue of the others, seen through the building's tissue-thin walls. Wren pinged them both with chest shots then strafed the scope down to scan Rashidi's path, catching movement on the third floor. It didn't look like armed response, someone running in the wrong direction to flee, but maybe headed for the trip switch.

Wren fired five times, and the figure collapsed.

"Second floor looks clear," Rashidi said.

"Two down on the seventh, two on the roof, one on the third," Wren answered. "Entering overwatch."

"Appreciate it, Commander."

Wren scrolled the building, tracking ahead of the IRT as Rashidi led them higher. In back of the squad a figure silhouetted itself briefly, maybe bobbing out of the elevator shaft before dropping back in.

Wren fired without thinking, the rest of the mag and clipped the guy's arm through concrete as he ducked back into shelter.

"Your floor, man winged behind the elevator," he reported.

"I see him," said Rashidi, sent his troops flanking. More rifle fire erupted then died away.

"Second floor clear, continuing the ascent."

Wren's heart pounded. He reached out a hand and

received another reload, another three seconds to switch out. It took his eye off the scope for a heartbeat, and when he looked again the trafficker on the seventh floor was in motion. Heading the same way as the first, west to the server racks.

Wren cursed and fired every round from the box, sawing a line through the wall to cut the guy down like a felled tree. He dropped.

Wren let a breath. "All three on the seventh are down."

"I heard that. They ran?"

"They ran."

"It's a pity. Third floor's clear. Anything else in store?"

Wren reloaded again, sweating now despite the cold. "I think you're clear."

The building looked quiet except for the IRT methodically clearing room by room. The building didn't have a big footprint. He swept the building again, saw nothing, then pulled out from the scope and blinked once long and slow before casting his eyes over the street.

Hot afterimages popped across the dark road. About time reinforcements appeared.

"We have incoming," came another voice in his ear, this one belonging to Sally Rogers, his CIA lieutenant poached from a rival department, and a brilliant field analyst. She was operating remotely out of Texas, with eyes in the sky via a LUNA surveillance drone at ten thousand feet. "Looks like two trucks inbound, they're big, eight-wheelers, maybe MKZT-6002 by the profiles. Military bearing, five men apiece."

Wren cursed under his breath. The MKZT-6002 was a beast, looked like the flatbed for a tower construction crane, but no crane attached. Squat and solid as a double-length Humvee, and not commonplace on the streets at all.

They were ready for this.

"Activate the second squad."

Somewhere below a second IRT squad fired up their UAZ van, ready to ram the inbound trucks. It'd barely make a dent on the eight-wheelers, though.

"Coming out of the northeast, boss," Rogers said.

Wren swung the scope over the building one more time, saw Rashidi on the fourth floor and advancing unopposed, then trained in on the road coming in from the north. No sign of the massive MKZTs yet.

"Estimate fifteen seconds 'til you have visibility."

They'd prepared for something like this. Not coming so fast, or with as much mass behind them, but he had redundancies in place. A Lada saloon below waiting to ferry Wren closer to any action, a second UAZ van weighted down with plate metal, ready to act as a ram or blockade a road.

"I'll take their engine blocks if I can," he said. "Get the ram vehicle ready to intercept."

"Boss."

Three seconds left, then the first of the squared-off MKZT-6002s came into sight, as big as a squashed garbage truck and racing at forty miles an hour. Easily three times the mass of his UAZ backup van, even loaded down with metal. Most likely it would be shredded by the bigger MKZTs.

Wren unloaded with the M82 rifle. He hit the glass windshield but sparked off, had to be triple-layer reinforced. He tagged the front grille but it was armored and didn't do a thing to slow the truck's momentum.

"Unable," he barked, reloading as the truck plowed on, chased by the second. "Hit it with the UAZ!"

Two blocks over, the UAZ rocketed out of a side street at the perfect ninety-degree vector, making up with velocity what it lacked in mass. The hit came wih a delayed crunch, just enough mass to jog the massive military vehicle to the side and send it careening up the curb to bury itself in a shuttered storefront.

Wren drilled twelve more shots through the windshield, digging enough holes to take out the driver and passenger and maybe coring the engine from above.

"Boss!" called Rogers.

He swung as he reloaded, watched the second MKZT-6002 closing on the building. He didn't have the angle now, it was almost directly below his vantage point. He fired shots that sparked off its roof anf bodywork, then it stopped at the front of the server building, shielding the entrance with its bulk.

"You have incoming, Rashidi!" He shouted down the line. "Rogers, give us a count of how many enter the building."

A second passed, and Wren stood, lifting the M82 off its tripod prongs to a shoulder lock, trying to get an angle. Via the thermal scope he picked out six figures inside the truck, but they weren't moving.

"I'm seeing no movement," Rogers said. "Boss, do you think-"

The truck started up. Wren's eyes flared. Not a single man had exited.

He scanned the building again, saw Rashidi on the sixth floor, almost to the core servers, and made the only leap possible as the MKZT raced away.

"Bomb, Rashidi! Get your men out!"

He barely heard the response. Dropped his M82 and snatched up the waiting fast rope, tossed it off the roof then threw himself after it.

Three big bounces carried him down six stories in seven seconds flat, then he was on the frosted sidewalk and unclipping. The Lada was right there as planned, door open, and he dropped into the passenger side.

"Go!" The car took off. Up ahead came the clanging crash

of gunfire, the moonlight splash of glass breaking as the IRT squad broke a way through and tossed fast ropes of their own.

"Exiting," came Rashidi's urgent voice as the Lada strained for velocity. Only two blocks away now and the driver breezed through a red light. Maybe there were figures rappelling fast down the building's side now, hard to tell.

Wren drew his Sig Sauer P320, .45 ACP eight-shell mag at the ready. There were barely two hundred yards left to cover with the MKZT charging west.

"Get out!" he shouted, looking up at the foreboding building as figures raced down the side like evacuating data trails. Nothing came back but whistling wind and the urgency of movement until-

"Team clearing the building, Commander," shouted Rashidi, with Wren maybe a hundred yards out. "I have-"

Then the building exploded.

Blasts rippled up from its base to its tip like a shockwave, dozens of fiery eruptions ripping through the structure like a vertical field of flowers blooming in dizzying fast-forward, each blowing out jets of cement dust and shrapnel.

The Lada skidded. The feed in Wren's earpiece roared to static. A second of crazy weightlessness followed as gravity took charge of the building, then it began to collapse, some two-hundred-fifty standing feet of ancient Russian engineering crashing down into a falling storm of masonry debris.

The Lada braked hard into a sudden bank of brick dust, striking the windshield like a tidal wave as the building vented its insides out. Shrapnel smashed spidery trails across the glass, a chunk of rock punched through and knocked out the rearview mirror. Dust puffed through the busted ventilation system, the brakes backwashed burning rubber, the Lada's momentum died out and Wren rocked back against the seat.

"Rashidi!" he shouted, already kicking his door open and charging ahead.

No answer came.

The earth shook like it had been hit by Lucifer's hammer, smoke and tumbling debris spinning through the dark. Ten yards on Wren stumbled on a chunk of concrete twisted with rebar but kept on, entering an avalanche of sloping rubble as the destroyed building found its new equilibrium.

"Rashidi!" he called, reached what had to be the curb, now buried some ten feet deep beneath the fresh flow of wreckage. A gusting wind pulled ribbony openings through the dust, giving Wren interlacing sightlines across the block where the building had stood.

All gone. A giant, groaning heap of broken concrete, hissing with ruptured gas lines and spurting water mains, all muted by the swaddling dust. Sirens pierced the shifting stillness, but distantly. Wren's heart pounded. He spun, trying to get a sense of where the team had exited, where they might have reached.

"Rogers!" he shouted. "Give me something."

"Winding back the footage," she answered. "Here, looks like they all made it out but got swallowed up by the rubble wave. Your five o'clock boss."

He staggered backward down the ruins. "Tell me!"

"Ten yards," she answered.

He reached the point, picked up a chunk of masonry and tossed it away, calling Rashidi's name.

Maybe some of them were alive. Some of them had to be alive.

Into the night he worked. Barely thinking about what had happened, about how the Blue Fairy had been more ready than he'd imagined, with a trip switch big enough to bring the entire building down. Scale, size, intensity, resources. The darknet was a trillion-dollar industry.

He kept working as fire crews filed up, police secured the area, earth-moving equipment was brought in to clear the roads and allow better access. Right alongside the emergency services he labored, accepting gloves and a mask when they were handed to him, swinging a pick when it was given, periodically calling Rashidi's name.

By the dawn it was done.

Five members of the IRT were alive. Dug out bleeding at the fringe of the wreckage, suffering from smoke inhalation and a dozen other injuries. Bloodshot eyes, dust plastered to their skin with cold sweat, but alive.

All except Rashidi. They found him last, closest to the building, where he'd been ensuring the safety of his team. His cold gaze burned into Wren's heart.

The Blue Fairy was going to pay for this.

Rashidi was laid on a gurney and carried away. Wren was left standing as they unearthed the dead traffickers. There was nothing to say. Smoke steadily rose, bulging out in a column that blocked the dawn light, and Wren's rage only grew with it.

They'd known. They'd been waiting for him.

His phone chimed in his pocket. He brought it up, found dozens of messages were waiting, all come in while he'd been digging. All of them images. He tapped one and it full-screened.

A stylized image of the Blue Fairy, black silhouette on a blue background, with twin children standing either side of her, holding her hands. Above their heads were his children's names.

Jake. Quinn.

Text ran along the bottom in block capitals.

SUFFER THE LITTLE CHILDREN, CHRISTOPHER WREN

FROM MIKE

Thank you so much for reading Saint Justice! I hope you enjoyed reading it as much as I enjoyed writing it. If you could take a minute or two to write a review on Amazon, I'd really appreciate it. Reviews make a huge difference, and I read every one.

I'd also love to have you on the Mike Grist newsletter, where you'll be first to hear when the next Girl 0 or Chris Wren thriller is coming.

www.subscribepage.com/christopher-wren

Mike Grist

ACKNOWLEDGEMENTS

Thanks to fellow authors Oliver Harris and Matt Finn for their encouragement and advice, to my Dad and Ailz for believing in Wren, and to my advance reader team: Britta Morrow, Bruce Simmons, Julian White, Chris Hooker, M. Jason Kelly, Meenaz Lodhi, Paul Henrichsen, Mike Keolker, Sue Martin, Steve Bonczyk & Barb Stoner. Of course, a big thanks to my wife Su for her steadfast support and invaluable comments.

You all helped make this book better.

- Mike

Made in United States
Troutdale, OR
03/01/2024

18096244R00181